MURDER AT WITCH'S HOLT

MURDER at WITCH'S HOLT

Roger Keevil

also by Roger Keevil

THE INSPECTOR CONSTABLE MURDER MYSTERIES

Murderer's Fête
Murder Unearthed
Death Sails In The Sunset
Murder Comes To Call
Murder Most Frequent
The Odds On Murder
No Bar To Murder
The Murder Cabinet
The Game Of Murder

THE COPPER & CO MURDER MYSTERIES

Honeymooner's Murder

MURDER at WITCH'S HOLT

a Copper & Co murder mystery

by
Roger Keevil

Cover design by Christopher Brooke
from an illustration by DM7/Shutterstock.com

Copyright © 2020 Roger Keevil

The moral right of the author has been asserted.

Apart from any fair dealing for the purposes of research or private study, or criticism or review, as permitted under the Copyright, Designs and Patents Act 1988, this publication may only be reproduced, stored or transmitted, in any form or by any means, with the prior permission of the publisher, or in the case of reprographic reproduction in accordance with the terms of licences issued by the Copyright Licensing Agency. Enquiries concerning reproduction outside these terms should be sent to the publisher.
mail@rogerkeevil.co.uk
www.rogerkeevil.co.uk

'Murder at Witch's Holt' is a work of fiction and wholly the product of the imagination of the author. All persons, events, locations, organisations and establishments are entirely fictitious or are used fictitiously, and are not intended to resemble in any way any actual persons living or dead, events, locations, organisations, or establishments. Any such resemblance is entirely coincidental, and is wholly in the mind of the reader.
But you knew that already, didn't you?

This book is dedicated to all those who, in difficult times,
try to make life a little better for their fellows

Chapter 1

"Not a lot of blood, is there, boss?"

"You're right, sergeant." Detective Inspector Dave Copper nodded in agreement with his colleague's observation.

"Which is a bit odd, seeing as how he's got a ruddy great arrow sticking out of his chest," continued Detective Sergeant Pete Radley. "Anyway, not much detecting to do to find out how he died. But you'd have thought he'd have bled more."

"The shortage of blood's not the only thing odd about this situation," remarked Copper, taking a step backwards and looking down at the dead body where it sat propped against the bole of an enormous and ancient oak tree. "What's he doing out here, presumably in the middle of the night, judging from when he was found, well away from the house, with bare feet and wearing just this long white robe?"

"Sleep-walking?" hazarded Radley. "Maybe that's his nightshirt."

"Pretty fancy nightshirt," responded Copper. "Great wide sleeves, and a whole lot of symbols of some sort embroidered all over it. Anyway, who do you know who wears a nightshirt?"

"I haven't actually asked around among the other guys at the station, boss," grinned Radley. "I could do a survey if you think it would help."

"Thank you for the offer, sergeant," replied Copper drily. "But for the moment, let's concentrate on the case in hand, instead of worrying about the sleeping habits of your buddies in the station canteen."

"Okay, boss," said an unrepentant Radley. "But you must admit, it's funny about the blood. Not being there, I mean. Like the dog in the night. I reckon that's one for your missus to sort out."

Copper turned to his colleague. "Sergeant Singleton," he said, with a slight edge to his voice, "will no doubt be carrying out her usual professional forensic examination as soon as she gets here from Westchester." A glance at his watch. "Which I dare say will be any time now."

"Don't you and Una ever find it a bit awkward, mixing work and personal life?" queried Radley. "I know I would."

"We manage remarkably well," smiled Copper. "Oh, and for the record, when we happen to be working together on a case, we prefer not to let the people involved know that we're married. Sometimes we get more information that way. So discretion, if you please."

"My middle name, boss."

"Anyway, we ought to get back up to the house. Questions to ask." Copper turned to the local uniformed officer hovering in the background. "Stay here with the body for the time being, would you, constable? The sergeant and I will be sending the forensic team down shortly, I expect."

"Will do, sir." The fresh-faced young officer gave a salute as the inspector and the sergeant set off along the path that led into the trees in the direction of the manor house.

*

"I got you a cup of tea, boss," announced Radley, as he pushed open the door and backed into the office, his hands occupied with a laden tray.

"And a little something for yourself, I see," observed Copper in dry tones, noting the tray's cargo of several bags of crisps and a plate bearing a pair of sugary doughnuts.

"Oh, one of the doughnuts is for you," said Radley, placing the mug of tea in front of his superior. "That's if you want it, of course."

"I wouldn't dream of depriving you, sergeant," smiled Copper. "I know you have this theory that, along with proteins and carbohydrates, doughnuts are one of the main food groups."

"A man's got to keep his strength up," protested Radley, his mouth full of doughnut. He was a chubby man around thirty, whose moderate height probably made him appear plumper than he actually was. Curly brown hair topped a round face that seemed forever ready to break into a grin, and his cheery and informal manner was often useful in obtaining vital information from unguarded suspects. "It's no easy life in C.I.D."

"Not regretting the move from Intelligence, by any chance? No second thoughts about the transfer?"

"You're kidding! Not for a second. No, I've got my feet well under this desk, so if it's okay by you, I'm staying. Mind you, it took a bit of getting used to at first. You know, what with us having been mates for so long, and then you go and get bumped up to inspector, and I got my promotion to sergeant, thanks to your old guv'nor."

"And now here we are," said Copper. Only a few years older than Radley, his elevation to a higher rank seemed somehow to have lent him an extra touch of gravitas, in slight contrast to his sometimes irreverent ways as a detective sergeant working alongside his former superior Andy Constable. However, the tousled hair and the occasional sparks of humour saved him from ever risking appearing severe.

"D'you know, at the start, the funniest thing was, figuring out what to call you. I mean, obviously it ought by rights to be 'sir', but that just sounded daft. And I couldn't go on calling you 'Dave' or 'mate', or else the Chief Super would have had my guts for garters if she'd caught me at it."

"And since 'guv' was out of the question – if you'd

ever called me that, I'd have been forever looking over my shoulder to check for D.I. Constable – I'm quite glad we settled on 'boss'. It makes it sound a bit less 1930s. Anyway, while we're on the subject of rank, I probably ought to give you some sort of official warning about the doughnut situation. You carry on putting away too many of those, and you're going to have trouble passing your next fitness assessment. And I don't want to have to go through the bother of getting used to a new bagman."

"You're probably right, boss," sighed Radley, reluctantly putting down the second doughnut.

"I definitely am," said Copper. "You said you're happy with your feet under that desk. Well, it's a funny thing about putting on the pounds, so they tell me, but you find that after a while, your arms seem to be getting shorter. So think on."

"Will do, boss," grinned Radley. The phone on his desk rang, and he gave a slight grunt as he stretched forward to answer it.

"See what I mean?" murmured Copper.

"D.S. Radley ... oh? ... where? ... hang on a second. Let me write that down ... got a postcode? ... great ... yes, he's here too. Do you want to speak to him? ... okay, I'll tell him ... yes, I expect he'll want to get over there straight away ... how about the Forensics people? ... okay, I'll leave that with you, then. Anything else, you can get us on my mobile." Radley replaced the receiver. "They've got a body for us," he declared, in response to Copper's enquiring eyebrow.

"Who, and where?"

"Out in the wilds somewhere. A place called Witch's Holt. I've never heard of it, but I've got the postcode for the satnav. Anyway, the Control Room seem to think we'd be interested."

"Then we'd better find out why," said Copper, shrugging into his jacket and picking up his car keys. He got to his feet and, followed by Radley, headed down the corridor in the direction of the car park.

*

"About another twenty minutes, according to the satnav, boss," said Pete Radley, as the car turned off the bypass on to a minor road heading out into the countryside. He scanned the fields, dotted with clumps of woodland, passing on either side. "This is all a bit rural for me. I'm much more of a townie."

"When you've been at this job for a while, you soon get to learn that there's just as much crime going on away from the towns as ever happens on some of the less savoury estates you hear about," replied Dave Copper.

"What, like taking and driving away the latest tractor without the owner's permission?" grinned Radley.

"You laugh," said Copper, "but I've known it happen. But the trouble was, the owner took it very amiss, because there was apparently some sort of long-standing feud between his family and the thief's, so he went after the perpetrator with a twelve-bore in his hand. It all ended very messily. So don't think of the countryside as some kind of rural idyll, because there can be all sorts of undercurrents. I've even known blood to flow in the aftermath of a village cake-making competition."

"Bloody hell, boss," said Radley. "Wonder what kind of witch's brew they've got in store for us at Witch's Holt," he added facetiously.

"No details when they called it through?" enquired Copper.

"No. They just said there had been someone found dead at a place called Holt Manor in the village of Witch's Holt, and that our detecting talents were required. Apparently the initial call was a bit sketchy."

"Well, I dare say we shall discover more when we

get there," said Copper, changing gear as the car began to climb a hill. Around them, the nature of the landscape was changing. From ordered fields behind neat hedges, some bearing crops in varying shades of green and gold while others held scatters of grazing sheep or cattle, the scenery now became wilder, with stretches of woodland overshadowing the road as it was forced to twist and turn around occasional outcrops of rock. The route emerged briefly on to an open patch of heathland, studded with untidy straggles of gorse and heather, before reaching the lip of a thickly wooded valley, into which the road suddenly plunged.

"We should be nearly there," reported Radley, looking at the satnav screen, "although I can't see any evidence of anything other than trees." As if to prove him wrong, moments later the car passed a sign at the side of the road. The legend, almost obscured by a heavy growth of moss, could just be discerned – 'Witch's Holt', with beneath, in much smaller letters, 'A magical place'. "Doesn't look that magical to me," remarked the sergeant. "There's no sign of anything, never mind a village."

A few moments later, in confirmation of the sign, a house appeared on the side of the road. It had obviously seen better days. Timber-framed and straw-hatted, what could have been the archetypal picturesque country cottage, with roses round the door, was guarded by an unkempt hedge with a slightly wonky gate and a front garden with a scruffy collection of hollyhocks, with door and window paintwork beginning to peel, and a thatch fraying at the edges. Further along the road crouched a row of brick-built labourers' cottages, their small dark windows seeming to bestow a surly glare on passers-by. Almost opposite stood the local pub, silent and unlit. 'The Black Cat' presented an attempt at a classical Georgian frontage to the world, with a small pillared porch and symmetrical sash windows ranged alongside and above, but from the side it was evident that the facade had been bolted on to an earlier Tudor building. Further cottages were visible up a small muddy lane at the side of the pub's yard.

"Is that it?" queried Radley. "Pretty grim sort of village. Not even a church."

"Ah," responded Copper. "In that case, it's not actually a village."

"You what?"

"Benefit of hours spend in the company of my old guv'nor," said Copper. "More odd facts than I ever learnt at school. And one of those was the fact that to count as a village, a place has to have a church. Otherwise it is classed as a hamlet."

"We did 'Hamlet' at school," declared Radley cheerfully. "Too much like hard work for me, but I loved the funny bit with the gravedigger and the skull."

"Be that as it may," sighed Copper, "we'd better forget Hamlet and Yorick, and concentrate on the apparently not-so-funny fact that we have a real dead body to consider. Wherever it is." He looked around. "Because we seem to have run out of village."

"Hamlet without the hamlet, eh, boss?" replied Radley, attempting not to smirk. "But we're on the right road. The satnav says the entrance to the place is just here on the right."

Following directions, Copper turned the car in through a pair of wrought-iron gates, smartly painted and gleaming with detailing in gold, past a sign in elegant script reading 'Holt Manor', with below it, the smaller legend 'Expanding the mind'."

"They seem to like their subtitles around here," remarked Copper, as he steered the car up the winding tree-overhung drive, the flanking undergrowth lined with rhododendrons and pink-flowered shrubs, before emerging on to a gravel sweep in front of an architectural cocktail. Part medieval stone-built manor house and part stately home, the building sported tall chimneys atop a muddle of roofs and a high tower with a crenellated crown. Lights gleamed from several of the leaded diamond-pane windows. The detectives made their way past the police car parked in front of the imposing stone porch and stepped into the flagged entrance passage, dim and wood-panelled. To the left, behind a wooden screen, the space could be seen to open out into a lofty hall with a roof of carved oaken beams above stone walls bearing a variety of armour, weaponry, and portraits of stern-faced individuals in the costumes of days long gone by. A massive stone fireplace adorned one wall, opposite a full-height oriel window whose stained-glass panes featured depictions of multi-coloured armorial shields, while a huge oak refectory table ran almost the entire length of the room. As Copper and Radley paused for a moment to allow their eyes to adjust to the gloom, they were met by a diminutive uniformed officer who stepped forward to greet them.

"D.I. Copper?" she enquired. "We were told you were on your way."

"Good. And this is my sergeant, D.S. Radley. And you are ...?"

"Khan, sir. P.C. Jazz Khan."

"Jazz?" queried Copper, eyebrows raised.

"Sorry, sir. Force of habit. It's actually Jasminder, but the guys at the station never manage to get their tongues round it, so they all call me Jazz."

Copper shrugged. "Sounds reasonable. Anyway, down to business. You were first on the scene?"

"Yes, sir. My partner and I were out on patrol a couple of villages away when the call came through from Control, so I put my foot down and we were able to get here quickly and secure the scene. And then I called it in, and told Control we'd need someone from C.I.D. Forensics."

"Smart work, constable," nodded Copper approvingly. "So where's this partner of yours?"

"He's keeping watch over the body until you and the forensics people arrive, sir."

"You seem to have everything under control, Khan. Well done. So, first things first." He turned to Radley. "You'd better start making some notes, sergeant." Radley obediently produced his notebook. "Right. Do we know who the victim is?"

"It's a man called Spelman, sir. Apparently he's the owner of the Institute."

"Institute?" queried Radley. "What kind of institute?"

"Not quite sure about that, sergeant," admitted Jazz. "People have been a bit vague."

"I dare say that will emerge," said Copper. "And where is the late Mr. Spelman to be found?"

"He's down in the holt, sir."

Copper looked puzzled. "I thought this was the Holt."

"No, sir," replied Jazz. "This is Holt Manor. The holt itself is just down the hill at the back."

"And what's a holt, when it's at home?" enquired Radley, pen poised.

"It's just a local word for a little wood, sarge," said Jazz. "Like a copse."

"I see," said Copper. "And that's where the body is."

"Yes, sir. By the Coven Tree."

"Coventry?" Radley was incredulous. "That's miles from here."

"No, sarge. The Coven Tree is a big oak in the middle of the wood. That's what they call it around here."

"How do you know these things?" wondered Radley.

Jazz smiled. "I'm a local girl, sarge. My dad runs the pharmacy in the next village, so I grew up in the area. Went to our village school with some of the kids from Witch's Holt. There are lots of stories, if you're interested."

"Maybe not the best time for a chat about local history," suggested Copper drily. "I'm more interested in the scene of the crime. Which is by this famous oak tree, you're saying?"

"Yes, sir. According to the person who found the body."

"And who was that?"

"One of the staff, sir. A woman by the name of Benz. She said she was out for her early morning run when she came across Mr. Spelman lying dead. And she had her phone with her, so she called 999 straight away. And we got here not long after that."

"Right. We'll need to speak to her soonest. Where is she?"

"Back here in the manor, sir. I thought it best to keep everyone together, so she's over there in the library with all the others." Jazz nodded towards a sturdy panelled oak door to the right of the passage.

"Others?" asked Copper. "What others?"

"All the rest of the staff and guests, sir. There's quite a houseful. I gather there was some sort of course taking place."

"Hence this Institute business, perhaps, sir, whatever that may mean," suggested Radley.

"Maybe," agreed Copper. "We shall have to find out what that's all about. But I suppose in the meantime, constable, we ought to take a look at our victim. How do we find him?"

Jazz pointed to the rear of the entrance passage. "If you go down that corridor there, sir, next to the foot of the stairs, it leads out on to a terrace. And there's a gravel path that goes down towards the holt. You can't miss it."

"Then off we go, sergeant. And you, constable, can continue to keep an eye on things here. Best not to let anyone of these people, whoever they are, go wandering about until we know rather more of what's what. And if the forensics team get here while we're gone, please point them in our direction. We'll head off down to this holt of theirs."

"The cops are off to the copse, eh boss?" chuckled Radley.

With a sigh, Copper turned and led the way towards the indicated corridor, Radley following in his wake.

Chapter 2

As the two detectives returned towards the rear of the manor, two women emerged on to the terrace, both clad in white overalls, sturdy-looking cases in their hands.

"Morning, girls," chirped Radley cheerfully. "Got all your boxes of tricks, ready to sort out our stiff, I see."

"Thank you, sergeant," said Copper. "A little more decorum with regard to our murder victim, I think." His voice softened, and he smiled in the direction of the leading woman. "Well, hello again. I don't think we expected to see each other quite so soon."

"Things do seem to keep cropping up to throw us together, don't they?" twinkled Sergeant Una Singleton, setting down her case and resting her hand momentarily on the inspector's shoulder. "Is this what they call being married to the job?"

"More than likely," agreed Copper with a grin. "Speaking of which, we have, as Mr. Radley so elegantly put it, a stiff for you."

"Sooz and I had a vague inkling that that might be the case," replied Una drily. "After all, I wasn't exactly dressed like this when I left the house this morning, was I?" she pointed out reasonably. "Anyway, I gather from the P.C. inside that we're on the right route to the site of the body. Correct?"

"Carry on down this path, sarge, and you can't miss it," said Radley. "You'll get to a clearing with a big tree in the middle, and that's where he is."

"Thanks," said Una. "Sooz and I will be on our way then. You remember my colleague Sooz, don't you, Peter?"

"Course I do," responded Radley. "We met at the wedding. Mind you, Sooz, you looked a bit different then," he grinned.

"I should think so," smiled Suzanne Heming. "For a start, Una was the only one who got to wear white that day." She looked down at her overalls. "It's never really been my colour, specially not in this glamorous style." She laughed. "Anyway, how are you? And more important, how is that baby of yours?"

"Still yelling the house down at nights," groaned Radley. "I only come to work to get some rest."

"No rest for any of us, I'm afraid," intervened Copper. "We have a death to investigate."

"We'd better make a start, then," said Una, picking up her case once more. She drew Copper aside slightly. "Any first thoughts?" she enquired. "What am I expecting to find?"

"It looks as if it might be a bit of a funny one, love," confided Copper. "Middle-aged chap in some sort of a long gown, propped against a tree with an arrow in him. Somebody's been playing Robin Hood, with unhappy results. See what you think."

With a brief peck on her husband's cheek and a beckoning nod to Suzanne, Una set off in the direction of the wood, while the two detectives watched them briefly before turning and re-entering the manor house.

*

Jazz Khan was still in position outside the library door as Dave Copper and Pete Radley re-entered the hall.

"Anything to report, Khan?" asked Copper.

"Nothing, sir," replied Jazz. "No movement. They're still all in the library as you instructed."

"Good. So, how many is 'all'?"

Jazz thought for a second. "There are twelve of them, sir."

"Twelve?" echoed Radley. "Strewth! That's me in for a dose of writer's cramp, once I've finished taking statements off that lot."

"Not to mention the possibility of anyone else who

may have been on the scene in between the last time the victim was seen and the discovery of the body," pointed out Copper.

"Actually, sir," intervened Jazz, "you don't have to worry about that. I gather from the woman I spoke to that the place is secured at night with the gates locked, so there shouldn't have been anyone else here. And I don't think the locals would want to set foot here after dark anyway."

"So, it's just the twelve," mused Copper. "Plus the dead man, of course. Thirteen in all."

"That makes a baker's dozen," commented Radley.

"Yes," responded Copper absently. A speculative light was in his eyes. "Interesting number, bearing in mind where the man was found." He shook himself slightly. "Well, better get on with it." He crossed the hall to the library door.

As the inspector and the sergeant entered the room, to find the occupants seated around on chairs and sofas, a host of faces turned towards the newcomers. The vast majority of those present, Copper noted, were female. "Good morning, ladies ... and gentleman," he began. "My name is Detective Inspector Copper, and this is Detective Sergeant Radley." Warrant cards were produced. There was a murmur of reaction. "And as I am sure you are all by now aware, a dead body has been found on the premises in suspicious circumstances, which we are bound to investigate. So our first task will be to establish who each of you is, and what is the nature of your presence here. Now, as I understand it, the dead man, a Mr. ..." He turned towards Radley.

"Spelman, sir," prompted the sergeant.

"Mr. Spelman," continued Copper, "was, I believe, the owner of this Institute, as I've had it described to me. Presumably that meant he was in charge. So, in default of Mr. Spelman, can I ask which of you would be the appropriate authority here?"

Two people on opposite sides of the room stood simultaneously. "I suppose I am," declared a woman with cropped red hair, at the same time as the only man in the room stated "That would be me" in a firm transatlantic accent.

Copper permitted himself the ghost of a smile. "Well, I imagine that can't be true of both of you. So," addressing himself to the woman, "perhaps, madam, you'd like to identify yourself." He gave a mute indication to Radley that he should begin to make notes.

"I'm Charlotte-Anne Connor," said the woman. "Mr. Spelman's personal assistant. His second-in-command, if you like. So if there's anything you want to know about the Institute, just ask me."

"I shall certainly be doing so," replied Copper. He turned to the man. "And you, sir?"

The man looked coldly at the woman who had just spoken. "Sorry, Charlotte-Anne, but I think you're outranked here. I'm Rudolph Day, inspector. Rudy for short. And I'm the co-owner of the Institute. Which means, I think, that this lady works for me. Since I certainly appear to have been paying her wages."

"I see," said Copper calmly, noting the tension in the air. "Well, of course, I shall need to speak to both of you. But perhaps, as apparently the most senior person here in terms of authority, I ought to begin with you, Mr. Day." He looked around the room. "I wonder if there's anywhere where our conversation could be a little more ... private?"

"There's the small study through there," suggested Rudy, pointing to a door in the corner of the library.

"That sounds fine," agreed Copper. "And Sergeant Radley, perhaps you'd like to call P.C. Khan in from the hall. She can be on hand if any of the ladies here should need anything. You know, just keeping up the good work she's been doing so far, until I've had a brief chat with everyone." A meaningful look indicated that the young officer's task would also involve preventing those present from leaving the room. "Then please join us in the study."

"Got you, sir." Radley just managed to stop himself giving a conspiratorial wink, before heading out into the hall. A murmur of voices could be heard before Pete and Jazz entered the library, as the others made their way towards the study door.

Copper unconsciously took position behind the substantial Boule desk, gesturing to Rudy to take a seat opposite in the only other chair in the room, as Radley hovered unobtrusively, notebook at the ready, just inside the door from the library. "So, Mr. Day," began the inspector. He surveyed the other. Fiftyish, he gauged, with a tall frame, slim yet muscular, with a head of thick dark hair in a modern youthful style, although turning grey at the temples. "You told us that you are the co-owner of the Institute."

"That's right."

"And forgive me ... the accent. American?"

"Canadian."

"I see Now, there have been several mentions of this establishment as 'the Institute'. So help me out here. What kind of institute are we talking about?"

"It was Castor's brainchild," said Rudy. "Sorry – that's Mr. Spelman."

"Castor, sir?" queried Radley, pen poised. "What, like the oil?"

"I think he preferred to think of it as like one of the Heavenly Twins, sergeant," replied Rudy, with the faintest hint of amusement in his tone. "But spelt the same, if you were wondering."

"Thank you, sir."

"And, the Institute?" said Copper, returning to his

enquiry.

Rudy took a breath. "Motivational courses, inspector. Castor had this theory that it didn't matter what your job was. You could be a trash collector or a nuclear scientist, but whatever it was, you could train your way of thinking and expand your mind, so that you could do that job the best way it could ever be done."

"Expanding the mind, sir," remarked Radley. "That's what it said on that sign we passed on the way in."

"So it did," agreed Copper. "So tell me, sir, how did this expansion take place?"

For the first time, there was a hint of evasiveness in Rudy's manner. "Oh, Castor had devised all sorts of techniques. Some of them were mental and some of them were physical. Some involved solitary meditation, I believe, and then there was some communal stuff. But, to be honest, ..." A slightly embarrassed-sounding half-laugh. "... I didn't really understand much of it."

"And yet," said Copper, puzzled, "you say you're a co-owner in the business. Because I assume this would be some kind of a business. From what little I know of such motivational schemes, they don't run themselves. And they're not usually operated as a charity. I've heard of some eye-watering fees being charged by people who just come and give a company's managers an hour's talk."

Again, there was a touch of evasiveness. "I'm not really the person to talk to in detail about all that," said Rudy. "I just put some money up at the start."

"Which would have been when, sir?"

Rudy paused in thought. "Maybe about ten years ago. And Castor found this place and bought it to set things up. Apparently it had been sitting here empty for years. But it was his baby. I'm not based here."

"No?"

"Oh no. A lot of the time these days I'm in Toronto.

That's my home originally. I'm in property. And that's where Castor and I first met."

"And can I ask how you met, sir? Just to get some idea of background, you understand."

Rudy seemed slightly nonplussed by the question. "Um ... introduced by a friend of a friend, I think." A weak smile. "You know how it is, inspector. But anyway," he hurried on, "after a while he explained this idea he'd had, and we put the money together for him to set up the Institute in this place. He moved back over, and I'm over here ..." Rudy searched for the words. "... from time to time. But I've never been hands-on. Much more of a sleeping partner." Rudy stopped short.

There was a long pause. "And when you say that, Mr. Day," said Copper eventually, "can I ask exactly what you mean?"

"Just what I say," replied Rudy. "Business." He clamped his lips firmly together.

Copper reflected for a moment. "Of course. So, in the context of this ... business, can I ask you if you are aware of anyone who might wish your partner harm?"

Rudy gave a shrug. "No."

"Including yourself?"

"Not at all. Why should I? Or anyone else?" Rudy looked calmly at the inspector.

"Well, I can think of a number of possibilities," returned Copper sharply. "A former employee with some sort of a grudge? Perhaps a former client of the Institute who felt that it hadn't lived up to its promises? Someone who might have felt threatened by embarrassing secrets which Mr. Spelman might have learnt in the course of some of the activities here? The plain fact is," he concluded with a touch of asperity, "that somebody wished Mr. Spelman ill, with the result that he is now lying dead in your grounds. And with or without your help, Mr. Day ..." A penetrating look. "... I intend to find out who."

*

"Did we detect a bit of wriggling on the hook, boss?" remarked Pete Radley, as the room's other door, leading out into the manor's entrance hall, closed behind Rudy, after he had been given strict instructions not to leave the premises.

"I think we did," agreed Dave Copper. "Although I'm not certain as yet as to precisely why."

"D'you know what I reckon?" said Radley. "I think our Mr. Day sort of let the cat out of the bag when he told us about being the sleeping partner in the business."

"You mean it wasn't just the business aspect in which he was Mr. Spelman's sleeping partner? Yes, I thought that came through fairly clearly," said Copper. "Not that their personal relationship necessarily has anything to do with anything. But I got a sniff of something else. For a start, it struck me that he ought to have been a little more astonished at Mr. Spelman's death. Irrespective of their relationship, I would have thought that he might have been somewhat more aghast at the fact that someone could wish Spelman ill."

"Well, we've got plenty of people to ask about that, boss," pointed out Radley. "Do you want me to get the next one in?"

"Do that."

"What about the woman with the red hair? If what was said earlier between her and Mr. Day is anything to go by, it sounds as if there wasn't too much love lost between those two. So maybe a different angle on things?"

"Excellent thinking. Let's have her in."

Charlotte-Anne Connor took the seat recently vacated by Rudy with an assurance that indicated that she was not feeling at all intimidated at the prospect of being questioned. Her whole attitude exuded confidence.

Copper estimated her to be around forty, with deep green cat-like eyes, smooth unlined features with just a subtle hint of make-up, and wearing an almost severe business suit in black with a white blouse, adorned only with a slim gold chain around her neck. The most startling aspect of her appearance was her flaming red hair, cut short in a feathered style which framed her face. She gazed at Copper expectantly. "So?"

The inspector was likewise not to be put off by the other's attitude. "So, Miss Connor ... it is 'miss', is it?"

"I prefer 'Ms.'," replied Charlotte-Anne in her unexpectedly deep voice. "But it really couldn't matter less. I'm sure you have far more important questions to ask me than that, inspector."

Copper was determined to remain unruffled. "Indeed, Ms. Connor. But first, let me express my condolences at the death of Mr. Spelman. You described yourself as his personal assistant, I believe. His second-in-command. So I imagine you must have been close."

"We worked closely together in certain ways, inspector, if that's what you mean," said Charlotte-Anne. "But if you're implying closeness in any other way, I'm afraid you're mistaken."

"You're saying that you and Mr. Spelman were not close in a personal way?"

"No," replied Charlotte-Anne. "If you were to think that, you would certainly be barking up the wrong tree."

"I see." Copper exchanged a brief glance with Radley, before continuing. "Then let's explore the nature of your working relationship with Mr. Spelman. How exactly did that function?"

Charlotte-Anne appeared to relax a little. "I suppose 'division of responsibilities' would best describe it, inspector. Castor more or less left all the administrative side of the Institute to me, while he was totally involved with the motivational aspects."

"Matters temporal and spiritual, as you might say," remarked Copper.

"I suppose so," agreed Charlotte-Anne. A slightly emotional expression crossed her face. "He really is ... was ... a very inspirational speaker."

"So, tell me more about this division of responsibilities. How did that work, precisely?"

"Castor devised all the courses," explained Charlotte-Anne. "He would give seminars to the group on how to maximise your feelings of self-worth. He devised a programme of individual assessments for the participants, so that he could tune into their personal spiritual needs and discover how their psyches could be nurtured. His theory was that a soul could be made to flower."

"Does that mean he had some sort of training or background as a psychologist?" enquired Copper, slightly bemused by the barrage of jargon.

"Not that I know of," replied Charlotte-Anne. "Castor explained that, with him, everything was instinctive. He knew he could tune into people's needs and set them on the right path for them. And he would tell them that their own personal flowers would burst from within."

"Ah," said Copper, managing not to roll his eyes. "But I gather that you did not involve yourself in these aspects of his work. So what was your rôle?"

"The organisation, inspector. I would place advertisements describing our work in the appropriate journals or on the net, and then liaise with those who replied in order to schedule them into our programme of courses at the Institute."

Pieces of the jigsaw clicked into place for the inspector. "And I assume that these courses are residential, which would account for the relatively large number of people present on the premises."

"That's correct. Each of our Seekers ... Castor called them Seekers after Self-Truth, you see ... is accommodated here at the manor, so that needs to be arranged."

"And would I be right in imagining that you might also be involved with the financial side of such matters? Your participants pay fees, no doubt."

"That's certainly part of my work, inspector," said Charlotte-Anne. "I handle all the financial affairs of the Institute. I have a background in accounting."

"Mr. Day plays no part?" queried Copper. "I gather he is a businessman as well as being financially concerned with the original establishment of the Institute. Does he not become involved at all?"

"He's scarcely here," retorted Charlotte-Anne somewhat waspishly. "And anyway, I think his interest level was always considerably lower than Castor's."

Copper registered the implication of hostility, but elected to ignore it for the moment. "So coming back to this division of responsibilities between yourself and Mr. Spelman, did that work out well?"

"Perfectly satisfactorily."

"There were no causes of friction between you?"

"None at all," declared Charlotte-Anne. "We each stuck to our own areas of activity, so everyone was happy. Why do you ask?"

"Because plainly," responded Copper, "somebody was not happy. Indeed, somebody was sufficiently unhappy with Mr. Spelman to bring about his death."

"With an arrow, Denise said." Charlotte-Anne sounded surprised.

"Denise being who? One of these 'seekers' of yours?"

Charlotte-Anne gave a contemptuous half-smile. "Lord, no. She's one of the staff. She's our fitness instructor."

"Fitness instructor?" Copper evinced surprise. "How does that fit in with all this psychological ..." The inspector just stopped himself in time from uttering something pejorative. "... thinking that seems to be prevalent?"

"According to Castor, it's all one and the same thing. *'Mens sana in corpore sano'* was one of his precepts. The power of the mind encompasses everything."

"Good to know," remarked Copper, half under his breath. "So, Denise is ...?"

"Denise Benz. She was the one who found Castor when she was out this morning. And she told us when she got back to the manor after calling the police. She said it was horrible." For the first time, a crack appeared in Charlotte-Anne's shell of self-assurance, and her voice seemed to tremble.

"Indeed," said Copper. "So you will understand why we need to ask how matters stood between Mr. Spelman and anyone else who might have had the opportunity to harm him."

Charlotte-Anne shook her head as if bewildered. "I can't think of anyone. Except ..."

"Except what?"

"Except ... except that it must have been one of the group. The people at the manor, I mean."

"And this would be because ...?"

"Because the estate is sealed shut at night. The front gates are locked after dinner. And Castor was fine then."

"Would that have been the last time you saw him?"

Charlotte-Anne nodded. "The last time all of us saw him. We all have dinner together in the Great Hall, you see – it's part of Castor's theory about developing a group ethos. But after that, everyone is free to do whatever they want."

"Including, Ms. Connor," observed Copper, "carrying out a murder." Charlotte-Anne seemed shocked at his blunt speaking. The inspector stood. "Well, I'll keep you no longer for the moment. But I dare say we shall need to speak again. In the meantime, I'd be grateful if you would remain within the manor." A nod to Radley, who ushered the interviewee out of the room and into the entrance hall.

Chapter 3

"She's got a bit of an edge to her, hasn't she?" remarked Pete Radley. "And about as much of a fan of our Mr. Day as he is of her, by the sound of it."

"As you say," nodded Dave Copper. "But as yet, no hostility in the direction of Mr. Spelman, which is really what we're on the trail of."

"And what do you reckon to all this airy-fairy New Age gibberish about 'seekers' and the power of the mind, boss? All this 'mens' whatever-it-was – which I never got to write down."

"'*Mens sana in corpore sano*'," quoted Copper. "It's Latin for 'a healthy mind in a healthy body', apparently. It's what Una says to me every time she drags me off to the gym when I'm not really in the mood to do anything other than collapse in front of the TV with a pizza. But let's get away from all this philosophical business and get back down to practicalities. We have a roomful of people next door, and I need some facts."

"So who's next, then, boss?" asked Radley.

"Well, since we've been talking about healthy bodies, we'd better start with the fitness instructor, since she's the woman who found our extremely dead body," said Copper. "I'm interested to know how that came about. So, let's have this Benz woman in and see what she has to tell us."

Denise Benz advanced briskly into the room and, somewhat to the surprise of the detectives, shook hands firmly with Radley, and then Copper, before seating herself. In her thirties and with neat blonde bobbed hair, tall and slimly-built but with a strong grip, and clad in a one-piece lycra body-suit and trainers, her movements were fluid and confident. "Good morning, inspector. You of course have questions for me, I think." The statement was made in a noticeably Teutonic accent.

After a momentary pause, Copper leaned forward. "Your name is Denise Benz?"

"Yes."

"Miss?"

A faintly derisive smile. "Of course."

"And would I be right in guessing that you're a German national?"

"That is correct."

"And you work here at Holt Manor."

"Yes."

'Lordy,' thought Copper to himself. 'This is like pulling teeth. This could take forever.' He took a deep breath and switched on what he hoped was an encouraging smile. "Perhaps you'd like to give me a little background. I've been told you're a fitness instructor. So how exactly does that fit in with what you do here?"

"This was all part of the theory of the Director."

"The Director?" interrupted Copper.

"Yes. Mr. Spelman. That is what he wished to be called. He said that you can not have positive thought processes if the body is sluggish, so there must be activity of the body as well as of the mind. He was very strict about this. So I am employed to devise a regime to bring this about. There is yoga. There are exercise sessions. And some sports. Because some of the women who come here are too ..." Denise seemed to be searching for the right word. "I could say that they do not impress me."

"I see. Now, I gather from the officer who first attended, that you were the person who discovered Mr. Spelman's body. Can you tell me how that came about?"

"Of course." Denise drew a breath. "I have a routine. Each morning my alarm wakes me at half seven."

"Sorry, miss, but can I just double-check that?" broke in Radley, looking up from his notes. "Timings might be important. You say you got up at half past seven?"

"Ah. No. This is a thing I still always say wrong," confessed Denise, looking embarrassed. "Because in German, we say *halb sieben*, which is 'half seven', but it means thirty minutes **to** the hour, not thirty minutes past. So *halb sieben* is what you would call half past six."

"Oh. Right. Glad I asked," said Radley, crossing out his offending note with a touch of irritation.

"So your alarm went off at six-thirty," confirmed Copper. "And then ...?"

"Then I did my stretches, put on my running clothes, and went out for my morning run. Just like I do every day. And I always go the same way. Out round along the line of the wall of the park until I get right down to the bottom, and then I come up the little valley, through what they call the holt, and back to the manor for my shower before breakfast. About forty-five minutes usually."

"Except, of course, that on this occasion, it was anything but usual," said Copper. "Can you tell us exactly what happened?"

"All was normal when I came up the valley and entered the holt. But when I came to the space where there is the big oak, I could see a man lying there. And I looked closer, and I saw that it was Mr. Spelman, and that he had been shot with an arrow. And that was a big shock."

"Naturally," sympathised Copper. "So what did you do?"

"I looked more close to see if he was still alive," continued Denise, "but I could see he wasn't. But I checked anyway for a pulse. I have first-aid training," she added. "It is part of my qualification in Germany as a fitness instructor. But it was clear he was dead, and because I had my watch on, I was able to telephone the police immediately." In response to Copper's enquiring look, she held up her wrist. "My watch is also like a handy - what you call in English a mobile - it has a telephone built into it," she explained. "It is a very good watch. From Germany."

"And you were alone at that point? There was no sign of anyone else?"

"Not that I could see. Everything was completely still."

"And apart from checking to see whether Mr. Spelman had a pulse, did you touch anything else?" asked Copper.

"No, nothing," Denise assured him. "Not even the arrow."

"I'm glad to hear it." Something in Denise's tone alerted the inspector. "But why the arrow in particular?"

"Because," said Denise, "except for the finding of the Director dead, it was the biggest shock of all. Because it is my arrow."

A moment of astonished silence followed her words, before Copper recovered himself, a sudden harder edge to his voice. "Your arrow? Explain, please."

"I make archery lessons as one of my sport activities, inspector. I was a junior champion when I was in school. So I have the bows and arrows as part of my equipment."

"Archery?" Copper sounded puzzled. "What on earth has that to do with expanding the mind, or whatever this Institute seems to be all about?"

"It is for the hand-eye co-ordination," said Denise. "For Castor, it was important that the hands and the eyes should be in tune with either other, for the making of a serious activity of the brain." It was noticeable that, as Denise became slightly flustered, the fluency of her English waned.

"And where is this equipment kept, Miss Benz?" demanded Copper. "Is it under your supervision?"

"No, inspector," confessed Denise. "It is under the stairs. In a storeroom at the back of the house, near to the door to the gardens."

"So anybody might have access?"

"Yes."

Copper sighed. "That," he stated, "could be extremely unhelpful. However," he continued after a pause, "let's resume by following what you did after you discovered the body."

"Nothing," replied Denise simply. "After I telephoned the police, I came back up to the manor, and there I found everyone gathered in the Great Hall for breakfast. So I told what had happened, and I had to stop them all going to see for themselves, because your police had told me to let nobody go near the body, so I ordered everybody to remain, and it was only few minutes afterwards that the car came with the officers. And we were all told to wait in the library."

*

"That one's a bit formidable, isn't she, boss?" remarked Pete Radley.

"Hmmm," responded Dave Copper, unwilling to comment further.

"But at least that explains the arrow."

"To an extent," agreed the inspector. "But not how it came there, or why. I mean, we have no inkling as yet as to why this Spelman chap was wandering about in the grounds, evidently sometime between dinner last night and breakfast this morning, barefoot and in his nightshirt, or whatever that robe thing turns out to be. And did it mean that somebody knew he was going to be there? Had he arranged to meet somebody? And were they, for whatever reason, lurking in the undergrowth, bow and arrow at the ready, with the intention of shooting him? And where's their motive? Nothing makes sense yet."

"It does seem a funny set-up, boss."

"So the only thing that's likely to clarify matters is to keep going with these interviews. I want to know more about how this place operates."

"There must be more staff," pointed out Radley. "I don't reckon the three we've seen so far could have been running the place on their own. Specially not with the partner off in Canada half the time, according to him."

"Good thought. Nip out and see who you can find."

"Will do, boss." Radley exited into the library, and his voice could be heard making the enquiry. After a few moments of low-voiced exchanges, he re-entered, ushering a young woman. "This is Miss Pine, sir," announced the sergeant, as the woman hesitantly took the seat facing Copper across the desk.

The new arrival could hardly have presented a greater contrast to her predecessor. She was short and almost scrawny, with a shoulder-length muddle of mousey brown hair with a straggly fringe, pinched features, and a dun-coloured cardigan which she clutched around her as she gazed timidly up at Copper through round wire-framed glasses. It was hard to guess her age – perhaps thirty, estimated Copper, although her style was that of a woman much older.

The inspector formed the immediate impression that, with one misplaced word, the interviewee might easily take flight, and he adopted what he hoped was a reasonable facsimile of his former superior's avuncular approach. After all, he had seen it work very well in the past. "Miss Pine," he began, with a friendly smile. "Am I right in gathering that you work here at Holt Manor?"

"Yes." The voice was high-pitched and thin.

"Good. And as you'll probably remember from earlier, my name is Detective Inspector Copper, and I'm investigating the unfortunate death of Mr. Spelman. So I'd like to ask you a few questions. If you feel up to answering them."

"I ... yes, of course, inspector."

"Good. So can we start with your full name, just so that my sergeant here can make a note of it?"

"Yes, it's Sue Pine ... well, Susan, really."

"And you're employed here at the Institute. In what capacity, can I ask?"

"I'm ... I was Mr. Spelman's secretary."

"I see." Copper thought for a moment. "Now, when we were speaking to Ms. Connor earlier, she described herself as Mr. Spelman's personal assistant. So how does this dovetail with you being his secretary? Does that mean that you worked for the pair of them?"

A slight sniff. "I suppose you could say that, yes. Of course, Castor ... Mr. Spelman, I mean ... he was very much the guiding spirit. He was a genius. There was nobody like him. And I can't think how on earth to carry on without ..." Sue tailed off, and pulled a scrap of tissue from her sleeve to wipe her eyes.

"You must have been very close," said Copper, his tone sympathetic.

"We were," snivelled Sue. "I mean, I had to be close to his way of thinking to carry out the work I did for him." The ghost of a tremulous smile. "Castor wasn't always the most organised person. I mean, he was brilliant at what he did, but he needed me to turn his thoughts into manageable material. Sometimes he would walk about here in the study, talking to himself and turning ideas over in his mind, and it was up to me to try and jot them down as he was speaking. Or sometimes I would come down to his desk to find it covered with scraps of paper where he'd woken up in the night with some sort of revelation and then come down to scrawl some notes, and I would try to make sense of his awful handwriting. Or he'd get me to look up things in the old books in the library, so I had to go through everything and make a catalogue. There's a copy next door, in case the Seekers ever want to look something up. But I was the one Castor relied on to turn all the material into scripts for the talks and seminars he gave. And then, of course, there were the other things ..." She broke off.

"Other things?" queried Copper.

"I mean the work I had to do for Charlotte-Anne," said Sue swiftly.

"Ah yes. She told us that she was much more involved with the administrative side of things."

"Well, if that's what she said ...," replied Sue, a hint of bitterness in her voice. "I mean, she should have been responsible for all the organising of the arrangements for the guests who come to the manor, but her part in that was mostly barking orders in my direction to book the advertising and to process the applications and to write to the guests and organise schedules and everything like that. I did all the real work, while she just concerned herself with making sure we got the fees. And she kept that very much to herself."

"Would I be right in gathering that you were not such an admirer of Ms. Connor's?" suggested Copper gently.

Sue's voice, which had strengthened during her remarks about Charlotte-Anne, reverted to its former reedy whine. "No ... I mean yes," she said. "Charlotte-Anne is alright, I suppose."

"But you were more of a fan of Mr. Spelman?"

"I suppose so, yes."

Copper reflected for a moment. "And how would you say things stood between those two? Personally?"

"Oh no, it was nothing like that," said Sue hastily. "No, they weren't involved at all. And anyway, Rudy was ..." She stopped abruptly.

"That wasn't exactly what I meant," said Copper. "I'm not enquiring about any romantic entanglements.

That is, unless they would have some bearing on Mr. Spelman's murder."

"Oh, I'm sure they wouldn't," insisted Sue.

"But what I was looking to find out," continued the inspector, "was in fact the reverse. Any causes of conflict between Mr. Spelman and Ms. Connor, or between him and anyone else for that matter, which might lead someone to wish him harm. Now, working closely with him as it appears you did, surely you would be the first person to become aware of any such thing."

Sue shook her head helplessly. "I can't think why anyone would want to hurt Castor. Everyone admired him so much, and he was so charming and inspirational and kind. There wasn't anything that you wouldn't do for him." She appeared to be blinking back tears.

"He seems to have had a very powerful personality," remarked Copper. "And powerful personalities don't always go down well with everyone they come into contact with. However, if you can't think of anyone who might have clashed with him in any way ..." He paused to allow Sue to comment, but when it became obvious that she had nothing further to say, he resumed. "Let's move on to more practical matters. When would have been the last time you saw Mr. Spelman?"

"Last night at dinner," replied Sue, "along with everyone else."

"Now that's the second time that dinner last night has been mentioned. Ms. Connor referred to it as well. So can you tell me please, what are the catering arrangements here at the manor? Is there a cook?"

"Oh no. This was another one of Castor's rules. He had a theory that the more everyone contributed to a communal effort, the better their spiritual connections developed, and so their understanding of the world and their fellow-humans blossomed. And this would lead them to becoming more fulfilled in whatever rôle they occupied. And so meals were always prepared by everyone together as a joint effort – staff and guests."

"Even if some of you were atrocious cooks?" enquired the inspector with a smile. "How did that work out?"

"Castor said that everyone had some sort of skill they could bring to the table," stated Sue primly, unconscious of any pun in her choice of words. "Meals are always very nourishing."

"And I suppose," hazarded Copper, desperately trying to keep any hint of judgement out of his voice, "you might all be on some sort of vegetarian regime?"

For the first time, Sue laughed. "Oh goodness no, inspector. Whatever gave you that idea? We cater for all diets. Castor wasn't some sort of weird fanatic, you know." Copper wisely chose to remain silent. "No, all the food is quite a normal selection of ordinary things. Except for the alcohol, of course."

"And which alcohol was that?"

"That's just it, inspector. There isn't any. Castor's opinion was that alcohol inhibited the clear workings of the mind ..."

"He's not wrong there," muttered Radley in the background.

"... and so there is never any on the premises. Castor was absolutely adamant about that. It's the same with tea and coffee."

"That's a blow," murmured the sergeant. "I could murder a cuppa." He fell silent in response to a stern glare from his superior.

"No, we all just drink herbal infusions," continued Sue. "I have camomile and honey, because it's said to be calming, but everyone has their own favourites. Castor had his own special mixture, which he never allowed anyone else to touch. Too precious, he said – it was designed to clarify his mind."

Copper's eyebrows rose, but he declined to comment. "So, coming back to yesterday's evening meal, you all prepared it together, and then you all ate together? Am I right?"

"Yes, inspector."

"And then what? Was there some sort of communal activity?"

"Oh no. Not last night. That was ... I mean, after dinner, we usually all go our own ways. Some people stay and chat. Some just go back to their own rooms."

"And you?"

"That's what I did, inspector."

"You didn't see Mr. Spelman again?"

"No. I went to my room and read for a while, and then I went to bed. And this morning, we were all gathering together in the Great Hall to prepare for breakfast, when Denise came in to tell us the awful news." Her voice wavered, and her hand with the tissue went back up to wipe her eyes. "And everyone was so shocked."

"I imagine they were," said Copper. "Well, I can see that you're upset, and if that's all you can tell us, I think we can let you go for the time being. Of course, I may wish to speak to you again later, so please remain within the manor."

"Of course, inspector. Where else would I go?"

Chapter 4

As the door to the hall closed behind Sue, Dave Copper let out a gusty sigh, leaned back in his chair, and stretched. "Four down, and goodness how many to go. Are you sure the numbers next door are actually coming down, sergeant? Or is it like that old silent movie joke where people are going out of one door and coming back in through another?"

"I don't think it's quite that bad, boss," grinned Pete Radley. "And I've got plenty of pages left in my notebook, so as long as my pen holds out, we'll be fine."

"Are you getting any sort of inkling as to what's going on around here? Because I have to confess, I'm not, so far."

Radley shrugged. "Not really. I mean, obviously there are some tensions, but nothing pointing in the direction of our murder victim. It seems he was a mixture of a visionary, a disciplinarian, and a saint."

"Yes, well, saints have been known to make enemies," observed Copper. He sat upright. "So, let's plough on and see if we can identify any."

"The good news, boss, is that there's just one member of staff to speak to, before we start getting into these so-called 'seekers'."

"Then fetch her in."

The smiling young woman who took her place across the desk was petite, with elfin features and short dark hair in a pixie cut. Her bright eyes sparkled with an alert expression. "Good morning, inspector. My name's Anna Logue, I'm twenty-three, and I stay here at the manor," she volunteered in a soft Scottish accent. "What can I do to help you?"

"Thank you for that, Miss Logue," replied the inspector, faintly amused at the other's ready willingness to assist. "Always good to have the basics. Although …

you say 'stay'. I thought you were a member of the staff rather than a guest."

Anna laughed. "Sorry, inspector. That's the Scot in me speaking. Where I come from, we say 'stay' where the English would say 'live'. Sorry to be confusing. But you were right the first time. I am staff, and I do live in. All of us staff do. I'm in the stables with Denise and some of the guests, and everyone else has rooms in the main house."

"Ah. Good. Thanks for the clarification. So can you tell us how you fit into the scheme of things here?"

"I'm I.T., inspector. Castor calls me 'The It Girl'." The smile faded. "That is, he used to."

"It sounds as if you and Mr. Spelman were on friendly terms," remarked Copper. "Did you work closely with him?"

"Oh, very. Closer than most, probably."

"So what is the nature of this I.T., Miss Logue?"

"Call me Anna, please. 'Miss Logue' sounds like my big sister Laura. She's a teacher, and very strict – not a bit like me." A soft giggle.

Copper began to warm to the latest interviewee. "Very well. Anna it is. So can you explain the job you were doing for Mr. Spelman? We've already been told that he had a personal assistant as well as a secretary. So I'm assuming that I.T. means some sort of computer work, but I don't see how this would differ from the jobs that the other two ladies would be doing."

"Oh, it's quite different, and quite separate, inspector. You see, Castor produced assessments of each of the individuals who came here, and because these were highly confidential, they had to be kept away from all the other everyday workings of the Institute. Not that he didn't trust Sue and Charlotte-Anne, of course. It's just that he said that certain information was sensitive, and it had to be kept restricted."

"But I still don't quite see ..."

"The thing was, Castor knew that there were loads of people who didn't believe in what he was doing. Scoffers, if you like. And there had been some, journalists mostly, who had tried to infiltrate the Institute by booking in for courses so that they could expose his secrets, as they would probably have put it. He'd even had attempts to hack into the place's original computers. So Castor employed me to set up an entirely separate system, not only to keep his client records secure, but also to carry out research into applicants before they even got accepted for attendance here. To make sure they were genuine."

"Wouldn't that amount to prying into people's private lives?" Copper sounded uneasy.

"Not really, inspector," Anna reassured him. "Castor felt he needed to know as much as possible about all his 'seekers', as he called them, so he could tailor what he did for them individually and help them find themselves. He needed to know their pasts. And everything was completely safe. It was all behind multiple firewalls, and only Castor and I had access through the passwords."

"Hmmm," mused Copper. "I hope your guests were reassured by that. If they knew, that is."

"I couldn't say, inspector. That would have been private between them and Castor."

"Right." Copper sat for a few moments, digesting the information, before starting off on a new tack. "So let's talk about yesterday. As far as I've been told, Mr. Spelman was last seen by everyone when you all dined together last night. The company then appears to have dispersed. And the next time we see Mr. Spelman is some time after seven o'clock this morning, when he is discovered dead in the manor's grounds. And I have a dozen people who could all have had access to the murder scene at some time during the night."

"Actually, that may not be quite true, inspector," stated Anna, to Copper's surprise. "I might be able to help you there."

"Indeed? How so?"

"Because of the accommodation arrangements. Like I said, there aren't enough rooms in the manor itself for everyone. Only seven, actually. Obviously, Castor had his own suite, and there are also the rooms used by Charlotte-Anne, Sue, and Rudy."

"Rudy didn't share with Mr. Spelman, then?" enquired Copper delicately.

"Er ... no. I think they used to but ..." Anna shrugged. "I don't know. Not my business. Anyway, that left three guest rooms. Everyone else is in what used to be the stables. I have a room there, next to the office where my computer is, and Denise's room is next to her fitness room, and then there are four more rooms for the guests."

"And what about the other offices? Where do Charlotte-Anne Connor and Sue Pine work?"

"Oh, they don't have offices of their own. They just use their own rooms."

"This is all good to know, Anna," said the inspector, "but I don't see how it helps me in considering who might have had the opportunity to kill Mr. Spelman."

"That," declared Anna triumphantly, "is because you don't know about my CCTV!"

"And what CCTV would that be?" wondered Copper, intrigued.

"It was all because of Castor's worries about someone from outside the Institute getting access to my confidential material," explained Anna. "So he got me to install a secret camera at the entrance to the stables, focussed on the corridor outside my door, so that we could see if anyone attempted to get access."

"And how does this help?"

"Because it runs 24/7," said Anna. "So if I check it, I can tell you when people returned to their rooms last night, and whether any of them left, and at what time."

Copper was delighted. "Anna," he said, "that is excellent. If what you say is right, this could be a very useful way of starting to rule some people out of consideration."

"Or of giving us a shortcut to identifying our murderer, boss," pointed out Radley. "If somebody turns out to have been prowling about in the middle of the night, you're going to be asking them some very pointed questions as to why."

"I am indeed," agreed Copper. He got to his feet. "So, Anna, can you take us to this computer room of yours?"

"Of course."

Anna led the detectives out of the study, through the Great Hall, and into a spacious and lofty medieval kitchen with a gigantic stone open fireplace, within which huddled an incongruous bright red enamelled range which looked to have been installed in the 1930s. A passage led to a heavy oak nail-studded door, which gave on to a cobbled stable yard, with a short covered way between the kitchen's back door and the entrance to the former stable block. Inside, the block had obviously been totally remodelled, with a central corridor with doors leading off it on both sides.

"And that's my camera." Anna pointed to a small device, scarcely visible as it nestled high in the junction of two dark timber beams. "My room's there," she said, indicating the first door on the left, "and my office is here." She punched a code into the lock of the second door, and led the detectives into a small room whose only furnishings consisted of a chair and a desk, on which sat a large desktop computer with its keyboard and monitor. Seating herself, she began clicking keys, and soon an image of the corridor appeared on the screen, with the current time shown in a lower corner. "So, when do you wish to see, inspector?"

"From the end of dinner-time last night, I suppose. Which would have been when?"

"Around ten o'clock, usually." More clicks, and a fresh time signature appeared. "There. Twenty-two hundred hours. So now we can watch the recording go forward."

"This is going to take forever if we have to watch a whole nights-worth, boss," groaned Radley.

Anna laughed. "Don't worry, sergeant. I can fast-forward it. See." Click. The time signature advanced much more rapidly.

"Hold it!" said Copper suddenly. "That's someone. Can you slow it back down?"

"Of course. There." The recording resumed normal speed. "So, this is just people coming to their rooms to go to bed. Just let me speed it up a little." Click. "That's Mrs. Cord there – she's one of the guests. And look – Mrs. Peel and Miss Barnes have come in together. Gossiping as always, by the look of it. Oh, there's me. And then you've got Denise not far behind me ... and finally Mrs. Icke. So that's everyone in and accounted for. And look, all by just after half-past ten."

"So can you now fast-forward it again," requested the inspector. "So that we can see if anyone left during the night."

The time signature rolled rapidly on with no trace of any movement on the screen, until finally Radley, gazing intently, abruptly yelled 'Stop!'. "There!" he declared. "There's someone. Can you wind it back?" Anna reversed the flow, and a figure appeared walking backwards into the shot. "Look at that, boss," said Pete. "We've got her!"

Copper smiled. "Sorry to burst your balloon,

sergeant, but you ought to take a look at the time on the screen." Radley looked closer, and groaned. "That's right," said the inspector. "Six thirty-nine a.m., and that is Denise Benz on her way out for her morning run."

*

"I'm rather pleased with that result," murmured Dave Copper to his junior colleague, as the two detectives followed Anna through the back door and into the manor house. "That's six potential suspects removed at a stroke. If they didn't leave their rooms during the night, there's no way they could have killed Castor Spelman."

"Unless," pointed out Pete Radley, "Denise Benz herself was the one who did it. Arranged to meet him at this famous oak tree with the aim of killing him, and then rushed back here with the dreadful news of her shocking discovery. How many times have you told me that the first person to find a dead body is very often the last one to see them alive?"

"Valid point, sergeant. But we'll soon know if there's any mileage in that from the post-mortem report. They should be able to give us a pretty good estimate of time of death."

As the group passed through the kitchen, Radley's eyes fell on a kettle simmering on the hob of the range. He gazed at it longingly. "You know, boss, I'm still gagging for a cuppa."

"Shame there's no such thing as tea in the house," replied Copper. "Only these strange infusions Sue Pine mentioned."

Anna, overhearing, turned with a twinkle in her eye. "You shouldn't believe everything you hear, inspector," she smiled.

"I seldom do," replied Copper. "How do you mean?"

"I mean, if you want or, as Sergeant Radley seems to, need a cup of tea, I might be able to do something about that."

"How come?"

"We haven't all drunk Castor's Cool Aid," said Anna. "Some of us have secrets. In my case, it's the fact that my dad Robert sends me food parcels. I mentioned to him that Castor wouldn't have tea in the place, so he lets me have a secret supply of proper Scottish tea bags, together with my favourite teacakes. I've got a wee kettle in my room so's I can have surreptitious tea parties. You're welcome to come and have a cup if you'd like, sergeant. You too, inspector."

Radley's face broke into an expansive grin. "Anna, you're a life-saver." He looked anxiously at Copper. "Could we do that, boss?"

Copper chuckled. "I don't see why not. A sergeant dying of thirst is no good to me. But we'd better be quick. The others cooling their heels in the library may be starting to get restive."

"Oh, you leave them to me," said Anna. "I can handle them. Wait here a minute." She disappeared swiftly through the door to the Great Hall, returning only a few moments later. "I've told them all that you've been delayed because something very important has come up, but you'll be back shortly, and they're all to stay put until you do. And your constable said that would be fine."

"Well done, Anna," smiled Copper. "Very resourceful."

"I've had another thought, inspector," said the young woman. "You know about the people in the stables. Would it be useful if I gave you a guided tour of the rooms upstairs? Who is where, that sort of thing?"

"That is very good thinking, Anna. I could do with more people like you on my team," remarked Copper approvingly. "Right, after you."

Instead of heading out into the hall and making for the main staircase as expected, Anna made her way to a small unpretentious door in the corner of the kitchen, which she opened to reveal a tiny twisting staircase. "Servants' stairs," she explained. "Shortcut up to the first floor." The detectives followed her, and the three emerged through another discreet door in the panelling to find themselves upstairs.

"So these would be the rooms occupied by the rest of the staff members and guests?" enquired Copper, surveying the corridor which opened to left and right.

"That's right."

"In which case, you'd better note these down, sergeant."

"Will do, boss."

"That's Sue's room just opposite," pointed out Anna, "and Charlotte-Anne's is next to it on the right. The loo's at the end, for the rooms that haven't got an en-suite bathroom. Then there's Castor's room here on the left, and next to it you've got what used to be Rudy's room, except that Mrs. Van der Voor has got it at the moment."

"Hang on," interrupted Radley. "I'm writing."

" And next to her, there's Miss Wakes, and then there's Mademoiselle de Roque ..."

"De what?" enquired Radley, scribbling frantically. "Sounds exotic."

"R..O..Q..U..E, sergeant. It's French," explained Anna. "At least, that's what she says. I'm not so sure."

"Intriguing," said Copper. "I look forward to meeting her and finding out."

"And finally," concluded Anna, "there's the room which Rudy now uses, which is the one right by the top of the main stairs. And that's it."

"Thank you, Anna," said Copper. "That could all be very helpful. Now ..." Looking at his watch. "About this tea ..."

"And I suppose there's no chance of one of those teacakes of yours?" ventured Radley. His eye fell on a bowl of fruit on a small side table halfway along the passage. "And I might nick one of those apples to be going on with."

Anna laughed. "I shouldn't try, sergeant, unless you fancy a very sudden visit to your dentist. They're not real."

"You what?" Radley took a closer look, and picked up one of the apples. "She's right, boss. This weighs a ton. What's it made of?"

Anna smiled. "It's carved onyx, I think. Just ornamental, and very bad for your teeth. You'd better settle for that teacake. Come with me." She vanished down the servants' staircase.

Some minutes later, whistles hastily wetted, the detectives again followed Anna back through the kitchen and into the main house. "I've just had a thought," said Copper suddenly, as they reached the entrance hall. "When we were talking to Miss Benz about the arrow which was found embedded in Mr. Spelman's body, she mentioned that her archery equipment was kept in a storeroom somewhere here. I wonder, could you show us where that is?"

"Of course." A few steps away, Anna threw open a door in the hall panelling and motioned the detectives inside.

To describe the room as a storeroom was to dignify it rather more than it warranted. Certainly, in a neat rack adjacent to the door hung a number of extremely professional-looking bows such as might be seen in international competitions, with their accompanying quivers, each containing a sheaf of arrows. Copper removed one to examine it. "Yes," he observed, "this looks pretty much the twin of the one we saw earlier." He looked around the room, the rest of which appeared to have been used as a dumping-ground for items of any and every sort. There were rickety racks of shelving bearing everything from dusty box files and old electric irons to piles of superannuated crockery and cardboard boxes containing a selection of light bulbs of different types and sizes. There were rolled-up carpets propped against a shabby dolls' house in one corner, while in another a battered old bicycle with no tyres was half-hidden behind a heap of gardening implements and trugs, with a large rusting metal toolbox lying open and spilling its contents on to the floor at the bottom, a pair of grubby old gardening gloves discarded on top of it.

"And, as Miss Benz told us, easily accessible by anyone," remarked Copper, sounding somewhat disgruntled as the three emerged once more into the hall. "Well, that doesn't help to narrow down our search in the slightest."

*

As he spoke, Una Singleton and her colleague Suzanne appeared through the door from the grounds.

"You don't look too happy, David," commented Una. "Things not going well?"

"You know what it's like, love," said Copper. "Still gathering straws, but nowhere near enough to start making bricks yet." A thought struck him. "But there is one straw you can help me with. Have you got any inkling of how long our murder victim may have been dead?"

"That's not really the sort of thing I want to speculate about before we've started on the post-mortem proper," replied Una reluctantly.

"Best guess?" coaxed Copper. "It could be really important."

"Okay," sighed Una. "If you want a ball-park figure, I'd say the man died somewhere between midnight and three in the morning. Would you say that's about right, Sooz?"

"Pretty much, from what we can tell so far," agreed her colleague.

"But don't quote me!" warned Una. "Official estimates once we've got him back to the lab. Which will be quite soon, actually. There doesn't seem to be anything else to find at the scene, despite our best efforts to go over it as closely as we could, so I've called for the van to come and take our dead man away."

"Good," said Copper. "But you're saying that the victim couldn't have died around, say, seven o'clock this morning?"

"Not a chance," affirmed Una.

"Thank you," said Copper with relief. He exchanged a look with Radley. "That's one suspect definitely off the list. Just the six, then."

Chapter 5

"Anna," said Dave Copper, "I don't suppose there would be any possibility that you might let us have sight of those background checks you did for Mr. Spelman on the current batch of visitors to the manor, would there?"

Anna looked doubtful. "I don't know how Castor would have felt about that, inspector."

"Ah, but here's the point, Anna. Or rather, two points. Firstly, Mr. Spelman is never going to know about it, and secondly, there might be some information in your files which could lead us to his killer. Which I imagine he would be in favour of. But you have my word, if there is information in there which turns out to have no bearing on this case, I shall forget it as soon as I've seen it. As long as there are no other implications, of course."

"All right, inspector. I'll see what I can do." Anna turned and headed in the direction of her office.

"You reckon there are some guilty secrets to discover, boss?" asked Pete Radley.

"I'd bet my pension on it," said Copper. "Why else have we got a dead man lying out in the grounds? It's plainly not a spur-of-the-moment piece of violence. There's some planning gone into this. So we've got those good old motives of hatred, jealousy and self-protection to consider. And for my money, self-protection is very often the winner hands-down when something's been planned."

"It sounds as if Spelman and Anna, between the two of them, were in possession of some potentially pretty powerful information," commented Radley.

"Agreed," said Copper. "And now Spelman's dead. Let's hope that doesn't make Anna a target. Well," he said, taking a breath, "let's get on with these interviews. Beginning with the remaining people who are accommodated in the manor itself. If the people sleeping in the stables are out of it, that's got to be our main focus. Who's on that list of yours?"

Radley consulted his notebook. "There's three of them, boss. There's what sounded like Mrs. Vanda Vore, although I couldn't quite catch what Anna said, and then there's a Miss Wakes, and finally this French woman de Roque."

"Then we'll have them in that order," decided Copper. He led the way into the library. "I'm very sorry to have kept you all waiting, ladies," he announced, "but there was an urgent requirement which needed to be attended to immediately. Wasn't there, sergeant?" He ignored the embarrassed throat-clearing from behind him. "But I'd like to press on now, so I'd be grateful if you'd join me in the study, Mrs. ... Vore, is it?"

An elderly woman with white fluffy hair, seated in an upright chair next to the window, rose. Stout but vigorous in her movements despite her apparent advanced age, she stepped briskly towards the detectives. "Actually, inspector, it's Van der Voor, to be more accurate, but I forgive you your mistake." The voice, strong and deep, held a touch of an accent which Copper couldn't immediately place.

"Then if you could join us through here, madam, we'll make a start." Copper held the door open for the woman, and the two seated themselves across the desk from one another, while Radley softly closed the door behind them and stationed himself unobtrusively in the background.

"Mrs. Van der Voor?" began Copper. "That doesn't sound like an English name, madam."

"Very delicately put, inspector," chuckled the other. "And you're right, although not completely. My name is Velma Van der Voor, and I'm half-Dutch, although my mother was English. I was born in the Netherlands, but I went to school in England when my family moved over here when I was young. But later I married a Dutchman, and I live in the Netherlands now."

"And what do you do, may I ask?"

"As a job, you mean?" Velma laughed. "What, at my age? Nothing, inspector. I have my little flat in Amsterdam and my cat, and I'm very happily retired."

"And your husband?"

"He died, inspector. A very long time ago now. All my family are gone. There's just me left." A shadow crossed Velma's face.

Copper nodded. "I see. I'm sorry. But then I'm a little intrigued, Mrs. Van der Voor, as to what brings you to Holt Manor. As I understand it, the courses run by Mr. Spelman at this Institute of his were mainly directed to improving people's lives through some sort of expansion of their consciousness, or some such theory, which enabled them to carry out their jobs in a better way. If you're living a life of retired contentment, as you describe it, on the other side of the Channel, what are you doing participating in the activities at the manor?"

"Yes, I suppose it is a little odd," agreed Velma. "But it was an odd coincidence that brought me here. I happened to see a film on the BBC – we watch the BBC a lot in Holland - about the code-breakers at Bletchley Park during the war, and it stirred up some memories. So I thought it would be interesting to see this old place just once more, for the last time."

Copper looked baffled. "Sorry, Mrs. Van der Voor. You've lost me. What has a film about Bletchley Park got to do with your visit here?"

"Ah." Velma smiled. "You don't know about the manor. Well, I'm not surprised. Very few people did."

"I'm still not getting it, Mrs. Van der Voor," said Copper, a faint edge of exasperation entering his voice. "Do please explain."

"I'm sorry, inspector," replied Velma. "Sometimes,

when you get to my age, you need to take your time. I was born in the same year as your Queen Elizabeth, and ladies of a certain age don't like to be rushed. But I think it's time for some history. You see, although I told you I was born in the Netherlands, and my family moved here a little later, that wasn't quite the whole story. We came to England when I was twelve because my father believed that we needed to. And he was right."

"Just a second," interrupted Copper. "If you were twelve, that would have been in 1938, if my sums are right."

"Correct, inspector. The year before the outbreak of war. My father saw what was coming. And so we moved to England."

"Which explains why you told us you went to school here. Oh, I understand. You mean that Holt Manor was some sort of a school at that time?"

"Not exactly." Velma gave a quiet chuckle. "That came later. No, I went to a perfectly ordinary school near where we lived. And when I left school, the war had started, and I took a job in a factory. We made munitions there. I was rather good at it," she added with pride.

"Fascinating though this may be, Mrs. Van der Voor, I still don't see where we're going."

"A little patience, inspector. We're almost there. Because when I was eighteen, some people came to the factory one day. They knew from the records that I was Dutch, you see, and they asked me if I wanted to help free my country. And of course, I said yes. I had no ties. My parents had both died in an air raid. So before I knew it, I found myself here at Holt Manor."

"I do believe light is beginning to dawn, Mrs. Van der Voor. The people who came to see you were, I assume, something official."

"Very official, and very secret, inspector. As was Holt Manor, at that time. In fact, I don't believe that its true identity was ever revealed completely, even many years after the war."

"And that identity was ...?"

"It had been requisitioned by the government early on in the war as a training school for the Special Operations Executive, inspector. I believe they called them 'Churchill's Secret Army'. They were training operatives who could be infiltrated into Europe in order to disrupt the enemy war effort. And my skills with munitions had been noticed. And so I was trained in all sorts of other skills – some of which I can't really talk about, even now, and some of which I hoped I would never need to use – ready to be dropped into Holland."

"What, by parachute?" Radley couldn't resist the impulse to interrupt. "As a secret agent?"

Velma laughed. "I may be a little old lady now, sergeant, but I was a mere wisp of a thing then. Just a young girl that nobody would suspect. And D-Day was coming, and we all had to be in place, ready to play our part." A deep sigh. "It was a terrible time. And I did what I had to do. But finally, the war ended, and everyone tried to get back to something like a normal life. And ... well, the years went past. And when you can see the end of your story approaching, you feel the need to go back and revisit some of the happier times. And you may not think it, knowing what we were preparing for, but we were happy here at the manor. We were all young, and alive, and none of us knew what tomorrow would bring, so we lived each day at a time. And so I thought, just once, I would come back." She gazed pensively at the floor for several long moments, but then looked up and gave a bright smile. "Of course, I'm here under completely false pretences."

"What reasons did you give for applying to be one of Mr. Spelman's so-called 'seekers'?" asked Copper.

"I looked up the manor on the net," said Velma, to

Copper's slight surprise. "Just to see what had become of it. And that's where I learned about the Institute. So I claimed that I lived in a home for the elderly," chuckled Velma, "and I said that I was responsible for organising their social activities, but that I felt that I was getting tired and inefficient, and needed a boost in my spiritual energy. Complete rubbish, of course, but the people here bought it. And they were probably happy to take my money, no matter how nonsensical it sounded. And so I booked in and ... well, here I am."

"I have to say, Mrs. Van der Voor," said Copper after a long pause, "I wasn't expecting anything like that. So tell me, since your arrival, have you had much to do with Mr. Spelman?"

"Only the same as everybody else, I would think," replied Velma. "Some group lectures during the day, and that one odd gathering in the evening. A couple of individual personal sessions. And then there were the fitness classes with Denise, but I managed to claim the privilege of old age to get out of most of them." A surprisingly impish grin. "Although I think I may still be fitter than one or two of the others. Naming no names." A hint of a wink.

"Just to check, had you met Mr. Spelman or any of the other guests before your arrival?" A shake of the head. "And did you, at any time since your arrival, become aware of any causes of tension between Mr. Spelman and any of the other residents at the manor? Any inkling as to why anyone might wish him harm?"

"None in the slightest, inspector," stated Velma, her face open and guileless. "Everyone seemed very supportive of him. Well, perhaps with one exception. I think there may have been some sort of falling-out between him and Rudy Day, which may be why I have been given the second-best room in the house. But I don't know any details."

Copper forbore to comment. "And on the subject of your room, can I just check on your movements last evening after dinner. Did you have occasion to leave your room at any point?"

"None whatever," said Velma. "Contrary to what you may have heard about old people, inspector, I sleep very soundly and long. I was in bed for eleven last night, and I didn't wake until around half-past seven this morning in time for breakfast. Which, I may point out, nobody seemed very much in the mood for after Denise had come back to the manor with the news about Mr. Spelman."

*

"Who'd have thought it, boss?" marvelled Pete Radley, incredulous. "That sweet old lady, a spy!"

"Evidently not so sweet," remarked Dave Copper. "Hidden depths, and an obvious talent to deceive. So were we, I wonder, on the receiving end of that skill? Not to mention the other skills she was rather cagey about. I can only imagine what they might have included."

"So you reckon she might have managed to lure Spelman out into the woods in the middle of the night on some pretext or other, and then done for him?" scoffed Radley. "And why would she have done it? She says she'd never met the guy before. What motive could she have?"

"I have absolutely no idea," confessed Copper. "Maybe Anna's researches will turn something up, although I can't think what. But on the grounds of means and opportunity, we can't rule her out. She could have made her way out of her room unobserved during the night, and she could easily have got hold of one of those arrows."

"Just like anyone else. So, I suppose you'll be wanting to bash on and see what other unlikely suspects we've got," grinned Radley. "Do you want me to haul the next one in?"

"Please do." The sergeant went to the door and, after a murmured exchange, ushered the next woman into the study. Copper indicated the chair opposite the desk. "Take a seat, Miss ...?"

"Wakes. Matilda Wakes, but everyone calls me Tilly."

Copper surveyed the woman as Radley, at a sign from his superior, re-opened his notebook and prepared to make notes. The only thing that struck the inspector was her thorough ordinariness. Average in height and with a slightly pear-shaped figure, she looked to be around the late thirties, with medium-length mid-brown hair caught back in a rather untidy pleat. Her face was neither plain nor particularly attractive, with brown eyes, unremarkable eyebrows, and thin colourless lips. She wore no make-up.

"We'd just like to ask you a few questions, and I hope you won't mind if my sergeant jots down some details. Now, as I understand it, you're here to take part in one of Mr. Spelman's residential courses?"

"That's right."

"And where have you come from to be here?"

"I live in Essex."

"And what do you do?"

"I work at the County General Hospital. I'm an anaesthetist." Copper glanced up at Radley, and managed to stifle his amusement at the sight of the sergeant, the tip of his tongue protruding between his teeth, apparently struggling with the spelling of Tilly's job.

"And what brings you here?"

Tilly thought for a moment. "It's a stressful profession, inspector," she began. "All the time you're dealing with people who have the most frightening situations to deal with, and the pressures are never-ending. It's not always easy to cope. Things don't always turn out the way you'd wish." She broke off for a moment and took a deep breath. "Anyway, a friend of mine had seen something on the net about there being places, like this one, who could help you evaluate yourself and re-adjust your levels of self-esteem." A faint smile. "Goodness, hark at me. I'm beginning to sound like the Director. So I suppose there must be something to be said for his system."

"And so this useful friend of yours pointed you in the direction of the Institute?"

"Yes. And I didn't want to come at first. But my friend nagged me into doing it, because she thought I was a bit of a mess, so I phoned up and spoke to Charlotte-Anne. And she was very persuasive. I mean, at the start I thought it all sounded like mumbo-jumbo. And it really isn't. Well, mostly not." Tilly pulled a face. "Some aspects are a bit odd."

"But now you sound as if you're a convert," smiled Copper. "Tell me, when you decided to come, was it for any specific reason?"

"No," said Tilly swiftly. "No, not at all."

"And it seems clear that you have become something of a fan of Mr. Spelman. So I'm guessing that there wouldn't have been any causes of friction between the two of you?"

"Why would there be?"

"You tell me," replied Copper blandly. There was no response. "Or how about between Mr. Spelman and any of the other people here? Have you seen anything during your stay which could indicate any problems between the Director and the other residents or staff? Any arguments?"

"Oh no. Castor was a very calm person. Soothing. He took away your worries."

"I see. Now tell me, coming to the events of the last twelve hours or so, when did you last see Mr. Spelman?"

"That would be at dinner last night," said Tilly. "We

all ate together, and then I had a short game of cards with Alisha - she's taught me how to play gin rummy – and then I went up to bed."

"Your room's here in the manor, I think?"

"Yes. I went up around half-past ten, I suppose, and I went to bed straight away. And, until my alarm went off this morning, I was dead to the world. Oh." Her hand went to her mouth. "That wasn't a very nice thing to say, was it?"

Copper waved aside the remark. "So, to confirm, you did not leave your room between going to bed last night and getting up for breakfast this morning?"

"No, inspector."

"And did you hear anything outside your room during that period which might have been anyone else moving about. You weren't awakened by any noises, by any chance?"

"No, inspector," repeated Tilly. "The doors are very thick. And I sleep like the dead."

Chapter 6

"So just one of what we're considering as our suspects to go, if my calculations are correct," said Dave Copper, as Pete Radley headed for the door to the library after showing Tilly out into the hall. "The exotic-sounding Mademoiselle de Roque."

Radley peered through the gap in the library door as he opened it just a crack. He turned to grin at Copper. "Oh, I think you can safely say that, boss," he whispered, before throwing the door wide and saying aloud, "Would you like to come this way, please."

The individual who subsided with self-conscious elegance into the chair facing Copper certainly exceeded the inspector's expectations. Tall and willowy, she wore her hair in a severely asymmetric bob in a striking purplish mahogany colour, and her face was artistically made up, with large eyes accentuated by thick sooty eyelashes and eye shadow in graduated tones of brown, exquisitely sculpted brows tilted up at the outer corners, and a vivid gash of deep red lipstick, all over a flawlessly even pale cream foundation. Her age was not easy to guess. A chunky gold necklace gleamed over a high-necked blouse, and a short emerald green jacket with exaggeratedly-padded power shoulders was worn above a black pencil skirt which was severely cinched in at the waist by a wide patent-leather belt, whose buckle design echoed that of the necklace. Long legs in sheer black tights and black patent high heels completed the ensemble.

Copper's eyebrows rose, and he cleared his throat. "Mademoiselle de Roque, I believe."

"Oh, please, call me Coco," replied the other, leaning back gracefully, crossing her legs, and gazing at the inspector through her eyelashes. Her voice was lighter than Copper expected, although the slight huskiness seemed to speak of numerous *Gauloises*, and the French intonation was lilting and pleasant.

"I think I would prefer to keep things rather more formal, since this is a murder investigation, mademoiselle," said Copper, a little stiffly.

"Oh. Well, in that case, at least call me 'Miss'. I have lived in England for so long, and you English can never get the pronunciation of 'mademoiselle' right." Coco gave a light throwaway laugh.

"Very well, 'Miss' it is. And may I ask what you do?"

"Oh. You have not heard of me. That is a shame." A Gallic shrug. "But then, not everybody has. But I think I am known to those who matter." And in response to Copper's invitingly raised eyebrow, "I am a fashion designer. One of the best. Those people who know say I am at the top. And also I write for magazines and newspapers."

"And you're French, I'm told."

"Yes, that is correct. I am from Paris. That is where I learned all about fashion to begin with. I have been apprentice at some of the great houses. But I came to England many years ago, because the English scene, it is so much more exciting than the French. Vibrant, I could say, and open to new ideas. And I began to produce some of my own creations, and I became noticed, and now I make commissions for people who want something special. Did you see what the winner of Best Actress wore at this year's awards in London? That was one of mine."

"I'm impressed, miss," said Copper. "But what you say leads me to wonder, with such success under your belt, why you should be attending a course here at the Holt Manor Institute. I would have thought, with no disrespect intended to the other guests here, that the procedures here were more intended for those people who were feeling something of a sense of failure in their lives, or at least the need to improve their mental state."

Coco leaned forward. "Well, I will let you into a secret, inspector. I came here because I was invited."

Copper was surprised. "Really? What, by Mr. Spelman, do you mean?"

"I do."

"So you're telling us that you knew him before?"

"That is right, inspector. But only a little. You see, he had come to me because he wanted something designed. Something out of the ordinary. Some robes, in fact, for ... some special purposes he had. And so we spoke on the telephone and he explained what he wanted. I sent him my designs, which pleased him very much, and so I made them for him. And as a thank-you, he invited me to come here to see them being worn, and also because he suggested that his methods might provide me with even more insights into what designs I could create. And so, of course, I accepted his invitation."

The inspector's interest was sharpened. "One moment, Miss de Roque. You mention robes. Tell me, would one of those you designed for him have been a floor-length style in white, with wide sleeves and a number of embroidered motifs scattered all over it?"

Coco sounded amazed. "But yes, inspector. How did you know?"

"Because I have to tell you," replied Copper, "that when Mr. Spelman's body was found, he was wearing just such a garment."

"What?" Coco seemed aghast. "Are you saying that Castor was killed wearing one of my creations?"

"I'm afraid it appears so, yes."

"But this is ... astonishing." There was a light in Coco's eyes which Copper couldn't quite fathom. "And when it is in the news ... I suppose there will be much publicity."

"I think that's probably unavoidable, miss."

Coco leaned back. "Well, I will have to manage somehow." There was an indefinable air of satisfaction in her voice.

"Now I need to ask you," resumed Copper, "since you were acquainted with Mr. Spelman beforehand, whether there were any causes of conflict between you. Was there, for example, any sort of clash between you over your designs for these ... robes of his?"

"Not at all, inspector. He loved them." Coco was firm.

"And would you know of any problems between Mr. Spelman and anyone else?"

Coco shook her head. "No. Why, were there problems?"

"That's what I'm trying to discover, miss," said Copper. "As yet, with remarkably little success," he added, half to himself, in irritation. "And finally, I'm told you're accommodated in a room here at the manor. I'm wondering if you can add anything to the accounts we've already had about the events after dinner last night."

Coco shrugged. "I don't know what you've been told, inspector. All I know is that after dinner, some of the others stayed downstairs for a while, including Mr. Spelman, but I went up to my room. I wanted to check on my media – I have many followers, you know. But I assure you, Mr. Spelman was alive and well when I last saw him, and I don't know any more until I came down this morning to hear what Denise Benz was saying."

*

"Can I sit down for a bit, boss?" requested Pete Radley. "Only my back is killing me, standing there all this time."

"Yes, our Mr. Spelman seems to have been a bit frugal with his furniture in this room," agreed Dave Copper. "Quantity-wise, anyway. Although I suspect this desk cost a pretty penny. So go ahead, take the weight off for a minute. After all, we seem to have come to a sort of natural hiatus."

"What, between our suspects and the also-rans?" queried Radley. "You got to admit, boss, we've got a right mixed bunch here. There's half the United Nations, what with Canadian, Dutch, and French, and then you've got characters ranging from Miss Bossy Connor to that little mouse of a secretary. And mostly women, which is a bit unusual."

"Don't forget that old cliché about the female of the species, sergeant," smiled Copper.

"I won't, boss," said Radley. "But you must admit, it's slightly odd that there don't seem to be any men attending this Institute of Mr. Spelman's. Do you suppose they were actively discouraged, for some reason? Does the fact that we've got a dozen women here – well, with the exception of Spelman's partner – does it mean that there was something a bit iffy going on? Although I can't think what. I mean, I can't imagine anyone having unsavoury designs on the Dutch lady. Or the French one, for that matter. She's a bit too overpowering for me."

"It's certainly a pretty wide variety of womankind, sergeant," chuckled Copper. "And we rule nothing and nobody out until we have the full picture."

"I suppose that means you want to get on with it." Radley heaved himself to his feet with a quiet groan. "No rest for the wicked."

"No rest for us until we've identified the wicked," Copper corrected him gently. "Four left, if I remember rightly."

"You do, boss." Radley flipped open his notebook. "And it just so happens that I made a note of them as Anna was showing us that security video of hers. So you have Mrs. Cord, Mrs. Peel, Miss Barnes, and Mrs. Icke. Any particular order you'd like them in?"

"No. We'll just start at the top and work down."

As Radley was reaching for the door handle, the mobile in his pocket rang. "Hold on a second, boss ... Hello ... oh, hi, Una ... yes, he's here. Just a second." He held out the phone to the inspector. "It's your good lady in Forensics, boss."

"Hello, love ... Yes, we're still ploughing through people here. How's things at your end? ... Wow, that was quick. We never saw the coming or going of them ... What, already? You and Suzanne don't hang about, do you? ... Look, I can't get away just yet. I'm in the middle of interviews ... Do I really have to be eyes-on? I mean, I'm perfectly happy to take your word for things. And you'll be doing some pictures anyway, won't you? ... So you can get on with the rest of the p.m.? ... Then that's fine. We'll get over to you as soon as we've finished up here." Copper clicked off the call and handed the phone back to his colleague.

"What was that all about?"

"News on Mr. Spelman," replied Copper. "They've got him back at Westchester and they've started work on him, and Una reckons there are already some things we ought to be aware of. Interesting, she says. So she requests our presence as soon as convenient."

"We'd better be nippy then, hadn't we, boss? I mean, Una's pretty damn good at her job, isn't she? If she says something's interesting, that usually gets our attention." Radley paused once more. "Just one question before we crack on, boss. How come you never have your phone with you when we're out? Why do they always have to get you through me?"

Copper chuckled. "It's mainly because I've never got around to changing my ringtone."

"What, you mean that laughing thing?"

"'The Laughing Policeman', to give it its proper title." Copper smiled fondly in remembrance. "I remember the first time it went off when I was out on a job with my old guv'nor. He wanted to know what on earth I was playing at. But then I told him the story about my old grandad, how he'd loved the song and always done it for us kids at parties, and he let me get away with it. Except that one day I happened to be lurking at the back of a very high-powered press conference being conducted by the Assistant Chief Constable, and the blasted thing went off at full volume. I'd forgotten to mute it. So harsh words were said, as you can imagine. But I can't bring myself to change it, so I just don't bring the phone when I'm out on the job. Simple."

Radley shrugged. "Not that I mind being your answering service. Happy to help. Anyway, as you told me Mr. Constable used to say to you, shall we get back to our muttons?"

"You have been paying attention," laughed the inspector approvingly. "Okay, let's have the next one in."

The woman who next took her place across the desk from Copper was middle-aged, motherly, and plump, with a round cheerful face whose friendly open expression held the promise that she would be a good listener. She wore a beige twinset teamed with a tweed skirt, her whole appearance somehow conveying an impression of unremarkable reliability.

"I'm sorry you've been kept waiting so long, madam," began Copper. "Mrs. Cord, isn't it?"

"That's right, inspector," nodded the woman. "Maia Cord. And don't worry about the wait. I mean, none of us is any hurry, are we? I'm happy to take all the time in the world in order to get the right outcome."

Copper was surprised at the other's ready helpfulness. He was far more used to interviewees who twitched and fidgeted and couldn't wait to get out from under his searching gaze. "That's very good to hear, Mrs. Cord," he said. "Co-operation is a very valuable commodity, and my job would be a great deal easier if I received rather more of it."

"I couldn't agree more, inspector," said Maia. "Mine too."

"Oh?" Copper was intrigued. "So what job do you do, may I ask?"

"I'm a marriage counsellor in Westchester," replied Maia. "Although nowadays, we're more correctly known as 'relationship consultants'. Because, of course, not everyone gets married these days. In fact, more than half my clients come from non-conventional partnerships, which is not necessarily a problem, and it's invariably the children who suffer the most when break-ups happen, whether the parents are married or not. So my colleagues and I do our best to repair the damage in a threatened relationship. Or rather, to help a couple to find the strength and the courage to repair the rift for themselves."

"That sounds like very valuable work," said Copper admiringly. A tiny frown creased his brow. "But there's just one thing puzzling me. It sounds rather as if your work is very much an echo of what we've been told is what this Institute of Mr. Spelman's is all about. Developing understandings and fostering inner strengths, all that sort of thing. So I'm wondering what brings you here, when you seem to be covering a lot of the same ground."

Maia smiled. "It's a very good question, inspector," she said, "and one that I'm not sure I can answer. The truth is, someone very much higher-up in our organisation seems to have got word of what the Institute was doing – in fact, one of the girls I work with thinks that one of the bosses had been here in search of some kind of spiritual improvement – and the word filtered down that someone from my section should attend a course here to see if we could enhance our services. I don't know." She shook her head in despair.

"Trendy millennials! You'd think they'd have better ways to spend our budget. Anyway, I was the one fortunate enough to be chosen."

"You sound," observed Copper, "as if you are not entirely convinced by the whole process, Mrs. Cord."

"Oh, some of what Castor Spelman says makes a great deal of sense," said Maia. "And if I hadn't already been perfectly well aware of how some people think, and what you can do to help them to broaden their thought horizons, I might have found it useful. But some of the more fanciful stuff is, quite frankly, for the birds. You wouldn't catch me spouting it in a month of Sundays. And one of the activities – well, the less said about that the better." She tutted, but then broke into a smile. "But I could do with losing a few pounds," she added, "so some of the sports sessions are quite fun."

"Including the archery?" broke in Copper.

Maia's face fell. "Yes. Wasn't that awful? Denise told us that Castor had been shot with an arrow when she burst into the Great Hall with the news this morning."

"And tell me – I haven't thought to ask any of the other guests, but had everyone participated in Miss Benz's archery class?"

"Yes. Some of the staff too, but certainly all the guests. Including me, of course."

"With any particular degree of success?"

Maia chuckled. "Not so's you'd notice, inspector. Most of them couldn't hit a barn door at five paces. Actually, I quite surprised myself. I wasn't too bad, but of course, nowhere in Denise's class." She reflected. "Rudy was quite good, but I suppose he'd probably had plenty of practice over time. And I was actually really surprised at Velma. You wouldn't think a woman of her age could pull a longbow, but she turned in a pretty good performance. And I think Coco was just afraid of breaking a nail!"

Copper considered for a moment. "A thought occurs to me, Mrs. Cord. With your training involving looking into the relationships between individuals, I would imagine that you would be perfectly placed to pick up on any tensions between any of the people here. I wonder, can you help me out with that?"

"What, you mean, was I witness to anyone threatening to kill Castor Spelman?" enquired Maia. "Sorry to disappoint, inspector, but that's the sort of thing that regularly gets said in my office when situations become overheated. I don't have any such thing to report here, I'm afraid. And in any case, these things tend to be said in the heat of the moment, and the threat is very seldom meant. One learns to take such things with a large pinch of salt. Unless, of course, there is some history to take into account. I'm not aware of anything of the sort here. And casual passing remarks don't even register on my scale."

"Ah well, it was rather a forlorn hope," said Copper good-humouredly. "So, just before we finish, can I ask you if you could verify the sequence of events in the manor at the end of last evening. You all finished dinner together, I think?"

"Yes. That would have been about ten o'clock. And then people tended to drift off in various directions. Some went upstairs straight away. I think Castor may have come through here into his study. Oh, I remember Tilly started a game of cards with Alisha, which I watched for a bit, but then I went over to my room in the stables and got into bed with a book. I'm afraid it's a guilty pleasure of mine," she confessed. "There's nothing I enjoy more than a good piece of soppy chick-lit. The way these people go on with each other – well, I just laugh from beginning to end."

Chapter 7

The next arrival was a middle-aged woman, brisk and efficient in her manner, with a direct gaze and mid-length iron-grey hair swept back neatly from her face. She took the seat facing Dave Copper, smoothed the skirt of her grey business suit, folded her hands neatly in her lap, and looked expectantly at the detective.

"I'm Sheila Peel, inspector," she stated without preamble. "Mrs., if you need to know. And you have questions."

Copper was slightly taken aback at the direct approach. "Indeed I do, Mrs. Peel. And I suppose the first of those would be to ask what you do."

"I'm a lawyer, inspector. Most specifically a tax lawyer. Chiefly for individual clients, but also very often for businesses. As I'm sure you can imagine, the dividing line between the two is quite frequently rather blurred."

"I'm afraid my knowledge of the world of taxes is very sketchy," admitted Copper. "In fact, not to put too fine a point on it, I find tax forms utterly baffling."

"Oh, I'm sure, with a little application, inspector, you'll find they're not," replied Sheila, her tone smoothly condescending.

"Well, I suspect I'm probably not alone," said Copper, making a superhuman effort not to let his hackles rise, "but fortunately all these matters are taken out of my hands by the finance department which pays my salary, so I don't have to have any direct dealings with H.M.R.C. Which I imagine is not the case with yourself."

"That's true. Many of my clients have what I might describe as a complicated relationship with Revenue and Customs. So they rely on me to smooth the path and help to disentangle them from any problems that may arise."

"And reduce their bills?" suggested Copper. "I dare

say they count on your being able to do that for them."

"Where it is justified," responded Sheila in prim tones. "But I think, inspector, we're rather straying from the path. I don't quite see what this conversation has to do with your investigation into the unfortunate death of Mr. Spelman."

"Unless, of course, your presence here would be accounted for by the fact that you might be involved with the tax affairs of the gentleman or his Institute," pointed out the inspector. "Might that be the case?"

"It would be highly improper for me to reveal or discuss the tax affairs of any of my clients," said Sheila haughtily, but as Copper directed a steady challenging gaze at her, she softened. "But I understand why you ask. And since Mr. Spelman was not in fact one of my clients, I suppose I can tell you that no, I am not here in my professional capacity. At least, not in that respect."

"Then in what respect would it be?" enquired Copper, intrigued.

Sheila sighed. "It was felt by one or two of the senior partners in the practice that my attendance here might be helpful in ... shall I say, smoothing relations with both some of my clients and the civil service officials I have to deal with."

"Oh?"

Sheila was clearly embarrassed. She coloured. "It had been suggested that, on occasion, I may have been a little more confrontational than was appropriate in my dealings with others. And perhaps a more empathetic approach might sometimes produce better results."

"You mean," smiled Copper, "that very often one can catch more flies with honey than with vinegar? One of the celebrated Hercule Poirot's favourite mottoes, I believe. Not that I read much detective fiction, you understand – it's usually hopelessly far-fetched - but from my own experience, I can attest to the truth of the saying."

"Well, that was the partners' opinion, certainly," said Sheila. "So it was felt that, on what they'd heard, from goodness knows where, of the Institute's work, that the fees invested in my coming here would be well recouped by the practice in the long run."

"And do you believe that's correct?"

"We shall have to see, shan't we, inspector?" Sheila seemed reluctant to give anything away. "But certainly, some of the things said here have given me something to think about. As for others ... well, I'll reserve judgement."

Copper renewed the smile. "Now one thing I won't ask you, Mrs. Peel, is whether there were any confrontations between yourself and Mr. Spelman during your time here. We have enough evidence to reassure us that you couldn't have been responsible for his death."

"Not that I think you could honestly blame me if I were," said Sheila unexpectedly. "I mean, I'm not one to criticise. The questions I raised during the first general meeting were perfectly reasonable, in my opinion. But I can't say that Mr. Spelman's reaction displayed the sort of zen-like calm which he was advocating for the rest of us."

"Really?"

"Really. In fact, he seemed to take my quite innocent queries as some sort of attack on himself and his theories. And he said, very rudely I thought, that if I had come here in some sort of spirit of mockery, I was totally at liberty to remove myself from the premises."

"I have to say, Mrs. Peel, that I am surprised," said Copper. "From all I've heard of Mr. Spelman, aggression seems to have been the last thing I would have expected from him."

"Well, you live and learn," retorted Sheila waspishly. "And of course, my first instinct was to reply in kind, but I managed to restrain myself. The thought occurred to me that, if I were to return to the office and report how things had developed, my status in our law practice could well have been diminished. I think the partners would have taken rather a dim view, and my career prospects could have been damaged. So I returned as soft an answer as I could manage, in the hope that it would divert Mr. Spelman's apparent wrath."

"And did it?"

"Quite the contrary, inspector. Mr. Spelman seemed to take delight in pointing out that, as a tax lawyer, I was probably constitutionally incapable of seeing the good in anyone. In fact, I believe he deliberately set out to turn the others against me. Not that he succeeded of course. Well, mostly not. There are still one or two who seem reluctant to speak to me."

*

"Well, that's altered the pattern a bit, hasn't it, boss?" remarked Pete Radley.

"It has," concurred Dave Copper. "From a succession of people with no apparent motive to wish Mr. Spelman ill, some of whom have plenty of opportunity, we now have the first person who might conceivably have wanted to take revenge on him for the public slights she tells us she received, but the evidence shows us that she couldn't possibly have done it."

"But I suppose the good thing is that we now know that there was another side to Mr. Spelman that we hadn't been told about before," pointed out Radley. "It seems he wasn't such a fluffy bunny as everyone has wanted us to believe. And if he managed to rub Mrs. Peel up the wrong way – which I admit doesn't sound as if it was too difficult – might he have done the same thing with someone else? With results that were a bit less restrained than hers?"

"Hold that thought, sergeant," said Copper, "while you wheel the next one in here."

The young woman whom Radley showed into the study next seemed like a breath of fresh air after the tense atmosphere engendered by Sheila Peel. She was young and pretty, in her early twenties, with blonde hair falling in curls to shoulder level, a pink-and-white complexion, and large blue eyes which echoed the colours in her floral blouse. "Miss Alisha Barnes, sir," announced the sergeant.

"Ah," responded the inspector. "The card-sharp in the company."

Alisha blinked at him uncertainly. "I'm sorry, inspector?" She seemed nervous.

"Don't worry, Miss Barnes," said Copper. The young woman was obviously in need of reassurance. "It's simply that Miss Wakes mentioned to us earlier that you'd been teaching her how to play gin rummy. And in fact, that was how you were occupying your time yesterday evening after dinner. Which I believe must have been the last time you would have seen Mr. Spelman."

"Yes, that's true," nodded Alisha. "And I can't help thinking how, only a little while later, someone else must have ..." She tailed off, blinking rapidly once more, this time in order to keep back the tears which threatened to spill from her eyes.

"I'm afraid you're correct, miss," said Copper. "And the unpleasant fact is that this someone else must have been a member of the company who were staying at Holt Manor last night." Alisha caught her breath. "Oh, you needn't worry that we think you may have been responsible," the inspector reassured her. "We're quite happy to say, from what we know already, that you could not have been involved. So I can at least set your mind at rest on that score."

"But that means," persisted Alisha, "that it must have been one of the others."

"And I need your help in finding out who that might have been," coaxed Copper in his most avuncular manner. Clearly, this witness would need to be handled delicately. "Do you think you'll be able to do that?"

Alisha gulped slightly. "I'll do my best, inspector," she quavered.

"Good. Now I'll call you Alisha, if I may," said Copper, leaning forward confidentially. "And I'm going to let you into our way of thinking. Obviously, we have to assume that the person who killed Mr. Spelman must have had some sort of grudge against him. It seems possible that their feelings may have emerged in conversations, either involving him, or about him. I wonder, can you recall any such thing?"

"Not really," said Alisha helplessly. "Actually, I never had that much to do with Mr. Spelman. Personally, that is. I mean, I went to his talks, of course, and he was always somewhere around when we were doing Denise's fitness activities, but we hadn't actually got to the part where I was supposed to have an individual assessment session with him. That was meant to be later today." She gazed at Copper, her eyes seeming bigger than ever. "Oh dear."

"And can I ask," said Copper, intervening swiftly to forestall the tears which threatened to brim over again, "how it is that you've come here to the manor? What was it that you aimed to achieve by attending?"

Alisha sighed. "Confidence. I get a bit nervous sometimes, and I'm afraid that it stops me doing my job properly."

"And what job is that?"

"I'm an estate agent. Well, trainee, really. Our head office is in Westchester."

"A local, then. Like Mrs. Cord."

Alisha shrugged. "Maybe. I don't know her. But I don't spend much time at the head office anyway. I'm based at the Dammett Vale branch."

"And what is it that you do? House sales? There are some very large houses around the Vale, aren't there?"

"Yes, inspector. But that's not mainly what we do. Our office mostly deals with agricultural property. A lot of the farmers in this area rent their farms from the large estate owners, and it's not always easy when you're in the middle of some difficult negotiations about renewals. Or sometimes a family just dies out, or the younger generation don't want to take on the farm, so there's the need to find new tenants. Or else two farms might get consolidated, and then you've probably got a set of farm buildings which are surplus to requirements, so they're sold off or rented out. Or outbuildings get converted into residential."

"It sounds as if you're quite on top of it, Alisha," remarked Copper admiringly.

"But sometimes I get flustered when I'm talking to a client who knows far more about working the land than I ever could," confessed Alisha. "So my manager thought that a bit of motivational toughening-up would do me good. And he heard about the work here at the manor, and ... well, here I am."

"And during your time here, you've never seen or heard anything that might lead you to think that there could be some sort of tension between Mr. Spelman and anyone else?" Copper sought to confirm.

"No. I mean, there was one time when Maia Cord was trying desperately not to laugh at what Mr. Spelman was doing, but I don't think he knew. He was too involved. But there wasn't anything said at the time, because it would have broken the atmosphere, so I don't think he can have noticed."

*

"Right, then, sergeant," instructed Dave Copper. "Let's have the last one in."

Pete Radley opened the door to the library and beckoned to its final occupant. "Last but not least, boss," he muttered to his superior, before the last interviewee strode through the door and plonked herself down facing Copper. Clad in denim dungarees over a shapeless grey sweater, she was in her mid-forties, estimated the inspector, sturdily built, with an untamed mane of crinkled black hair and sharp brown eyes.

"Now, what can I do to help you, inspector," she asked in forthright tones. Her accent was decidedly Midlands.

"Firstly, let me apologise for keeping you waiting so long."

"Oh, don't you worry none about that," said the woman. "I spend half my life hanging about. That's 'cos I'm a woman with lots of patience!" She guffawed, somewhat to Copper's surprise. "Sorry, inspector. That's just a joke we have around the office. I'm supposed to say 'clients', but half of them have got so much wrong with them that they seem more like patients to us on the team."

"Team?" enquired Copper. "Which team would that be?"

"I'm not explaining very well, am I, inspector? I work in the social services department of the council."

"The local council?"

"No, Greater Midlands Council. I'm not from round these parts, as you can probably hear. I was born near Dudley. What they call the Black Country." The woman chuckled. "Because of the pollution, in case you were wondering."

"Ah. Right. I understand. Now, the thing is, Mrs. ... sorry, my sergeant forgot to remind me of your name."

"It's Sheryl. Sheryl Icke, although all my mates call me Cher. That's on account of the fact that I look so much like her!" Another robust guffaw. "You know – tall, thin, pale complexion, long straight hair, brilliant singer."

Copper smiled weakly to acknowledge the joke, but made no remark. "And is that Mrs. Icke? Miss? Ms?"

"It's 'Mrs', inspector." Another unrestrained chuckle. "It had better be, or else my husband and my three boys are going to be asking me some very funny questions."

'And there's another good reason for never judging a book by its cover', thought Copper to himself. "So, on to the subject of questions, Mrs. Icke," he said aloud, "I need you to tell me about the events of the past twenty-four hours here at the manor."

"You want to know if I murdered Castor Spelman," stated Sheryl in forthright tones. "Go ahead and ask. I didn't, of course. About the only thing I've ever murdered is one of Cher's songs at the karaoke evening down the pub." The unrestrained laugh returned, before Sheryl's face turned more sombre. "You mustn't mind me, inspector," she said. "I've just got a bit of a colourful sense of humour." She regarded Copper with a twinkle in her eye.

The inspector declined to take the bait. "So, if you didn't murder Mr. Spelman, might you have any inkling as to who did? I would imagine that, if you're involved in social work, you must come across all manner of people, and you must need to be able to learn how to interpret some of their moods and actions."

"That's actually very true," agreed Sheryl. "Most people don't realise that. They think our job is just to provide magic solutions to people's domestic problems. Really, it's more like being a mixture of psychologist and fairy godmother. That's one of the reasons I got signed up for this place. My line manager offered to find some money in our budget because she'd heard that the courses here are supposed to 'sharpen up your empathy so that you can give your clients better outcomes'. I'm quoting – she tends to come out with a lot of management-speak when she hasn't a clue what she's on about. How that's supposed to sort out a carer for somebody is anyone's guess."

"So how far has the psychologist in you got in empathising with your fellow-guests?" enquired Copper with a smile. "Have you noticed any clashes of personality? Any tensions between individuals which might have led to the current situation?"

Sheryl shook her head dubiously. "Nothing that would imply someone wanted to murder Castor Spelman, inspector."

"And how about the fairy godmother?" asked Copper facetiously. "Any magical insights?"

"Magic? From me?" scoffed Sheryl. "Not likely! And as for the rest of it, what a load of tosh that was."

"What was?" wondered Copper, puzzled.

"All this ceremony rubbish. Wafting about in a robe and chanting about the spirits of the earth. And I'm sure some of them took it seriously."

"Mrs. Icke," said Copper, "I do not have the faintest idea what you're talking about." He sounded completely baffled.

"What? You mean nobody else has told you about it? Too embarrassed, I expect."

"Then why don't you tell us?"

Sheryl took a deep breath. "It was a couple of evenings ago. At dinner, as we were all just finishing, Castor stood up and said that he had a new experience for us which he believed would help to open our minds. He said Witch's Holt was a unique place, especially that night at the full moon. He told us that, because of the history of the manor, and its location on a ley line, whatever that is, there were unseen spiritual powers which we could draw on. And he said that the number of people present was no accident."

"Thirteen," mused Copper under his breath. "I did wonder ..."

"And so he said we would all meet in a few minutes down in the holt, at an old oak he called the Coven Tree. He disappeared upstairs, and the rest of us were all given black gowns, like the ones students wear, and Charlotte-Anne handed out some lanterns and led us down to this place in the wood. She got us to form a circle, and then suddenly Castor appeared out from among the trees in a long robe and started to chant some nonsense about ancient wicker, whatever that may be, and we were all supposed to join hands and do replies to his chanting so's we could be in tune with the earth. I caught Maia's eye, and she was trying her best not to laugh, but I think some of them were quite caught up in it. Anyway, mercifully it didn't go on too long, and Castor sort of faded into the undergrowth and the rest of us came back up here and went to bed. There wasn't a lot of talking. Like I said, I have a feeling that a lot of people were embarrassed."

Chapter 8

Pete Radley could scarcely contain himself until the study door had closed behind Sheryl Icke. "Witchcraft?" he exploded. Incredulity was etched across his features. "Are they kidding me?"

Dave Copper couldn't help but be amused at his colleague's reaction. "I'm very much afraid they're not," he chuckled. "And now we know what was meant by the various oblique references from some of our ladies."

"Yes, but seriously? Witchcraft? It's the twenty-first century, for crying out loud. I mean, I know the country is full of people dressing up as witches and whatnot at Halloween, which these days is just an excuse for a fancy dress party, but honestly, witchcraft? Prancing about in the woods at midnight? They have to be joking."

Copper continued to smile. "You may not have noticed, but the twenty-first century hasn't severed quite as many links with the past as you thought. Haven't you seen the number of people who get together at Stonehenge at the summer solstice? That's all connected with ancient earth-worship. And would you like to guess when the last trial for witchcraft took place in England?"

Radley shrugged. "I don't know. Sixteen hundred and something?"

"Nineteen-forties." Copper laughed as Radley's jaw dropped. "And the law wasn't repealed until the nineteen-fifties."

"How on earth do you know this stuff, boss?" enquired the sergeant.

"I happen to have a very well-read wife," replied Copper. "Una was telling me a while back about a case in one of her reference books where there were elements in a murder case relating to witchcraft. Or, to be more accurate, Wicca."

"Oh, what like in that old film, 'The Wicker Man'?"

wondered Radley. "I saw that on TV. But wasn't that all about some policeman getting locked up inside a big wicker figure and sacrificed, while everybody else danced around in a circle? I don't much fancy the thought of ending up like that. And Sheryl Icke did talk about wicker, didn't she?"

"I'm sure we don't need to have any worries on that score," Copper reassured him. "And anyway, it's not that sort of wicker. It just sounds the same. Wicca, I think, is what some people think of as white magic. Tuning into the spirituality of the earth, by all accounts. So in fact, it's not a million miles from what Castor Spelman seems to have been going on about during these courses of his. Nothing at all to do with pointy hats and black cats, or any of the other daft things people think of when you mention witches."

"But is there any chance that Spelman's death could have been some sort of weird sacrifice?" speculated Radley.

"I certainly hope not," replied the inspector. "We've heard nothing to indicate any such thing. It sounds more to me as if this ceremony malarkey Sheryl talked about may have just been a bit of set-dressing. One of Mr. Spelman's more esoteric ideas to drive his message home. And anyway, the ceremony wasn't last night, was it? It was a couple of days ago. There certainly couldn't have been an assembly of the coven ... oh good grief! Listen to me!" Copper sounded aghast at his own choice of words. He drew a deep breath. "These people couldn't all have got together at the required time last night on account of the CCTV evidence. So there's another explanation. And probably a much more conventional one. At least, I hope so," he added under his breath.

"So where do we go from here, boss?"

Copper stood. "I think the first thing we do is accept Una's invitation, and go and find out what she has to tell us regarding the body. You never know, it may provide answers which will stop us talking in the realms of fantasy about sacrifices and covens. Then, with that under our belts, we can come back and carry out some searches. Maybe there's something helpful to be found in people's rooms. And I dare say we can be persuasive enough not to make them insist on seeing a search warrant." He made his way back into the library, to find the young officer still in position. "P.C. Khan, thank you for keeping an eye on our company of residents."

"Happy to help, sir."

"Good. Because I'm going to enlist your help a little further. Sergeant Radley and I are just off to Westchester to get some more information from Forensics, but I'd be grateful if you would stick around here and make sure none of our potential suspects go astray. Is there any problem with that?"

"As long as I can clear it with my station, sir."

"I'm sure there'll be no difficulties there." Copper turned to Radley. "Sergeant, can you get on to Khan's superiors and sort that out?"

"Will do, boss." Radley turned away, pulled out his mobile, dialled, and began murmuring into it.

"And I have a suspicion that we've abandoned your colleague who was keeping watch at the murder scene. Well, it appears that Forensics are happy that there's nothing else to be gleaned from there, so he can abandon his vigil and come back in the warm with you. The poor chap's probably got thoroughly chilled and bored by now."

"Don't worry, sir," said Jazz. "I'll pop down and find Brad and bring him back, and I'll make him a coffee to thaw him out."

"Not here, you won't," declared Radley, hanging up from his call. "There's none on the premises. Orders from the Director, we were told."

"That's okay," said Jazz. "There's a petrol station a mile or so away on the Westchester road. They've got a machine for takeaways." She smiled. "Local knowledge, sir. Always useful. We quite often go in there when we're out this way for a quick snack and a loo-break. So Brad can nip along and get us a couple of drinks while I stay on point here."

"Your organisational skills continue to impress, Khan," smiled Copper. "Well, I shall leave you in charge. We're off – back later." He led the way out towards the car on the manor's forecourt.

*

"I've not been here before, boss," said Pete Radley, as the inspector pulled into the car park of Westchester's police headquarters, housed in an ultra-modern building sheathed in mirrored glass, interspersed with cladding panels in bright red and gleaming steel, adjacent to the county town's railway station. "It's all a bit smarter than our old station, isn't it?"

"It is that," agreed Dave Copper, as he strode past the quirky old-style blue police lamps flanking the entrance doors, and into the building with a flash of his warrant card at the attending officer at the front desk. The detectives crossed the marble floor of the echoing atrium, and Copper led the way into a waiting lift, pressing the button for the sixth floor. "And you wait until you see the Forensics Department."

"Wow," muttered Radley, as the lift doors re-opened. "This is a bit of all right."

His admiration was justified. The contrast with the old premises occupied by the forensic team, a gloomy subterranean burrow often referred to by the other officers at the station as 'The Bat-cave', could scarcely have been greater. There, walls painted in a dull muddy green flanked dimly-lit passageways with floors covered with ancient-looking linoleum. Here, the opening lift doors revealed a brightly-lit corridor between a series of open-plan offices whose windows gave views over the roofs of the town below. At the end of the corridor, the inspector made his way through a double swing door into a large laboratory dazzling with the gleam of spotlights, stainless steel, and brilliant white work surfaces. Operatives, singly or in murmuring pairs, were dotted about at benches or workstations, intent on their observations and analyses of the items before them. Floor-to-ceiling windows along one wall gave an uninterrupted vista over the suburbs below, which gradually petered out into a patchwork of greenery as the countryside beyond faded towards a hazy horizon.

At the end of the room, Sergeant Una Singleton looked up from where she was seated at a workstation, making entries into a computer. "Detective Inspector!" she greeted Copper cheerfully, as the other occupants of the room glanced up briefly, before returning to their tasks. "And D.S. Radley. Thank you for coming to join the party. You're here to take a look at our latest guest, I assume?" she smiled.

"With an invitation couched in such charming terms as Sergeant Radley described, how could we refuse?" replied Copper, risking a conspiratorial grin at his wife.

"Then you'd better come this way, hadn't you?" said Una. "We've given him a private suite all to himself. And Suzanne is just finishing up a little housekeeping in there." She rose, crossed the room, and pushed open a door in a wall of frosted glass, beckoning the detectives to follow her. Inside, the centre of the room was occupied by a shining steel table on which rested a figure draped in a white cloth. To one side, to the sound of running water, Una's colleague Suzanne Heming was just finishing drying her hands.

Suzanne elbowed the tap off and turned to

welcome the visitors. "Hello again, inspector. And sergeant. Come to see what we've got for you?"

"I was intrigued by the slightly mysterious summons," replied Copper. "And apparently Mr. Radley has never had the opportunity to visit these hallowed halls where you high priestesses perform your magic, so we're both in a learning pattern."

"We'd better make a start, then," said Una. "We've already looked him up and compiled the start of a dossier." She consulted a sheet of paper. "Castor Spelman, British, age 50. Well-nourished male in apparent good health, nothing flagged up in his NHS files, no records on the national police computer." She moved to the table. "And here's your murder victim." She took one corner of the sheet covering the body and drew it back completely. "Pretty good-looking for his age," she added. "All things considered."

Castor Spelman lay on his back. The dead man was completely naked, his skin pale and waxy, with hands and face having a slightly darker tanned appearance. The classic post-mortem Y-incision, running from the front of each shoulder towards the centre of the chest, and then downwards towards the groin, had been closed with an exceptionally neat line of stitching.

"That," observed Copper, "is a very tidy piece of handiwork. Yours, I assume, Suzanne?"

"It certainly is," smiled Suzanne. "We can't let our guests leave our custody looking scruffy, can we? It wouldn't be respectful. Anyway, at least it means that those needlework classes at school didn't go to waste."

"Why else do you think the Westsea Players' programmes list '*Sooz Heming - wardrobe mistress*'?" commented Una.

"And I see you've got him out of his Wee Willie Winkie costume, Sooz," remarked Radley.

"Which, by the way, was all he had on," said

Suzanne. "No underwear."

Radley shrugged, grimacing. "Didn't particularly need to know that. So, moving on, that robe thing did have some pretty smart embroidery on it. Bet you clocked that with your professional eye, Sooz. So if we run out of murder victims, we can always get you to stitch up a suspect," he quipped. "Sorry, boss. Only kidding," he added hastily in response to his superior's faint growl of disapproval.

"And moving on from the subject of Suzanne's handiwork, admirable though that may be," said Copper, "what else are we looking at? Other than the obvious, of course." He indicated the puncture wound in the dead man's chest. "That's clearly where he was shot."

Una smiled. "'Clearly' is a word we try not to use too much around here. Jumping to conclusions is a very dangerous thing to do in our job. And that would certainly have been the case here."

"How so?" enquired the inspector. "There's a dead man lying with an arrow in his chest, and you're saying that he wasn't shot and killed by it?"

"That's right."

Copper was baffled. "So what am I missing?"

"To be fair," said Una, "there's no way you could have known. Not by what was visible at the scene."

"So, enlighten us."

"We removed the arrow," began Una. "And then, because it's routine procedure, we checked the puncture wound for depth and dimensions. Not for any special reason. It's just what we do."

"And ...?"

"And we found a very interesting thing. The arrow wasn't what made the hole."

Copper did a double-take. "Hold on a sec. Let's just check the context of this. They are having archery classes at Holt Manor, run by a German former junior champion, or so she tells us. Everyone has a go at shooting the arrows, apparently with varying degrees of success. We are then called to a murder scene where a man lies dead, transfixed by one of those very arrows. But you tell me that the arrow isn't what killed him?"

"Ah. I didn't quite say that, David," smiled Una. "But no, he wasn't actually killed by the arrow. It would have brought about his death by extending the initial puncture to the lung, and I won't go into the technicalities about blood penetration and drainage, except he was already dead when the arrow went in. Because the original hole was made by something else. And the arrow was subsequently introduced into it."

"So he was stabbed in the chest first, and the arrow was then pushed into the wound?"

"Precisely."

"Sounds to me as if our murderer was aiming to be a bit cunning, boss," Radley observed. "Maybe trying to throw the blame on to somebody else. And to make our fitness trainer the most obvious suspect."

"Entirely possible," mused Copper. "Because who would think that our supremely talented forensics team would have the skill to spot their crafty ruse? Congratulations, ladies. Which then brings me on to the next question. If the arrow wasn't the initial weapon, what was? Any idea?"

"A very clear idea, as it happens," said Una. "Picture a slim shaft, circular, about five millimetres in diameter, about fifteen centimetres long, broadening out at the tip into a flattened shape about ten millimetres wide and just over one millimetre thick." She looked expectantly at her husband.

After a few seconds, it clicked. "A screwdriver!" declared Copper. "The murderer stabbed him with a screwdriver."

"That they did," confirmed Una. "And the weapon

penetrated the heart, killing the victim immediately."

"Which is why there was so little blood flow," realised the inspector. "And then the killer pushed the arrow into the hole with the intention of disguising what had happened. But not quite deeply enough to cover the evidence of the screwdriver?"

"That's my reading of it. And in fact, on examination of the area immediately surrounding the puncture wound, there are traces of bruising which are almost certainly the marks left by the base of the handle of the screwdriver as it came into sudden contact with the surface of the skin, even through the thickness of the robe fabric."

"You said there had been some planning gone into this, boss," said Radley. "It sounds as if the whole setup was even more deliberate than we thought. It wasn't just somebody lurking in the undergrowth waiting for Spelman to turn up for some sort of midnight rendezvous in the woods in order to take a pot-shot at him."

"Also," added Copper, "although it's probably stating the obvious, you don't get close enough to stab somebody with a screwdriver unless you're reasonably well-acquainted with them. But since the residents of the manor were all linked with one another, that doesn't really get us anywhere." He pondered for a moment. "Here's a thought. Does our victim have any sort of defensive wounds? I mean, is there any evidence that he attempted to fight off this attack?"

"None at all," replied Una. "The stab wound and its immediate surroundings are the only damage."

"Does that mean," enquired Radley slowly, "that there's also no evidence that Mr. Spelman was coerced into being where he was? Who goes trotting out into the woods in the middle of the night with bare feet in just some fancy robe? I mean, if he'd been dragged or pushed, or even carried, you'd get some kind of bruising somewhere, wouldn't you?"

"That, sergeant, is a very good point," said Copper approvingly. He turned to Una. "Well?"

She shook her head. "Nothing. There is no evidence to suggest that he was there other than of his own accord. And certainly not carried – there's leaf-litter on the soles of his feet consistent with his having walked through the wood."

"Then what on earth was he doing there? And why did he calmly let himself be stabbed?" murmured Copper to himself. He gazed unfocussed out of the window in abstracted thought.

"Sooz might have an answer to that," said Una after a long pause. "She's the one who looks into the toxicology."

"Sorry, what?" Copper dragged his concentration back into the room. "Look, can we make up our minds? I thought you'd already told us that the arrow wasn't what killed him. I want to move on from the archery aspect of it."

Una laughed. "Not toxophily, David. We're not talking about bows and arrows any more. I said toxicology. Sooz's department. Nasty chemicals in Mr. Spelman's system."

Copper grinned ruefully. "Sorry, love. Wasn't listening properly. Note to self – wash ears out. So, Suzanne, let's have it. What nasties did you find?"

"I've got all the stomach contents over there on the bench," said Suzanne, pointing, "if you want to take a look."

Copper held his hands up in protest, looking faintly queasy. "Thanks all the same, but I'll give it a miss."

"Me too," added Radley. "The sight of other people's lunches tends to make me lose mine."

"Quite enough information, sergeant," responded Copper. "But, like you, I'm more than happy to have the verbal details."

Suzanne chuckled. "Sorry, gentlemen. Sometimes I can't resist a little ghoulish teasing. But here goes. We'll start with the basics of what I didn't find. There's no trace of illicit drugs of any kind in Mr. Spelman's system, nor even of any of the common prescription or non-prescription drugs, such as paracetamol or anti-histamines. Nor were there any traces of alcohol."

"No surprise there, boss," said Radley. "Not after we were told that he wouldn't have booze on the premises."

"Evidently the late Mr. Spelman treated his body as a temple," observed Copper.

"So, moving on to the stomach contents," continued Suzanne, "I can tell you what his last meal consisted of. There was a vegetable soup, followed by a kind of chicken casserole with cous-cous, and the main course was followed by a mixture of fresh fruit and cream. The whole lot consumed, judging by the state of digestion, between three and four hours before death."

"Well, that accords with what we already knew," said Copper. "The whole company had dinner together. We know that. And I'm guessing that, because everybody ate together and presumably had the same, there's nothing dodgy in the meal?"

"That's right," said Suzanne.

"So that's it? We know they wouldn't have finished off the meal with coffee or tea. So how come Una says you might have an answer to our puzzle? Surely there's something else."

Suzanne gave a quiet smile. "And so there is. I was saving the best for last. Because this wasn't, in my opinion, consumed with the meal, but between one and two hours afterwards. It was an infusion."

"That'll be one of those weird herbal jobbies that Sue Pine mentioned," pointed out Radley. "She told us that Spelman had his own special mix."

Suzanne's eyebrows rose. "Did he, indeed? Well, I doubt if this particular mix was Mr. Spelman's deliberate choice. Because nobody in their right mind drinks oleander tea."

Chapter 9

"What on earth is oleander tea?" queried Dave Copper.

"That's just it," replied Suzanne. "There's no such thing."

Copper sighed in exasperation. "Could somebody please tell me how come Mr. Spelman drank something that doesn't exist."

"Oleander is a garden plant," explained Suzanne. "It's fairly ornamental. It's mostly got pink or white flowers on a bush with woody stems and small pointy leaves like spear heads. In fact, many people, if they've been on holiday to the Med, will have seen them growing all alongside the road."

"Oh, I've seen those," said Pete Radley. "I went to Crete once with the lads on a stag do. Mind you, we weren't noticing the vegetation. We were mostly there for the ..."

"I don't think we particularly want to know details of your unsavoury holiday experiences," interrupted Copper. "Carry on, Suzanne."

"Peter's right," said Suzanne. "And the Mediterranean countries plant them deliberately along the roadsides to discourage animals from straying on to the roads. Because the oleander is deadly poisonous. All parts of it. Anyone such as a child ingesting as little as one leaf could find themselves in severe trouble."

"What kind of trouble?" wondered Copper.

"Blurred vision, irregular heartbeat, confusion, faintness, digestive symptoms ... I could go on. With enough intake, death."

"So," said Copper slowly, thinking it through, "if someone were to make an infusion, as you mention, from oleander leaves ..."

"Which would not be at all difficult," put in

Suzanne. "Chop some up, add boiling water."

"... and then cause it to be consumed by their victim, that person could well be in a confused and disoriented state?"

"Very probably."

"And susceptible to suggestion? '*Not feeling well? Here, let me help you*' – that kind of thing?" But not necessarily physically incapacitated to start with? Still capable of moving under their own steam, maybe with a little guidance?"

Suzanne nodded. "It's quite possible. What do you think, Una?"

"You're more of an expert in these matters," said Una, "but from what I know, I think you could well be right, David."

A satisfied smile began to steal across the inspector's features. "Then I think you may have answered that particular riddle, Suzanne. And Sergeant Radley was absolutely right when he said that there was a great deal of preparation gone into this murder. Even more than we originally thought. So here's our scenario – somebody, one of our manor residents, has it in for Castor Spelman. They decide to do away with him, and they have the knowledge, from who knows where, to brew up the fatal potion." He broke off. "Oh good grief. I'm getting suckered into this blasted witchcraft story."

"Witchcraft?" echoed Una, perplexed.

"Tell you later," said Copper. "Anyway, the murderer contrives to get Spelman to drink this witch's brew – oh lord, I'm at it again – with the result that they are able to manoeuvre him down to the Coven Tree in the middle of the night and, armed with the screwdriver and the arrow, leave him dead on the ground." Nods all round. "So, two crucial questions. Who? And why?"

*

"Only one thing to do, boss." Pete Radley broke the

silence as the rest of the group digested Dave Copper's assessment. "Get back to Holt Manor and keep asking questions."

"Absolutely right, sergeant," concurred the inspector. "And it's not just answers we're looking for. I think there could well be evidence to find. You two ladies may well have checked the murder scene and pronounced it clean, but with what we now know, we need to take a look at the premises with a much more critical eye than I'd anticipated. Una, are you and Suzanne clear to come back with us and do a run at anything else that we may think relevant?"

"Happy to help," nodded Una. "Just let me delegate a couple of things." She moved to the door of the room, opened it, and called "Darren!" A young man in a white coat appeared. "Darren, Sooz and I are going back out to our latest crime scene. Can you deal with a couple of things while we're away?"

"We'll be off," interrupted Copper. "See you at the manor shortly?" At Una's nod, he motioned to Radley, and the two detectives made their way back to the lift and out of the building.

*

The wheels of the car crunched on the gravel of the Holt Manor drive as the inspector pulled up next to the patrol car still sitting in position outside the front entrance. "Do you want to bash on straight away, boss," enquired Radley, climbing out, "or would you rather wait for the others to arrive?"

"No need," smiled Copper, as the sound of another car approaching was heard, and the Forensics Department vehicle pulled up alongside. "Well, you two didn't hang about," he added, as Una stepped out of the passenger seat. "I thought you'd be way behind us."

"Not with Sooz driving," replied Una, slightly shakily. "When time is tight, she's a bit like Jehu in the

Bible - she driveth furiously."

"Then we'd better not let her skills go for nothing," said Copper "We'll make a start." With the others following, he led the way into the manor, to find Jazz Khan and her colleague stationed in the entrance passage. "Hello again, Khan," the inspector greeted her. "Any developments to report?"

"Nothing, sir," replied the young P.C. "I thought it would be okay with you if I let people go off to their own rooms or wherever within the manor, but nobody's left the premises."

"Good," approved Copper. "We'll be carrying out some searches, with the support of the forensic team. This is Sergeant Singleton, who is in charge of that side of things." The two women exchanged nods.

"Before we start, D... Inspector," said Una, "there's something you mentioned back at HQ that you never got to expand on, and it might have something to do with what we may be looking for. What on earth was this mention of witchcraft?"

"Ah. Yes. A rather odd tale told by one of our witnesses," replied Copper. He swiftly gave a précis of what Sheryl Icke had said about the ceremony in the glade in the woods. "But other than the name of the village ... sorry, hamlet, before Sergeant Radley takes it into his head to pick me up on it ... I really can't see any relevance. Other than the fact that they call this oak where Spelman was found 'the Coven Tree'."

"Um ... sir ..." Jazz spoke up hesitantly.

"Yes, constable?"

"Sir, there is actually quite a bit of history around here."

"I remember you said something about there being a lot of stories," recalled the inspector. "But seriously?" At the disappointed look on Jazz's face, he relented. "Okay, so what might there be that relates to talk of witchcraft at the manor?"

"Well, for a start, sir, there's the Witch's Cave."

Copper raised his eyes heavenwards. "Of course there is," he sighed. "Why wouldn't there be? So, Khan, tell us more."

"It's down in the gully in the woods, sir," said the young officer.

"You mean near where the body was found?"

"That's right, sir. Well, just a bit further down, beyond the Coven Tree."

"That'll be the gully that Denise Benz said she came up as part of her morning run, boss," pointed out Radley.

"So, potentially on the radar," said Copper. "And what is the story of this cave, Khan?"

"They say it's where the local witches used to meet in the old days, sir. All us local kids were told tales about black magic and curses, and warned to stay away. Of course, that was probably just to stop us from trespassing on the estate ..."

"Specially with what was going on back during the war, boss," chipped in Radley.

Jazz looked slightly puzzled at the observation, but carried on. "Of course, we didn't take any notice – you know what young kids are like. So everyone sneaked in for a dare at some time or another. There's a bit of wall you can climb over down at the bottom of the gully. Not that there's much to see – just a crack in the rocks which opens up into a small cave inside. No cauldrons with green steam coming off them or anything like that," she said, with a slightly embarrassed smile. "But just spooky enough for us kids to try to make each other jump."

"Well," said Copper, "I suppose we'll need to take a look, just in case. At least," he added with a chuckle, "we can be reasonably sure that there won't be any witches around the place these days." The chuckle died away as he was struck by the look on Khan's face. "Constable –

something you wish to say?"

Jazz blushed slightly. "It's just ... no, it's stupid, sir."

"Come on, out with it," insisted the inspector.

"She isn't really ... I mean, it's only silly children's talk, sir."

"What? And who?" demanded Copper.

"It's Mrs. Hexham," said Jazz. "Old Mother Hexham, the locals call her. They say she's the last remaining witch in Witch's Holt, sir. She looks the part, it's true. She's really old, and she's got long straggly hair and a pointy chin, just like in cartoons. And she's got a cat. She lives in the last cottage at the end of the village."

"I noticed that place when we first arrived, boss," remarked Radley. "Ratty old dump, I thought. Needs a bit of magic to smarten it up."

"Are you telling us that this Mrs. Hexham may have something to do with the case, Khan?" enquired Copper.

"Oh, I'm sure she couldn't have, sir," protested Jazz. "I doubt if she gets about much now. I mean, she was ancient when I was young, so I can't see her climbing over the wall to get to the cave these days. She must be getting on for a hundred."

Copper sighed. "Then, on balance, let's say that it's reasonable not to add her to our list of suspects. We have enough to consider as it is. So, back to business." He reflected for a moment. "Una, let's you and I go and take a look at this cave, just to rule it out, with luck. Khan, do we need you to show us the way?"

"No, sir. You can't really miss it. Just go past the Coven Tree and down the gully."

"Good. In that case, sergeant, why don't you take Suzanne through to the kitchen, and she can make a start on trying to locate the source of this poisonous brew of hers?"

"Will do, sir. It's through here, Sooz." Radley led Suzanne towards the Great Hall, while Copper and Una made their way out of the back door in the direction of the grounds.

"Oh. Hold on, love." A thought occurred to Copper. "It's going to be dark in that cave." He jogged back to the car, collected a pair of torches, rejoined Una, and the couple carried on down towards the gully.

"And here we are," said Una, indicating the crack in the rock wall which Jazz had described. She stepped into the darkness and switched her torch on, Copper following tentatively in her footsteps. He switched his own torch on and played its beam around the interior of the cave, revealing walls of dark red sandstone streaked with damp and featuring patches of algae.

"Not so spooky after all," he remarked, with something sounding suspiciously like relief in his voice. "Just like Khan said – no cauldrons with green steam, or anything like it. But I can see why the local children might like to scare each other with tall tales of witchery."

"I wouldn't be so quick to dismiss them if I were you," said Una, pointing her torch upwards. "See those sooty deposits on the ceiling? Somebody's had a fire going in here at some time, although I wouldn't care to say how long ago. Could be decades. Centuries, even." She deflected the light downwards, and its beam fell on a recess at the back of the cave. She stepped forward and peered at the illuminated section of cave wall, intent on making a closer inspection. "Now that's interesting," she declared. "Do you see those?" She indicated a series of grooves and circles scratched into the stone. "I think I know what those might be."

"And what's that?" enquired Copper.

"Witches' marks," replied Una. And in response to Copper's exclamation of incredulity, she continued, "Feel free to scoff, but I saw a programme on television not too long ago where they were talking about just such a thing as these." She pointed. "That circular symbol is the most common type – the one that looks like a six-pointed flower. They're called hexafoils, which means six leaves, and they're supposed to deflect evil. You mostly find them on medieval buildings, around doorways or fireplaces. They prevent evil forces from entering your house, or the barn where you store your grain."

"You're telling me that these hexafoil things are actually supposed to ... what, foil a hex?" Copper sounded as if he couldn't believe what he was saying.

"If you lived in a village like this in medieval times, that's exactly what they were meant to do," smiled Una, amused at her husband's astonishment. "And maybe not so medieval. You heard what P.C. Khan was saying about the stories among the locals - the local witch in the creepy old cottage. Well, perhaps there is some sort of lingering superstition." She inspected the marks again. "I can't say for certain how old these are. They definitely aren't recent. But maybe this place was actually believed to have been a meeting place for witches in times gone by, so the marks were made here to keep them away."

"And do you reckon Castor Spelman might actually have bought into this hocus pocus?" asked the inspector.

"I couldn't say," shrugged Una. "That's your department. But one thing I can tell you." She scanned the cave interior once more with the beam of her torch. "I can see no evidence of any recent activity in here. So whatever explanation there may be for the man's murder, it doesn't lie in this cave."

"Then let's get out of here," said Copper.

*

Back up at the manor, the couple entered the kitchen, coming face-to-face with Radley and Suzanne who were just about to make their way out towards the Great Hall.

"Any luck?" asked Copper.

"Not a sausage so far, boss," reported Radley. "Sooz

and I have been through all the store cupboards in here, and there doesn't appear to be anything that she's got worries over."

"We've found plenty of herbal infusions of all sorts," confirmed Suzanne. "In fact, more kinds of tea than your local supermarket."

"Some of which I wouldn't drink for ready money," put in Radley. "Just a sniff of them was enough to put you off for life."

"But they were all reasonably conventional, if you like that sort of thing," continued Suzanne. "There wasn't anything that you'd be unlikely to find in your average high street health food shop. And in any case, apart from a couple of single ingredients like camomile and mint, which were in plain little jars, the vast majority were in nice neat tea bags, so I can't see that there would have been any opportunity to tamper with them."

"Well, it's good to rule out that possibility," said Copper. "But in fact, I'm not totally surprised. Because don't you remember, sergeant, we were told that Mr. Spelman had his own special concoction which nobody else was allowed to touch. And if it's not to be found here, maybe we can find it in his room. Perhaps Anna Logue isn't the only one on the premises with a crafty kettle. With a nice little pot of something alongside, which has been substituted by our murderer with the offending oleander leaves."

"Oh!" Suzanne let out a sudden exclamation. "Oh, I'm so stupid!"

"Why?" wondered Una, concerned. "What have you done?"

"It's what I haven't done," said Suzanne, an expression of irritation on her features. "And that'll teach me not to look where I'm going. Idiot!"

"I don't understand," smiled Una, beginning to be amused at her colleague's words. "What are you talking about?"

"It's when we got here," explained Suzanne. "I was so keen not to waste any time that I pretty much had my foot right down all the way."

"I know," said Una with feeling. "Which is why I had my eyes closed most of the time."

"And I might as well have done the same," said Suzanne. "But fortunately, I must have had at least one eye open. Because as we were coming up the drive, I must have subconsciously noted the plants on either side. And I've only just realised what I saw. In amongst all the other bushes, there they were. Oleanders!"

"That's going to be where they came from then, boss, isn't it?" declared Radley. "Job done."

"It certainly seems pretty obvious," agreed Copper.

"Just a moment, though," demurred Una. "Obvious isn't what we do in forensics. Now I don't know if all oleanders are the same, or if there are distinctions between the different strains. I'd like to be positive that these oleanders on the estate chime with what Sooz found in her toxicology analysis. So what I suggest is that you, Sooz, escorted by our trusty Sergeant Radley, go and get some leaf samples from these plants, and then when we get back to the lab you can run a test to make sure that the plants here and the toxin are like for like."

"'*To make assurance doubly sure*'," said Copper. At Una's quizzical eyebrow, he explained, "It's a quote from Shakespeare. It's what the guv used to say. You know, belt and braces, just to be certain."

"Mr. Copper, you are full of surprises," smiled Una. "Okay, Sooz – if you and Peter would like to do that, we'll go and check on things in Mr. Spelman's room." She glanced sideways at her husband. "If that's all right with you, inspector."

"An admirable plan, Sergeant Singleton," responded Copper with an answering smile. "So let's get to it."

Chapter 10

Back in the entrance passage, the group found Jazz Khan and her young uniformed colleague perched on hard chairs, looking somewhat disconsolate. On the floor beside each sat an evidently empty takeaway coffee cup. The two came smartly to their feet, and Jazz stepped forward.

"Still nothing much happening here, sir," she reported. "It's all been very quiet. Everyone seems to be keeping pretty much to themselves."

"And that's probably no bad thing," responded Dave Copper. "We'll be carrying out some further interviews later, and that means there'll be less chance of anyone coordinating their stories. If they need to, of course," he added. "I'd better start by having a word with Mr. Day, since he's presumably the main person in charge. Do you happen to know where he is?"

"He was going into the study, the last time I saw him, sir."

"Good," said Copper. A thought struck him. "Khan, you and this young chap have been here since pretty much first thing, haven't you?"

"That's right, sir."

Copper looked at his watch. "And I bet you haven't had anything to eat, have you?"

"Well, actually, no, sir." Jazz glanced sideways at her companion. "Brad didn't think to get anything else when he went for the coffees."

"That is not good." A sigh. "Sergeant Radley, do you suppose we can contrive to continue our investigations without the support of our uniformed colleagues?" Copper quirked an eyebrow in Radley's direction while remaining solemn-faced.

Pete Radley responded in kind. "It'll probably be tough without back-up, sir, but we'll have to make the best of it." A smile hovered at the corner of his mouth.

"There you are then, Khan," said Copper. He broke into a laugh. "You two can buzz off. Get yourselves back to that petrol station and grab yourselves some sandwiches. I can't run the risk of two of our officers flaking out through lack of sustenance."

"Thanks, sir," replied Jazz. "If you're sure?"

"Go!" commanded the inspector, mock-sternly.

"Yes, sir. Right away, sir. But if you need us again, we're in the area, and our shift doesn't finish for hours yet. So ..."

"Go!" reiterated Copper with a further laugh, and the two young uniformed officers escaped without a backward glance.

"I do love to see the command structure of the Force at its most impressive," chuckled Una. "Authority being admirably exercised."

"That's enough cheek from you, Sergeant Singleton," grinned Copper. "Remember you're speaking to a senior officer."

"As if I'd dream of forgetting it ...sir," dimpled Una.

Suzanne cleared her throat. "Don't mind us, you two," she said, "but isn't there meant to be some sort of investigation taking place? Just saying."

"Good point," said Una. "So why don't you carry on as I suggested, and disappear into the bushes with Peter in search of the offending oleander foliage? In the meantime, David and I can do that check on Spelman's room."

"Once I've cleared it with Mr. Day, of course," pointed out Copper. "I don't want our case compromised by any charges of illegal searches."

As Suzanne and Radley made their way out of the front door, Copper and Una passed through the library, ignoring the enquiring looks of the two or three people scattered about the room, and tapping on the study door, before responding to the muted 'Come in' from inside the room, to find Rudy Day seated at the desk, apparently lost in thought. He looked up warily. "Something I can do for you, inspector?"

"There is, Mr. Day," said Copper. "We've had some information come our way, thanks to the researches of our forensic colleagues ..." A nod in the direction of Una. "... and it would be very helpful if we could follow that up by taking a look at Mr. Spelman's room. That's if you would have no objection, of course."

Rudy looked uneasy. "Don't you need some kind of warrant before you search someone's premises, inspector?" he enquired.

"Indeed we do," replied Copper blandly. "That's if the search is compulsory, naturally. Normally that's the case where the owner of the premises has something to hide. I'm sure that wouldn't be the case with you, Mr. Day." An open smile, which somehow failed to reach the inspector's eyes. "As a rule, we like to rely on the cooperation of the public. But of course, I can always obtain a warrant if you insist." The threat, delivered in the silkiest of tones, was nevertheless clear.

"Er ... no, that won't be necessary," said Rudy. "No, you can go ahead if you need to."

"That's very helpful, Mr. Day," smiled Copper. "In fact," he added, pressing his advantage, "can I take it that this permission extends to the rest of the building?"

"Um ... yes, of course." Rudy seemed to become aware that his reluctance was creating an unfavourable impression. "Of course, inspector," he repeated, sounding more positive, "you must search wherever you please. Do anything you must to find out who killed poor Castor. Shall I show you up to his room?"

"Thank you, Mr. Day. And don't trouble yourself. I know the way." Copper turned without explanation and led the way out of the study, leaving Rudy looking concerned.

"And that, love," murmured Copper, as the couple climbed the stairs, "is how you exercise authority." He grinned at his wife.

"Neatly done," smiled Una. "So, which way to the master suite?"

Castor Spelman's room was, like the manor house itself, a curious mixture. The bones of the original medieval building could be detected in scraps of gothic masonry around the windows, while Tudor linen-fold panelling covered two of the walls. A third was hung with what looked like a genuine eighteenth-century tapestry, caught back to reveal a door which gave on to a bathroom, while the ceiling was painted in an extravagant rococo style featuring cherubs bearing overflowing cornucopias up towards presiding deities seated above in the heavens. The furnishing was likewise an odd miscellany. There was a massive dark oak double-fronted wardrobe behind the door to the hall landing, and the entire room was dominated by a large four-poster bed with hangings of purple velvet, held in place by fat gold tassels, providing a contrast to the minimalist chrome armchairs and a sofa table topped with smoky glass.

"If I had to judge Castor Spelman's character from this room," remarked Copper, "I would say that there were some weird contradictions going on."

"Judge not," replied Una, "although it doesn't exactly all hang together, does it?" Her eye fell on an object on a low table between the windows. "But that," she added, pointing, "is something else, and very much in tune with what we've already seen."

"How do you mean?" enquired the inspector. "What is it?"

The object was a brown earthenware pot some fifteen inches high, rising from a small circular base into an extremely wide belly before narrowing again to a tall neck. On the surface facing the couple could be discerned the stylised features of what could be seen as a sinister and threatening bearded face.

"That," explained Una, "is a Bellarmine."

"And what is a Bellarmine, when it's at home?" asked a puzzled Copper.

"Otherwise known as a Witch's Pot," answered his wife.

Copper sighed. "Wouldn't you know it? Well, come on, love – tell all."

"It was on a television programme," began Una.

"Same one as the one about those marks in the cave?"

"Same one. Different period of history." Una went closer to examine the ceramic. "These started around the sixteen-hundreds, if I remember correctly, so therefore much later than the cave markings. And they're named after an Italian cardinal named Bellarmino. That's supposed to be his face."

"Unpleasant looking chap, if it's anything like a good likeness," commented Copper, stepping alongside Una and peering at the design on the pot. "And what was his claim to fame?"

"I think he was much opposed to those people who wanted to break away from the traditional church. I can't remember the precise details, if I'm honest. And I'm not sure how the pots came to be given his name."

"Was he mixed up with supernatural doings of some kind?" enquired Copper. "Isn't that the period when people were doing a lot of witch-hunting? Did he go about putting curses on people? So is this pot the same as those marks – did it keep the witches away?"

"Not exactly," said Una. "The thing about these pots is, they were supposed to reverse a curse back on to its sender. Suppose your enemy put a curse on you so that, for instance, some crucial part of your anatomy dropped off ..." She glanced sideways at her husband, her eyes twinkling.

Copper blinked. "Now that's a prospect I prefer not to think about too closely," he grimaced.

"Quite so. You wouldn't be too keen. Our marriage would definitely not be enhanced. So you'd do something about it. And into one of these pots you would put certain significant items ..."

"Such as?"

"Oh, all sorts. Hanks of hair. Animal bones. Pieces of paper with incantations written on them. Human fluids."

"Bloody hell."

"It needn't necessarily be blood," said Una. "Other bodily fluids would do just as well."

"Yuk." Copper pulled a face. "Too much information."

"You did ask. Anyway, once you had carried out these procedures, the usual thing was to conceal the pot somewhere significant. They've been found bricked up inside walls or hidden away up chimneys. And then the curse would bounce back against the person who had ill-wished you, and you'd be as right as rain," finished Una with a triumphant smile.

"Well, who knew? Every day's a school day," remarked her husband. "It's like being back in the old days with the guv. With a rather more attractive teacher, of course, love," he added, depositing a peck on his wife's cheek. "So what's this witch's pot doing at Witch's Holt? Or is that a stupid question? More important, what does it have to do with our case? Did Castor Spelman fear being on the receiving end of a curse?"

"Except, of course, that he wasn't," pointed out Una practically. "He was on the receiving end of an arrow, or rather, a screwdriver followed by an arrow. Not much supernatural about either of those. And he wasn't cursed in order to put him in a fit state to be attacked – he was drugged. Which is the reason we're in his room."

"And I'm wasting your time by making you give me history lessons," said Copper contritely. "You're absolutely right, love." He chuckled. "You know, all this talk of spells and witchcraft reminds me of one of the early cases I did with the guv. That one was all about a clairvoyant, and there was a lot of talk about the Carrie Otter books – you know, that schoolgirl magician – which some critic or other had apparently described as 'a load of old warlocks'. I have to say, I can see his point." Una gave an answering laugh. "Anyway, back to business. Let's get searching. Divide and conquer?"

"Excellent suggestion. Do you want to have a look around in here while I take the bathroom? That seems the most likely haunt of anything in the drugs line."

"Sounds like a plan to me. Go ahead." While Una disappeared into the bathroom, Copper began a search of the bedroom. There was, in truth, little capacity for concealment. The bed, gently rumpled from occupation from one side only, the inspector noted, showed no signs of any struggle. The matching bedside tables, carved oak bearing small red-shaded lamps, yielded nothing that seemed significant. On one stood an untouched glass of water and, alongside it, a paperback biography of Winston Churchill. The other held a smart speaker, live but silent, on its lower level, while on the top surface a self-winding watch from an extremely expensive and well-known maker rocked rhythmically to and fro in its cradle. There were precious few decorative items about the room – a small oil painting of what might have been the manor in its original medieval incarnation hung on one wall, with an almost aggressively modern collage of steel wires and geometric shapes on another, while an arrangement of dried flowers and foliage stood on a side table. The inspector crossed to the wardrobe, opening one door to reveal a mostly perfectly ordinary selection of expensive-looking suits, shirts and trousers, with a rack of shoes beneath, the whole rendered unusual by the fact that, at the end of the rail, there hung four or five long robes in a variety of colours, all elaborately embroidered, and all strikingly similar in style to the garment worn by the dead body.

"How are things going?" enquired Una as she re-entered from the bathroom.

"Nothing much so far," replied Copper. "Except these." He indicated the hanging robes. "Our Mr. Spelman doesn't seem to have been a man to stint himself, particularly in the realms of fancy ceremonial garb. I'm guessing these probably set him back a pretty penny. I shall have to check with Coco de Roque."

Una frowned slightly. "Have I heard that name before somewhere?"

"Maybe. Depends whether you're up with your *haute couture*. Apparently she's some sort of fashion designer – top of the game, according to her - and she made that robe the dead man was found wearing."

"And she's here?"

Copper nodded. "She was present for this course Spelman was running. Whether that's significant or not, we shall have to see. Anyway, how have you got on?"

"Not spectacularly, I'm afraid," admitted Una. "Apart from the fact that the bathroom is an Art Deco vision in mint green and mirror tile, there was precious little to find. Towels on one side only of the double towel rail. A double-fronted wall cabinet with one side empty, and the other side containing only a few conventional toiletries, all of them normal commercial brands which showed no signs of having been tampered with. One bottle of designer cologne, which I happen to know is eye-wateringly expensive. And a single toothbrush." She raised an eyebrow.

"I think we may safely say," said Copper, "that Mr. Spelman was in solitary occupation. No sign of anyone else sharing the room. Evidently what we were told about love's middle-aged dream having faded appears to be borne out by the evidence. Anyway, I'm almost finished here. Just the other half of the wardrobe to go." He opened the second door, and stood back with a satisfied sigh. "And here we are."

The interior of the cupboard was fitted with shelves, which at top and bottom held folded sweaters, underwear, belts and other small items. And on the middle shelf sat the kind of tray found in many hotel rooms, with two cups and saucers, a teapot, small plates, cutlery, and a small electric kettle. Alongside the kettle stood a screw-top glass jar, empty of contents.

"How nice to be proved right, just once in a while," smiled Copper.

"How so?"

"Don't you remember? I said downstairs, when Suzanne came up with her sighting of the oleander bushes, that I wondered if there might be such an arrangement in Mr. Spelman's room, so that he could brew up his own special concoction whenever he wanted to? And now, here it is. And I'm betting that this jar is what his private mixture was housed in. Except that now, it's empty."

"And I will take charge of it right now," said Una, producing a plastic evidence bag from her case and placing the jar within it. "There's almost bound to be some residual traces of the previous contents, even if it's been washed out in the meantime. And the sooner I get back to the lab to do some tests, the sooner I'll be able to tell you."

"That sounds like a very good plan," replied Copper. "In fact, shouldn't you take the whole kit and caboodle? Kettle, cups, the lot? Maybe someone planted the nefarious mixture in that jar and left Spelman to make his own lethal brew in his own good time, but that doesn't accord with what we presume was the scheme to get him out into the gardens. So there's also the possibility that he had a late-night visitor who very kindly brewed up the concoction for him at the crucial moment, in which case, surely there's scope for some giveaway fingerprints."

"You know, you can be so annoyingly clever sometimes," smiled Una, as she delved once more into her case for more evidence bags, as well as a larger bag to place them all into.

"It's a gift," grinned her husband.

"And for that, you can lug all this. And as soon as we're back at the department, I'll get on with doing the finger-printing while Sooz does the analysis on the jar."

"Sounds good to me," said Copper. He glanced out of the window. "Because by happy coincidence, I can see Suzanne and Peter coming back towards the house, and from the body language, I'm guessing that she's pleased with what she's found. Let's go back down and meet them."

Una and the inspector reached the foot of the stairs just as Suzanne and the sergeant came in through the front door.

"Any joy, Sooz?" enquired Una.

"I hope so," said Suzanne. "I've taken samples from half a dozen different bushes, so we should be able to get a pretty good analysis of what is what. All I need now is to get back to my bench and start work."

"That's perfect," said Una. "And we've discovered a jar which seems the most likely candidate to be the container of the mix which drugged Mr. Spelman. So if it's alright by you, David, we'll head back to the department and make a start."

"Couldn't be better," agreed Copper. "Call me when you get anything."

"Of course."

"Let's get going then," said Suzanne, producing the keys to the forensic team's vehicle. "I'll have us back to Westchester in no time."

"Oh no you won't!" retorted Una, seizing the keys. "I've had quite enough close brushes with death for one day, thank you very much. We shall be heading back to the department at a much more sedate pace. And I shall be driving."

Chapter 11

As the forensic team's vehicle disappeared down the drive of Holt Manor, Dave Copper turned to his junior colleague. "And then there were two."

"Ah, but the best two, boss," replied Pete Radley with an answering grin.

"Modesty forbids," smiled Copper. "And with a dozen people to interview, half of whom seem to be in the frame as potential suspects, I think we ought to get on with it."

"Where do you want to start, boss?" enquired Radley, producing his notebook from a pocket. "I've got a list of all the people in the place. Do you want to do it alphabetically, or what?"

The inspector reflected for a moment. "No. Let's begin with the ones that we're ruling out on account of Anna Logue's very useful CCTV. We know that the residents of the stables couldn't have had the opportunity to get out during the crucial period, but that's not to say that they don't have useful information to give us. Now, as I recall, there were a couple of them in the library a little while ago. We'll check them out first."

As the detectives entered the library, they found Maia Cord and Sheila Peel sitting on opposite sides of the room, each casting an occasional surreptitious glance at the other, as if wondering whether they were sharing the space with a murderer. "Good afternoon, ladies," began Copper. "Once again, I do apologise for having left you so long in limbo, but I'm afraid that enquiries into a murder necessarily need to take their time."

Maia Cord rose to her feet. "But are you any closer to knowing who killed Castor, inspector?" she asked, concern written over her face.

"I can only tell you that we are still gathering facts," replied Copper, unwilling to divulge information unnecessarily. "And in order to do that, I'd like a further word with each of you. In private. And perhaps I could conveniently start with you, Mrs. Cord." He looked around. "The only question is, where? Perhaps Mr. Day wouldn't mind if we commandeered the study again."

"He's not in there," volunteered Sheila Peel. "He came out a few minutes ago, saw we were here, and then muttered something about going upstairs."

"Odd," said Copper. "I've just come down, and I didn't meet him."

"Maybe he went up those sneaky back stairs, boss," suggested Radley. "Perhaps he heard you coming down and didn't want to be seen."

Copper shrugged. "It's possible. Anyway, the point is, the study seems to be free, so I see no reason for us not to use it." He crossed to the door and held it open. "After you, Mrs. Cord." As he resumed his former place behind the desk and invited Maia to seat herself once more in the chair facing him, Radley quietly brought one of the upright chairs through from the library and sank on to it with something resembling a smile of relief, producing his notebook and preparing to make notes.

"To be frank, Mrs. Cord," began the inspector, "I don't believe that everybody has told us everything they know. And that includes you."

Maia appeared startled at the directness of Copper's approach. "But I have, honestly, inspector. You asked if I knew of any threats spoken against Castor Spelman, and I didn't. I told you that. And I really couldn't have had any reason to threaten him myself. I'd never met him before. So why would I want to harm him? It doesn't make sense." Her voice rose.

"Relax, Mrs. Cord." Copper smiled at Maia's growing agitation. "You aren't being accused of anything. In fact, very much the reverse. You see, we have positive evidence that there is no way you could have been involved in Mr. Spelman's murder. So you needn't have any fears that you are in any way a suspect."

Maia let out a deep breath, and the tension visibly left her body. "But then I don't understand," she said. "What else can I possibly tell you?"

"I think I can probably call on your professional instincts, Mrs. Cord." Copper leaned forward confidentially. "You're a specialist in relationships. Now plainly, this whole group of people seems to have been constructed very much as a community. I'm guessing that you will all have spent much of your time together, if not in close proximity, then certainly in the vicinity of one another. And under those circumstances, people talk. Am I right?"

"Yes, we did function as a group most of the time," agreed Maia. "Although Castor did hold these one-on-one sessions with people. Individual assessments, he called them. So they were private conversations. I'd have no idea what went on there."

"But surely," suggested the inspector, "there would have been other one-on-one conversations, as you call them, between other members of the group, or between Mr. Spelman and various individuals. Not everything took place behind closed doors, did it?"

"Well, no. Of course not."

"And my thinking is, that it would be unusual if sometimes, things were overheard that weren't intended to be. Somebody could, for instance, have been on one side of an open door and, without meaning to eavesdrop, they might have heard what was said on the other. Now when we spoke earlier, I think you said something about passing remarks not registering on your radar, but I'm not certain that's true. In your work, I suspect that passing remarks can probably be interpreted as having great significance. And that's why I say that your professional instincts might provide useful information for me. I'm not looking for direct threats. What I need is a better insight into the relationships between the people here at the manor. Because one of them is most certainly a killer, and I believe you can help me to discover who that could be. If you can only dig back through your memory." Copper sat back and regarded Maia expectantly.

There was a long pause as Maia gazed past Copper and out of the window, evidently deep in thought. Eventually, she gave a small smile. "It's the habit of discretion, inspector," she said. "I've become so used to keeping to myself the things that people say to, or about, one another, that it's become second nature to me not to repeat them to a third party."

"And I understand that," replied Copper, "but of course, in this instance, you're not being asked to break professional confidentiality."

Maia seemed to make up her mind. "Do you know, inspector, I never get the opportunity to have a good gossip, so I'm not sure I know how to do it." She laughed shakily.

"But there's something you've thought of?" hazarded Copper. "And does it by any chance involve Mr. Spelman?"

"As a matter of fact, it does."

"Then why don't you tell us about it?"

"It's actually like you said," said Maia. "About the door, I mean. You see, it was between sessions, and I was at a bit of a loose end for a minute, so I thought I'd come into the library to see if I could get myself something to read. I told you about my guilty pleasure reading soppy chick-lit, didn't I? Well, I'd just finished the only book I'd brought with me, and I'd noticed that there was a section on the shelves where people who'd been here before had left their own books that they'd finished and didn't want any more. I wondered if there might be some old rubbish there I could swap for my own book. So I went back to my room, picked up my book, and came through next door to see if I could find a replacement. And my luck was in, because there was a book by one of my favourite authors, so I picked that up and put mine in its place. And just as I was about to go back to my room, the study door opened, and I could hear voices."

"And these voices were ...?"

"They were Castor Spelman and Rudy Day. I suppose I'd been half-aware of them, because I could hear muffled talking through the door, although I didn't pay much attention. But then the door was opened, I suppose by Rudy, and they must have been on the tail end of an argument, because I heard Rudy say 'I wish I'd never got involved with you', and then Castor replied 'And don't think you can get out of it that easily, because I've got you tied up more ways than you can think'. And Rudy shouted 'You've got no idea what I can do', and then he slammed the door before storming off."

"And how did Rudy react when he saw you?" wondered Copper. "He couldn't very well miss you."

"Actually, he could," confessed Maia. "Because he was obviously about to walk out once he'd delivered his parting shot – you wouldn't believe the number of times I've seen that happen, inspector - and I knew I'd be so embarrassed if he knew I'd overheard, so I just ducked down behind the sofa, and he never knew I was there. And when the coast was clear, I just scuttled back to my room."

"I see." Copper thought for a moment. "So Mr. Spelman's personal relationships weren't running entirely smoothly, by the sound of things. But you didn't hear him say anything else to Mr. Day at that point?"

"No," confirmed Maia. "Oh!"

Copper was alerted. "'Oh'? What does that mean?"

"It means I've just remembered something else I

heard," said Maia.

"Involving Mr. Day?"

"No. It was Castor."

"Speaking to someone else?"

"Yes. It was that secretary of his, Sue Pine."

"And in what way is this of interest?" enquired Copper.

"I really don't know," admitted Maia, " but it just struck me as out of character at the time."

"How so?"

"I went into the kitchen yesterday to make myself a cup of tea – well, one of those things they call tea. I can't say I actually much like the taste of any of the ones I've tried so far, but there's always the hope that you'll strike lucky eventually, isn't there? Anyway, just as I got there, Castor came out of a little door in the corner of the kitchen. It quite surprised me, because I had no idea that there was a door there. I thought it was just a cupboard, but in fact it's a little staircase. Anyway, he burst out of there in quite a rush, and he was followed by Sue, who seemed to be trying to hold on to his arm to keep him there. But he shook her off, and turned back to her, and he said, quite roughly, 'You're just wasting your time and mine'. Almost a snarl, it was. Totally out of character with the way he'd been presenting himself to everyone during the sessions. Not at all like last thing last night, when apparently Sue went into his study, and Sheryl told me all she could hear was him having a good laugh, so they must have got on sometimes. Anyway, back in the kitchen, he noticed me, and just switched the snarl off, quick as a flash, and gave me the most charming smile, and walked out into the Great Hall. And I would have said something to Sue, but she just turned tail and went back up the way she'd come. And I brewed up a cup of nettle, liquorice and comfrey tea, which tastes just as disgusting as it sounds, before going off to Denise's next class."

*

"Interesting turn of phrase from Mrs. Cord there," mused Dave Copper, as the door to the hall passage closed behind Maia.

"What's that, boss?" asked Pete Radley.

"When she said that Rudy Day delivered a parting shot at the end of his row with Castor Spelman. Because she'd already mentioned that Rudy was quite adept when it came to those archery classes of Denise Benz's. He'd had plenty of practice over time, of course. But it would have meant that he had the skill to deliver a well-placed arrow into Spelman in the half-light of the early morning in the clearing in the woods." Copper chuckled. "It's a beautiful theory. Shame it's complete rubbish."

"Why? Sounds quite good to me."

"And it would be, if only Spelman had actually been shot," observed Copper. "Except that he wasn't, of course. He was screwdrivered to death. The arrow was an afterthought." A moment's reflection. "Although it couldn't have been, because the killer would have had to come armed with it when luring or manoeuvring, or whatever it was they did, to get the victim out to the Coven Tree. So we're definitely back with your previous theory – this was a well-thought-out murder."

"Better get on with finding this thinker, then, hadn't we, boss?" said Radley, jumping briskly to his feet. "Shall I get the next one in?"

Copper smiled. "Fresh enthusiasm, eh? That's what I like to see in a detective."

"It's not just that, boss," confessed Radley. "My stomach's starting to rumble. It seems forever since breakfast, and that teacake of Anna's didn't fill much of a gap. I thought a bit of work would take my mind off the nadgers."

"Seems to me we should have got Khan to bring you back some sandwiches while she was at it," remarked Copper. "It appears I'm surrounded by officers suffering from the pangs of hunger. But work has to come first." Radley looked crest-fallen. "But here's a compromise for you. We'll scoot through these interviews, and then we'll see if there's something to be found in the kitchens to fortify us."

"Works for me, boss," said Radley. "I'll bring that other woman through."

Sheila Peel seated herself opposite Copper. Her initial calm appeared to be back in place, seemingly in no way ruffled by the spiky turn which her first interview had taken, although the inspector thought he could still detect an inner tension. "I imagine, inspector, that after our earlier conversation, you've probably managed to construct some sort of motive for me to murder our host," began the lawyer.

Copper was somewhat surprised by the challenge. He smiled. "As it happens, Mrs. Peel, nothing could be further from the truth. In fact, I'm perfectly happy to tell you that we have evidence that there is no way that you could have been responsible for killing Mr. Spelman."

Sheila's eyebrows rose. "Really?"

"Really. So no matter how convenient your clash with Mr. Spelman may have been in providing you with a reason to dislike him, the facts are clear. You had no opportunity for murder."

"Oh." Sheila seemed if anything faintly disappointed. "Well, I suppose that's reassuring to know."

"But it's not your altercation with Mr. Spelman which now concerns me," continued the inspector. "But rather any tensions between him and others which you may have been aware of, even though you may not have been involved."

"There was certainly an occasion when I heard myself mentioned," volunteered Sheila. "I don't know if that's what you're looking for."

"That would depend on what was said, and to whom," replied Copper. "Suppose you tell me the details."

"It was sometime around teatime a day or two ago. It was actually a rather nice afternoon, and there was a gap in the schedule for me. Well, I say that – I'd actually engineered a twisted ankle so that I could get out of one of Denise's fitness sessions. Aerobic exercise and I don't get on too well together."

"Tell me about it," Radley muttered, but then buried his nose afresh into his notebook at a disapproving glance from his superior.

"I was sitting on one of the stone benches out on the terrace at the back," continued Sheila, who appeared not to have noticed the interruption. "There's quite a suntrap, just in the corner of one of the surviving medieval buttresses. And I could hear someone approaching around the corner of the building, evidently in the middle of a conversation."

"And you were mentioned, you say?" asked Copper.

"Not by name," said Sheila. "It was Castor who was speaking, and he said 'Maybe I should get the books checked. After all, we've got a lawyer on the premises'. Of course, that drew my attention straight away. And the other person replied that there wasn't any need for that, and she could explain everything to him if he gave her the chance."

"And who was that other person?"

"Well, just then, the two of them came round the corner, and I saw that it was Charlotte-Anne Connor. And Castor, who seemed to be rather hot under the collar, was just about to say something else when he noticed me sitting there, so he bit off whatever it was he was about to say, and grunted something about things not being over by a long chalk, and he'd have it out with her later. He then stalked off indoors, and Charlotte-Anne sidled back round the corner, as if to pretend that she'd never been there in the first place."

"So you heard nothing more? You couldn't gather what they'd been discussing?"

Sheila shook her head. "Not positively, inspector. But, of course, in my profession, when you hear mention of the books needing to be checked, it's difficult to discount the possibility that someone is talking about some kind of irregularity or fraud."

"Fraud, eh?" mused Copper. "That's certainly cropped up as a motive for murder in past cases. As well as being a criminal act in itself, of course."

"Oh goodness!" suddenly exclaimed Sheila. "Fraud! How silly. I wonder why I didn't remember it sooner."

"So you do believe that the two were discussing some kind of financial fraud?" queried the inspector.

"Oh, not that," retorted Sheila impatiently. "No, the other fraud."

Copper blinked uncertainly. "I'm sorry, Mrs. Peel. I don't follow. How many frauds do you think were taking place around here?"

Sheila smiled apologetically. "Sorry, inspector. I'm not making myself very clear, am I? No, it was just the mention of the word that reminded me."

"Of what exactly?"

"It may have been yesterday – I'm not sure. There's an odd dislocation of time around this place, inspector. You're never quite sure what is when. Which was actually the point. You see, I'd somehow mislaid the schedule which I'd been given, and I needed another copy, so I was looking for Sue the secretary. Somebody told me that she might be in her room, which they said was upstairs in the old part of the manor where I hadn't been before. So I was climbing the stairs when I heard Castor speaking, and I thought 'Good. I can ask him which is Sue's room', and I got to the landing just in time to see him nose to nose with the French woman."

"Coco de Roque?"

"That's the one. 'Coco' indeed! Ridiculous name, obviously made up, but then she just exudes falseness, in my opinion. The fashion world is so bizarre, isn't it? Anyway, Castor had his back to me, and I was just in time to hear him saying quite clearly 'I can smell a fraud a mile off. You're finished!' Most aggressive, which seemed odd, because from what I'd understood, she was here at his invitation because of some work she'd produced for him."

"And did Miss de Roque respond?"

"Not a word. Because just as she was drawing breath to do so, she caught sight of me. And Castor turned to see what she was looking at, and then disappeared into what I assume was his room without another word. I just asked Coco if she knew where Sue's room was, in as normal a voice as I could manage, pretending that I hadn't heard a thing, and she pointed it out to me and then wafted past me and down the stairs."

"So, again, you didn't hear any further details which would shed light on the reason for Mr. Spelman's remark?"

"I'm sorry, inspector," replied Sheila. "I'm just as much in the dark as you are."

Chapter 12

"Not quite as much in the dark as we were before," said Dave Copper, as he sat in thought after Sheila's departure.

"In what way, boss?" asked Pete Radley, returning to the room after ensuring that Sheila was safely out of earshot. "Neither of those two had anything concrete to tell us, other than bits and pieces of chat."

"On the contrary," said Copper. "And bits and pieces are the building blocks of a solid case. You ought to know that by now. For a start, we've got definite confirmation, over and above the vague hints we'd had before, that Castor Spelman's relationship with Rudy Day was on the rocks. And Rudy was apparently keen to extricate himself, so did Castor's evident unwillingness to unravel the bonds make Rudy look for more definite steps to take?"

"And talking about relationships, boss, it doesn't sound as if the boss-and-employee relationship between Castor and Sue was the smoothest ever," said Radley. "I mean, not like ours, obviously." He grinned. "It sounds as if she'd done something which he didn't approve of. If your boss starts mouthing off because you've mucked up his precious schedules, or whatever she did for him, you're going to be a bit miffed, aren't you?"

"Not the strongest motive for murder I've ever heard," observed Copper. "But this talk of fraud – now that's another kettle of fish. People get into serious trouble for that kind of thing. And although I can see why Charlotte-Anne Connor's name might be relevant in that context, I can't see what earthly connection she could have had with Coco de Roque. They seem an unlikely pair to have been in cahoots with one another."

"Still more questions then, boss."

"More questions to ask, certainly," said Copper.

"And since the various ladies in question don't seem about to present themselves in an orderly queue for interrogation, we'd better go looking for them."

The search didn't take long. As the detectives emerged into the entrance passage, they caught sight of Sheryl Icke in the Great Hall, staring pensively out of the oriel window. The light from the stained glass fell on her, casting an almost ethereal harlequin glow over her which, Copper reflected, was totally at odds with her no-nonsense character. "Mrs. Icke," he hailed her, causing her to jump slightly. "I wonder if we might have a word."

"Of course you can, inspector," she answered, advancing into the room from the window recess. "Do you know, I was miles away, thinking about all this murder business. But I'm all yours. What can I tell you?"

"Shall we sit down?" suggested the inspector, and seated himself on one of the benches at the refectory table, gesturing for Sheryl to take the imposing carver chair at the head of the table, as Radley positioned himself further down the bench.

"Castor's chair," marvelled Sheryl. "Very posh. Although I bet some people wouldn't be so happy putting themselves in a dead man's place."

"Actually, Mrs. Icke," said Copper, "going back to what you said, thinking about Mr. Spelman's murder is exactly what I was hoping you would do. Or to be more precise, I hoped you might be able to think of something more than you've already told us about the events of the past few days. I don't necessarily mean anything to do with Mr. Spelman directly."

"Then what?"

"I wondered if you might have overheard something helpful, by way of conversations between any of the other residents of the manor. Something which might throw some light on the way people may have been thinking."

Sheryl thought for a moment. "There was one thing I did hear. Not that it was any kind of threat, of course. It was more of an observation. But it did involve Castor."

"I'm all ears." Copper gave a discreet nod to Radley to take notes.

"We were all coming back from the gardens after one of Denise's classes with the bows and arrows. And I think pretty much everyone was there, and we were all talking about how we'd done. And I had to laugh, because I was complete rubbish. I said to Tilly, it's a wonder I didn't kill somebody, which she didn't seem to find particularly funny, but then, some people have no sense of humour, do they? Anyway, I had to stop, because the lace on one of my boots had got loose, so I had to sort it out, and that always takes ages. I mean, look at them." She leaned back and hefted one foot up on to the table. "You'd think a woman of my age would have more sense than to wear great clumpy things like these with lacing halfway up the shin. But my husband loves them. He bought them for my birthday. Says they make me look like a biker chick." Sheryl smiled fondly. "Soppy great lump." She seemed to realise that she was straying from the point. "Anyway, I'd stopped to sort out this bootlace. And I was crouched down at the side of the path, probably half-hidden by one of the bushes, and everyone else carried on past me. But Castor and Sue were bringing up the rear, and just as they got to me, I heard her say something like 'Love can turn to hate, you know'. And he gave her a look, and said 'You mean Rudy?', but then she seemed to back off, and I thought I heard her mutter 'I'm not saying any more', and then she went off in a sort of a scurry and overtook everybody else and disappeared indoors."

"And how did Mr. Spelman react?"

"He didn't really," said Sheryl. "He just carried on and caught up with someone else, and I can't remember who, but they just seemed to be chatting as if nothing had happened. So then I finished tying up my lace and set off after them all. That was that, really. Is that the sort of thing you were after?"

"Difficult to say before we have the complete picture, Mrs. Icke," said Copper. "But perhaps it's another straw in the wind. Anything else occur you that might be of interest to us?"

Sheryl looked dubious. "Not really. I mean ... well, it only registered with me because it seemed relevant to what I do every day."

"And what was this, exactly?"

"It was at dinner one evening. You see, the way it works is, we all pitch in to get the meals ready, and then some of us take it in turns to serve up. And it was something that Velma said that struck a chord."

"Mrs. Van der Voor, that would be?"

"That's right, inspector. Actually, she was sitting exactly where you are now. We don't have fixed places – we just plonk ourselves down in the first gap we come to. Anyway, I was taking some dishes of vegetables round, and just as I came up behind Velma, I heard her say 'You have to learn to have no feelings. And believe me, I speak from very bitter experience'. But then I leant in to put the dish on the table, and Velma looked up and saw it was me, and she stopped speaking immediately. Of course, I didn't say anything, because I had no idea what she was going on about, but it just seemed to me that it sounded like the way my job pans out some days. And as I was going, I just heard her say 'Sometimes you have to do what you have to do." But I couldn't tell you what it was all about."

"And can you remember who it was Mrs. Van der Voor was speaking to?" enquired the inspector.

"Of course," said Sheryl. "Actually, there's a coincidence for you. It was Sue."

"Where to next, boss?" murmured Radley in a low voice, as the detectives retreated to the far side of the Great Hall, while Sheryl resumed her musings, gazing out of the oriel window towards the drive and gardens.

A sudden crash from the direction of the kitchen made both officers jump. "I think we've got our answer to that," replied Copper, recovering with a smile. "Let's go and find out who seems intent on demolishing the place."

In the kitchen, the two discovered Alisha Barnes on hands and knees, picking up large pieces of glass from the floor. Slices of lemon lay in the midst of a puddle of water, full of dangerous-looking smaller shards, while on a nearby work surface stood a large glass water dispenser, evidently the companion to the broken vessel, whose liquid contents included floating slices of cucumber.

Radley sprang forward. "Here, let me help you with that, miss. You'll cut yourself to pieces if you aren't careful."

Alisha turned a tearful face towards him. "Oh, I'm so clumsy. And I was just trying to be helpful, because the lemon water had almost run out, and Mr. Spelman is always saying that we have to keep ourselves hydrated, because otherwise our nervous system dries out and that produces tensions, and I came in here for a drink and I saw that the dispenser needed topping up, and I wanted something to do anyway, because it's awful just sitting around wondering what's going to happen and thinking over and over again about the murder, and my hands were shaking and I dropped the jar ..."

Radley held up a hand to halt Alisha's babble. "Don't you worry about it, miss. You just leave everything to me. Now, is there a dustpan somewhere around?" The young woman pointed wordlessly to a cupboard. "Good. Then I'll take care of this lot, and you just go and have a little word with the inspector here. You look as if you could do with a sit down. All right?"

"I'm so sorry, sergeant." Alisha seemed ready to resume her outpourings, before Copper stepped in and put an arm around her to draw her to her feet.

"Just you leave everything to Sergeant Radley, Alisha, and you come and sit quietly here with me." Copper guided Alisha towards a pair of bentwood chairs at the far end of the kitchen.

"It's all going round and round in my mind, inspector. I keep thinking of Mr. Spelman lying dead out in the cold, shot with an arrow, and it scares me. What if someone else gets killed?"

"I don't know of any reason why that should happen," Copper reassured her. "You mustn't let your thoughts go in that direction. In fact, one of the things that helps people who are upset in the aftermath of a killing is not to think about it, but to talk about it." Alisha's watery-eyed look was full of doubt. "Take my word for it. We find it helps. Not just you, but us as well. Because the more we know, the sooner we are going to be able to catch whoever did this, and the sooner we can set your mind at rest. Does that sound sensible?"

Alisha nodded tremulously. "But I don't know what more I can tell you, inspector. I never really got that close to Mr. Spelman, so I never heard him say anything to anyone that they might not have liked."

"Perhaps not, Alisha," said Copper. "But my hope is that you might have heard someone else in conversation, and you might have picked up some sort of snippet which could point us in the right direction. Anything at all. It could be anyone, guests or staff." He regarded the young woman expectantly.

"Well," she eventually said reluctantly, "I suppose there was one time that Mr. Day said something, but I don't know how helpful it is."

"Then tell me what it was, and I can be the judge of whether it is or not," coaxed the inspector.

"Actually, it was in here," said Alisha. "It was before lunch the other day. It was my turn to help getting things ready, but I'm not very good in the kitchen. Well, you can tell." She gave the faintest of smiles. "So I'd been given the potatoes to peel. You can't really go wrong with that, can you? And I was sitting here in the corner, with a bowl of potatoes on one side and a bowl of water on the other to put them in, when Rudy Day and Charlotte-Anne Connor came through from the Great Hall, going towards the stables. They were deep in conversation, and I just don't think they noticed me."

"And what were they talking about?

"It was sort of about what I do, I think. Property, that is. At least, that's what it sounded like. I mean, when I first came here, I did think that a house like this would cost a huge amount if it ever came on to the open market. I suppose I couldn't help myself – it's the estate agent in me. Although I can't think how you'd begin to value it. I mean, I don't know if the medieval parts are listed, because if they were, it could alter the valuation and you can't just change things if you want to because you need to get all sorts of permissions, and not everybody's up for that and it can take ages anyway, and I'm not sure if the newer part is properly historic as well, because there are a lot of country houses which look as if they're Tudor but they turn out to be Edwardian and built by some factory owner, so you have to be careful with descriptions ..."

"I think we're rather getting off the point, don't you, Alisha?" interrupted Copper, managing to stop Alisha's ramblings in mid-flow.

Alisha bit her lip. "I'm sorry, inspector," she apologised. "I always talk a lot when I'm nervous. My boss is always going on at me about it. He thinks it doesn't go down well with the clients. It's one of the reasons they thought the course here might be good for me."

'And he's probably not wrong there,' thought Copper to himself. "I believe you were just about to come to the part where Mr. Day and Ms. Connor were speaking," he gently reminded Alisha.

"Oh yes. It was Rudy who seemed to be in the middle of something, and as he came in he was saying to Charlotte-Anne 'I know what this place is worth to both of us. Okay, there may be different reasons, but that's not what bothers me. What's obvious is that there's an obstacle.' And Charlotte-Anne said something about being very careful, and Rudy said it didn't matter what had been done in secret before, as long as things went right in future. But then they went on through the back way towards the stables, and I didn't hear any more."

"And you thought that they might have been discussing the value of the manor? Perhaps with a view to the property being sold? Maybe even without Mr. Spelman's knowledge? Because obviously, both of them would be involved to some extent if there were that kind of thing in the wind."

Alisha shrugged helplessly. "I honestly don't know, inspector. That was the first thing I thought of, but that's probably just me, on account of my job. But it could have been anything, really."

"But it certainly gives us something to think about," said Copper. "No information ever goes to waste. Perhaps I'll need to speak to those two again to find out what secret this conversation was about."

Alisha's eyes suddenly opened wide. "Secret?" she echoed in a half-whisper. "Oh goodness."

Copper's attention was immediately alerted. "You've remembered something?"

"Yes," replied Alisha. "From last night."

"And did this have anything to do with Mr.

Spelman?"

"No. I mean, I don't know. It might have. But I couldn't have known that at the time, could I, inspector, so it can't be my fault, can it?" Alisha collapsed once again into tearful agitation.

Copper put a restraining hand on the young woman's arm. "Calm down, Alisha. Just tell me what you mean, and try to be clear. And don't forget, we know you couldn't have been responsible for what happened during the night, so let's have no talk of anything being your fault. So, what happened? What secret?"

Alisha took a deep breath. "It was something Velma said. You see, I'd been playing cards with Tilly, and we'd finished because it was getting late, and I went to put the cards away in the library cabinet where they belong. It took me ages, because I dropped the cards and one of them went right underneath the cabinet, so I had to go out to the hall to get a walking-stick out of the stand to try to reach it, which I managed to eventually, and when I came back to where we'd been playing, I came up behind Velma who was talking to Tilly."

"So where does this mention of a secret come in?"

"Velma said to Tilly 'Your secret's safe with me', and Tilly looked worried, but then Velma patted her on the shoulder and said something about being very discreet, and she'd say nothing, and anyway, she had her own secrets. She said 'I know more ways to kill a man than you could ever think of', and something like 'Nobody is alone'. But then she saw that I was there and said goodnight to both of us, and off she went." Alisha's hand went to her mouth. "Do you think that meant she was planning on killing Mr. Spelman?"

"Well, it would have been singularly indiscreet to advertise the fact beforehand," pointed out Copper, "so I can't think that can have been what she meant. But we'll have another chat with her later on to sort it out. In the meantime, you should try not to worry."

"If you say so, inspector," said Alisha, still a little shaky. "I think I'll go and have a lie down, if you don't mind. I'm starting an awful headache."

"It's the tension. That's what you came here to get rid of, wasn't it?" smiled Copper, adopting his most avuncular manner. "Go and put your feet up, and think no more about it."

Chapter 13

"I think we're amassing quite a collection of supplementary questions for our suspects," observed Dave Copper. "I'm always encouraged by talk of secrets. Whenever someone has something to hide, that's usually very fertile ground for providing motives."

"As long as we don't get so many motives that we can't sort one out from another, boss," said Pete Radley.

"Good point," said Copper, "although I'd rather have too many than too few. There's usually some way to discard the dross."

"So you'll want to crack on and winkle out some more, I guess," grinned Radley, consulting his notebook. "And by my calculations, the next one on our list is the slightly intimidating Denise Benz. I wonder where she's hidden herself away."

"Let's assume it's the most obvious place," suggested Copper. "If you were a fitness instructor and found yourself at a loose end, what would you be doing?"

"Working out?" hazarded Radley.

"Seems likely to me. Let's go and take a look."

As the detectives entered the stables, the clanking sound of metal on metal seemed to bear out the sergeant's guess. Pushing open the door to the fitness room, they discovered Denise Benz stretched out on the bench of an exercise machine, repeatedly pushing up a bar which was lifting a formidable stack of weights. Sparing the officers a brief glance before continuing, she could be heard counting "Eighteen ... nineteen ... twenty' on each gusty exhalation, before finally lowering the bar gently to its resting place. She sat up, wiped her face with the towel from around her shoulders, and looked expectantly at Copper. "You want something?"

"We do indeed, Miss Benz," said the inspector. "And we're sorry to interrupt you, but we have some further questions for you."

"More than before?" asked Denise. "I think I told you everything I know. I found the Director, and he was dead. What else could there be?"

"Well, that's what we're hoping you can tell us," replied Copper. "Not regarding your discovery of Mr. Spelman, but in the period running up to that. I don't mean this morning – I'm more concerned with the past few days."

"But it has all been normal," replied Denise. "The Director did his talks. I did my classes. There is not any more than that, I think."

"Ah, but we're slowly discovering that some of the things that have occurred have been far from normal, Miss Benz. We've learned that there have been conversations between some of the guests at the manor which have thrown an entirely different light on events here. I'm hoping that you may be able to contribute to the growing list of things we need to take a further look at."

"You mean that you want to know if I listened in to private conversations?" Denise sounded affronted.

"Not at all," said Copper. "But it's quite possible that someone may have said something to you, perhaps even in confidence, which might be useful to us. Now I understand that you might not wish to break a confidence, but I'm afraid that, in a murder investigation, we can't always observe all the niceties."

Denise appeared to consider for a moment. "So ask me your questions. I will answer if I can."

"Good." The inspector succeeded in producing a convincing smile of approval. "Now, when we spoke before, I neglected to ask you if you had had any disagreements of any sort with Mr. Spelman. Not that I have any reason to suppose that you had," he added hastily, as Denise seemed ready to bristle at the suggestion. "I am not looking for a motive for murder. Because I have conclusive evidence from more than one source that you cannot be implicated in Mr. Spelman's death. But this is a routine question I am having to ask everybody."

"And of course the answer is no," replied Denise curtly. "The Director and I were on perfectly good terms."

"But then I move on to the matter of the other people here, who might have clashed in some way with your ... Director. Were you perhaps aware of any conflicts? Any disagreements, however minor?"

"I have said, inspector, I do not listen to other people's conversations."

"Or has anyone reported such a thing in a conversation with you?" enquired Copper, determined to find a way past Denise's apparent unwillingness to co-operate. "One of your colleagues? Or one of the Director's seekers?"

There was a long pause. "There was maybe one thing. But I do not know what it meant." Denise frowned.

"I'm intrigued." Copper gave an encouraging smile. "Tell me more."

"It was at the end of one of my fitness classes. Nearly everybody had gone, except for that Coco woman. And I do not know why she bothers to come anyway, because she does not have the right clothes for proper work, and she just wears the floppy jogging trousers and the big t-shirt, and she can't hold the weights properly because of those stupid fingernails. I think she is what you call a waste of space."

"You're not a fan?"

"You could not say we are friends," admitted Denise. "And this was why it was a surprise for me. So she was last to leave, and I try to be pleasant to everybody, so I smiled to her and said that I hoped she would be able to be better at the next class, because the

Director always wants his guests to improve in all things. But then she came up to me, most close, and looked around to make sure that nobody else was here, and then whispered 'I'm in trouble. He knows. I need help, and I think maybe you're the only one who would understand.'"

"I assume she would have been speaking about Mr. Spelman," said Copper. "Did she explain what she meant by that?"

"No. And I did not understand. I said to her 'What is it you mean?', but before she could answer, one of the other women came back into here because she had forgotten something, and so Coco said 'Oh, it doesn't matter', and she went away very quick."

"But she was evidently worried about something? Something involving Mr. Spelman?"

"It is clear, yes. But do not ask me what it was."

"Why should she say she needed help, I wonder?" mused Copper. "Does that mean she felt herself to be under some sort of threat?"

"Doesn't that tie in with what we heard from Mrs. ...?" The inspector flashed a warning glance at his junior colleague's interruption. "I mean, what we heard from one of the other ladies?" finished Radley. "Spelman said to Coco that she was finished. That's a threat if ever I heard one."

"Which, as we've said before, doesn't exactly accord with the fluffy bunny image Mr. Spelman would have been anxious to convey," concurred Copper. "A definite lack of pleasant bonhomie."

"Oh, you think he was pleasant to everyone?" scoffed Denise. "No, he had his nasty side."

"But I thought you said that you and he were on good terms?" queried Copper.

"With me he was fine. Because I would not have tolerated any other thing. I am not weak, and he knew it," preened Denise. "But some others, he could be a bully to."

"Who then? I assume you must have some specific occasion in mind. So when would that be?"

"No, this was not one time. It was over a period, or so she said."

"And who would this be?"

"It was Sue," replied Denise.

"So I'd be grateful to hear how this emerged."

"It was after one of my archery classes," explained the fitness instructor. "Not with this group. It was a few weeks ago, but I do not remember exactly when. But I had just finished the class, and I asked Sue if she would help me to put away my equipment while the others came back to the manor for tea."

"Which wouldn't actually have been tea," put in Radley. "One of those horrible concoctions we found in the kitchen, I expect, boss."

"Hardly relevant, sergeant," Copper chided him. "Go on, Miss Benz."

"Sue had been part of the class," resumed Denise, "because all the staff take part at one time or another. And it is unfortunate for her, but she is mostly one of the worst. She does not have the talent for any sport – not like some of us." Denise looked smug. "And the Director was there on that day, and he had made a mock at her, because she was so bad at hitting the target. So when we came back to put the equipment back in the store cupboard, Sue seemed upset, and I told her not to worry about a little thing like being bad at shooting, and she said that it was not just that, and that Mr. Spelman was always criticising her for not doing something right. And she said it was not fair, because she always tried to please him, but it was never enough."

"She did describe him as a genius when we first spoke to her," recalled Copper. "She could hardly have praised him in higher terms. But evidently this wasn't mutual?"

"I think it wasn't. Sue said sometimes she wondered why she came to work here at all. She said she wasn't stupid, whatever some people might think. She told me, and I did not know this, that she had been an assistant teacher at one of the local schools, helping the children with their reading and science classes and other things, and she had given it up because she had heard about the Director's work and believed so much in it." Denise grimaced. "If I was not happy, I would have left a long time ago. But I am a strong person. Not everybody is. And now," she said, standing, "I must go and take my cold shower."

*

"She's certainly plenty strong enough in my book, boss," muttered Pete Radley, as the two detectives stood in the stables corridor and watched Denise disappear into her room. "I bet she'd have the strength to bury an arrow into some poor sap's chest. It'd probably come out the other side. And she's taller than me, too. Did you notice? She's butcher than some blokes I know. I'll tell you one thing – I wouldn't want to meet her on a dark night."

"And there is one aspect of the case we can be sure of," observed Dave Copper. "The fact that she didn't go out and meet Castor Spelman on the dark night in question, so her skills with her arrows are neither here nor there."

"I'll tell you one thing I couldn't fathom, boss. That thing Coco said to her, about her being the only one who could understand or help. What do you reckon to that?"

"I don't as yet. It's yet another thing on my list to ponder over. But in the meantime, we move on. I think it's just Anna Logue left on our first list, isn't it?"

"That's right, boss. Do you reckon she might be out here as well, beavering away at that computer of hers?"

"Only one way to find out." Copper rapped smartly

on Anna's office door, and was rewarded by a bright 'Come in!'.

Anna turned from her computer screen to greet the detectives with a cheery smile. "Inspector, sergeant – were you looking for me?" She laughed. "Sorry – stupid question. Why else would you be here?"

"We hoped we might tease a little more information out of you," admitted Copper.

"I'd invite you to sit down, except we've a wee shortage of chairs in here," said Anna. "We'd better pop next door to my room. It'll be more comfortable." She stood and drained the remaining contents of the mug in front of her, eliciting a faint groan of envy from Radley, which was not lost on his superior.

"I'll tell you one thing which would improve matters greatly for my sergeant here," smiled Copper. "If it's not too much trouble, could we persuade you to rustle up another cup of tea for him? The options on offer on the premises don't exactly appeal to him, and I fear he's on the verge of expiring from dehydration."

"And malnutrition," put in Radley.

"I'll tell you what, inspector," said Anna. "We'll sort Mr. Radley and yourself out with a proper brew, and then we'll go through to the kitchen and see what eats we can track down. Come on through next door."

The detectives perched on the side of Anna's bed as she busied herself with kettle and mugs. "So what was it you were wanting?" she enquired.

"We've been having a further chat with some of your colleagues and guests," said Copper, "and a number of facts have emerged which we're giving some more thought to. So I was wondering whether you might be able to contribute to our dossier."

"Well, dossiers are what I'm all about," said Anna, handing over steaming mugs to the officers. "Sugar?" Copper shook his head, while Radley muttered a rather shamefaced 'Three, please'.

"Got a dossier on Mr. Spelman, by any chance?" asked Copper, more in jest than expectation. "That might tell us everything we need to know."

Anna's brow creased. "Funnily enough, inspector, no. I'd never thought of that before. But the only things I know about him are what he told me so that I could build the website. I've never gone looking for anything else. But then, he'd never have asked me to research into himself, would he?"

"I dare say not. But I think you said earlier that he did in fact ask you to research into other people, didn't he, just to make sure that their motives in coming to the Institute were entirely above board."

"He did," confirmed Anna.

"So I'm wondering whether any of those researches you carried out might provide some sort of reason why someone would seek his death."

"Oh." Anna seemed struck by a sudden thought. "It's odd you should talk about death, inspector. Not Castor's, of course. But there were a couple of our guests where their story had a mention of death in it."

Copper leaned forward. "I'd be very interested to hear who. Do you have copies of these files?"

"Not to hand. I could print them off if you need me to, but I think I can probably remember most of the details."

"And these would have involved who?"

Anna collected her thoughts for a moment. "The first one I remember was Mrs. Van der Voor. Castor said she'd come from some home for the elderly in Holland, but he said he had an instinct that she wasn't quite as innocent as she seemed, so he got me to look her up. It took a bit of doing, but there isn't much you can't track down on the internet if you're persistent. And I was amazed at what I found. It turned out that, during the war, our dear old Mrs. Van der Voor was actually a spy!" Anna gazed wide-eyed at Copper to gauge the effect of her revelation, only to be disappointed at his lack of astonishment. "You knew!" she accused. "You knew all along."

"I confess," said the inspector. "The information doesn't come as a total surprise, largely because Mrs. Van der Voor told us as much. It was quite a large part of her reason for coming to the manor, although you'll understand her reluctance to broadcast the fact. But she didn't tell us a great deal more than the bare bones."

"Actually, it's quite a tragic story," said Anna. "I can see why she wouldn't want to go over it all in detail. It must have been very painful for her."

"In what way?" asked Copper. "Other than the obvious, being wartime, with all that that entails."

"I found some confidential government files in Holland. I had to do a bit of hacking to get into them, but I'd got quite intrigued by the story. Mrs. Van der Voor had been sent in behind enemy lines from here, and she was part of a resistance group who had been ambushed by the Nazis. Everyone else was killed, and she was the only one who survived, so no wonder she wouldn't want to talk about it. But the file got even more secret after the end of the war, and I couldn't get into it any further. And then the next thing I found was a few years later when there was a mention of her in a story about the war. It was part of a newspaper article, but it was all in Dutch, and it was a picture of a cutting so I couldn't use my translator on it, and I couldn't understand what it was all about. But obviously she settled down to a nice quiet life after all the excitement."

"And how did Mr. Spelman react to this news when you passed it on?" wondered Copper. "Was he excited?"

"Not exactly," replied Anna. "More thoughtful. He came and looked at the article and got me to print it off, and said he'd have to have a good long talk with Mrs. Van der Voor. He sensed there was more to tell. But whether he did or not, I never heard."

Copper turned to his junior colleague. "It's pretty clear why she didn't volunteer the whole story when we first spoke to her," he remarked. "But I still can't see that a piece of wartime history would have a bearing on this case."

"We'll be speaking to her again though, won't we, boss?" said Radley. "So maybe she can tell us what went on when this good long talk with Mr. Spelman took place."

"Let's hope so." Copper turned back to Anna. "You said there were a couple of guests where the question of death had cropped up. Who was the second?"

"That was Tilly Wakes," said Anna. "Nowhere near as interesting, I'm afraid. But still pretty sad in its own way."

"And what way was that?"

"You know she works in a hospital?"

"Indeed. She told us that. An anaesthetist, she said. I think that's right, isn't it, sergeant? I believe you made a note of it." Copper couldn't resist the gentle tease.

"Certainly did, boss." Radley gave his superior a broad cheerful smile, seemingly immune to the hint of mockery.

"So what was the story there?"

"She lost a patient. Well, of course, not her patient really, because she wasn't the doctor in charge. But the newspaper story said that there had been an official enquiry because a patient had died during an operation where she had been in charge of the anaesthetic, and the surgeon had denied all responsibility because he said that Tilly had made mistakes in her work. There were all sorts of accusations flying about, but it never seemed to come to any conclusion. There was no proof. It said the surgeon took a voluntary suspension for a while, and Tilly went on sick leave, but what the rights and wrongs of the whole business were, nobody seemed able to say."

"Miss Wakes did say that she was under a lot of strain with her job, didn't she, boss?" said Radley. "That's why she came to the Institute in the first place, so's she could figure out how to cope with it better."

"In which case, you'd have thought she'd regard Mr. Spelman more as some sort of saviour, rather than having any reason to want to kill him," observed Copper.

"But," continued the sergeant, "she'd also got the knowledge of how to knock the guy out. If she's handy with the anaesthetics, who better than her to give him a shot to zonk him out? Who knows what she's carrying around in her handbag?"

"In which case, she'd hardly need to go brewing some concoction from a garden plant," countered the inspector. "So just be grateful that Anna's made you a nice ordinary cup of good Scottish tea, and sup up. If Anna's got nothing more for us, we'd best be on our way."

"But don't forget, inspector, you're on a promise," laughed Anna. "I said I'd try to rescue Sergeant Radley from starvation, so come with me, and we'll raid the kitchen."

Chapter 14

In the manor's now deserted kitchen, Anna opened one of the large fridges to reveal shelves laden with all manner of fruits and vegetables, accompanied by numerous cheeses, tubs of plain low-fat yoghurt, and cartons of soya milk in various flavours, but it only took a few moments for Pete Radley's eye to light on something which elicited a grin of delight. "Pasties!" he cried in triumph. "Now that's more like it."

"I'm afraid they're vegan," said Anna. "I hope that doesn't put you off."

"I don't care what planet they're from," replied Radley. "If it's okay by you, I'm having one."

"As you will see, Anna, the wolf has been knocking extremely loudly at my colleague's door," smiled Dave Copper, as Radley seated himself at the kitchen table, tore back the pasty's wrapper, and began to munch. "With a bit of luck, I'll be able to get more work out of him, now that he won't be distracted by the pangs of hunger."

"Actually, boss, these aren't bad at all," said Radley through a mouthful of pasty. "You ought to try one."

"If only to stop you feeling guilty," said the inspector. And then, in an aside to Anna, "Although there's not much chance of that."

"And I wouldn't say no to one of those bananas as pud," added Radley. "Aren't they supposed to have loads of potassium in them? A man's got to feed his brain, hasn't he?"

A few minutes later, all traces of the impromptu feast having been cleared away, Copper stood. "No time to sit about, although we're very grateful for the emergency rations, Anna. But Sergeant Radley and I have work to do."

"Me too," said Anna. "I'm supposed to be putting a

list together for Charlotte-Anne so that she can contact future guests and cancel their arrangements."

"Then I dare say we shall see you later," said Copper. The detectives watched Anna head back towards her office, before the inspector turned to his junior. "And now I think it's time we took advantage of Mr. Day's permission, and carried out a few searches of the rooms upstairs."

"With you all the way, boss," said Radley, wiping the last crumbs from around his mouth. "Lead on."

As the two detectives climbed the main staircase towards the first floor – 'Plenty of creaks here' reflected Copper. 'You'd have a job sneaking up and down here without someone noticing' – Radley spoke up. "Any idea what we're looking for, boss?"

"Remarkably little," confessed his superior. "Other than a few so-far-inexplicable remarks from various people, we're not much further forward in narrowing the field. I think we'll just have to take the rooms in turn, and see what jumps out at us. Figuratively speaking, of course."

"I should hope so," said the sergeant. "An old place like this, you never know if there are going to be secret passages for people to lurk in. Here, do you suppose that's how they got Spelman out into the woods? Maybe there's some sort of tunnel leading from the manor down to that Witch's Cave."

"You, Mr. Radley," smiled Copper, "have been playing too many gothic horror video games. I think I'm going to have to have a word with your wife. She needs to restrict your intake. I'm more interested in considering the practicalities of this case, rather than thinking about fantasy fiction like Game of Kingdoms, or whatever it is."

"Yeah, right, boss. This case, with midnight magic rituals going on in the woods and an ancient witch living in a creepy cottage just down the road."

Copper laughed. "Fair point, sergeant. But I'm prepared to bet that there's a far more mundane motive than witchcraft here. So let's see if we can track it down." He surveyed the upper corridor stretching before them. "You made a list of the rooms up here, didn't you?"

"When Anna told us about them? Yes, boss." Radley delved in a pocket for his notebook. "Here we are. It's Rudy Day's room just here, and then Coco de Roque next to it. After that it's Tilly Wakes, and Velma Van der Voor is next to her. And then you've got Castor Spelman's room, but you've already covered that with Una, haven't you?"

"It might not be a bad idea to take a second look. You might spot something we didn't – fresh eyes and all that."

"No pressure then," grinned Radley. "Anyway, after Mr. Spelman it's Sue Pine, and finally there's his number two, Charlotte-Anne Connor at the end."

"Excellent," approved Copper. "Then we may as well start here and work our way along." He opened the first door.

The room occupied by Rudy Day was considerably less stylish than that occupied by his partner, although still comfortable enough. An Empire-style double bed with high headboard and footboard stood against one wall, and it was accompanied by a brocade-upholstered two-seater sofa and companion armchair with vaguely Egyptian design influences. An apparently genuine eighteenth-century mahogany clothes-press and a matching chest of drawers completed the furnishings, and a discreet door in the dove-grey panelling revealed a tiny shower room, all glass and chrome.

"Mr. Day doesn't seem to have had to rough it too badly after his change of room," remarked Radley. "This knocks spots off the hotel room that the missus and I had on honeymoon."

"Very much the antithesis of a honeymoon suite in this case," commented Copper, "if the situation is quite as we believe it to be. But the question is, is there anything here to add to our knowledge?"

"How about this, boss?" Radley indicated a mobile phone sitting on the small table at the side of the bed. "It's a bit daft, leaving his phone lying about. Most people I know have got their phones surgically grafted on to their persons. They can't let a minute go by without checking their Twoddle-feed. I know you're a bit different, but I can't think of anyone who hasn't got their whole life on their phone."

"Maybe Mr. Day is no different," mused Copper.

"What? You mean you want me to take a look at it and see if there's anything useful?" enquired Radley eagerly, reaching for the device.

"Certainly not, sergeant," retorted Copper severely. "That would be an illegal search, and completely outside our powers, unless we had a warrant." He gave his junior a steady and meaningful look. "I'm just going to have a glance in that en-suite. I'm sure there'll be something of interest in there. And I may be some time."

"Righty-ho, boss," grinned Radley. "I'll just stay here then, shall I?" he asked airily.

"You do that," said Copper. "I'm sure you'll occupy yourself somehow." The shower room door closed firmly behind him.

When the inspector emerged a few minutes later, it was to find his colleague sporting a broad smile, Rudy's phone in his hand. "Now, boss, you know you said ..."

"Never mind what I said," interrupted Copper. "Give."

"Our Mr. Day is not a very security-conscious person. For a start, the password to unlock this phone is 1234, which is about as barmy as you can get. It's the second most popular one on the planet, after 0000. It's just begging for someone else to get into it. So I did. Just a quick glance at his pictures, because it's amazing what pictures can tell you sometimes. And there we find several recent ones of some chap sitting in a bar with a drink, or else muffled up in some park or other, but the best one is a selfie of him and Rudy standing in front of Parliament."

"Maybe Mr. Day is giving a friend the conducted tour of London," suggested Copper.

"Oh no," retorted Radley, the smile growing even broader. "Sorry, boss, but you've got to admit, I'm good. I should have been a detective, you know. It looks a bit like our parliament, but it isn't. And there's a clue in the back of the shot." He held out the phone. "Take a look there."

Copper scrutinised the picture. He laughed. "Well done, sergeant. Eleven out of ten for observation. You're absolutely right. That is the maple leaf flag. This was taken in Canada. That's the Parliament building in Ottawa."

"And look at the date signature. This is recent. And these two look like very good friends, if you ask me. Proof if proof were needed that our Rudy could well want to be shot of Castor Spelman. He has other fish to fry."

"Starts to add up, doesn't it?" agreed Copper. "That's a very interesting straw in the wind. But let's not push our luck. Put that back, and we'll move on."

*

Coco de Roque's room would have been fairly plain, with oak-panelled walls, mid-Victorian furniture, and an ordinary modern double divan bed, if efforts had not been made to impart some style to it. A red chiffon scarf had been draped across the shade of a standard lamp. A fringed shawl in a swirl of peacock hues lounged languidly on the bed, with one corner falling to the floor in a puddle of multi-coloured silk. A vase of dried flowers had been augmented by a flourish of pink ostrich feathers, while a gold dressing-gown elaborately embroidered with writhing Chinese dragons lay casually discarded on an ottoman.

"I'm guessing that Miss de Roque likes her glamour," remarked Copper. "I suspect that it's on account of her occupation that this room has been … accessorised."

"I was thinking more 'tarted up', boss," said Radley.

"But I suppose we should expect no less from someone who obviously thinks of themselves as a fashion guru," said Copper. "Which Castor Spelman evidently bought into when he commissioned those robes of his from her, and then invited her down here to stay. So why, then, was there suddenly talk of fraud?"

"Here's a thought, boss. I mean, I haven't got a clue about fashion really – you just ask my missus. When we got married, she got me to do a great chuck-out of a lot of my old clothes, because she reckoned she wouldn't want to be seen out with me in some of them. I even had a job keeping hold of my lucky pants."

Copper raised an eyebrow. "Is this actually going somewhere, sergeant, or are we in for a discussion of your tastes in underwear?"

"What I thought was," ploughed on Radley, "what if Coco had been pinching designs from somewhere else, rather than making them up for herself, and Spelman somehow discovered it. He might think it devalued his precious magic robes. That would probably count as fraud, wouldn't it?"

"It might well," nodded Copper. "If there's any evidence of it. I suggest we have a browse. You take a look through that chest of drawers, and I'll check on the rest of the room." As Radley busied himself at the task, Copper took a look behind a folding screen in one corner of the room, to discover a washbasin with a wall mirror above it and a free-standing bathroom cabinet. "No en-suite luxury in this room," he called to his colleague. "We're down to your average B and B standard, by the look of it. Anything interesting at your end?"

"Not really," said Radley, joining him. "Very little in there, actually. It's pretty sparse. Most of the drawers were empty. Just some tights and a few pairs of big knickers, which I didn't look at too closely, although it did strike me that they weren't the sort of posh pants you'd think the lovely Miss de Roque would wear. Much more Bridget Jones."

Copper opened the cabinet. "Well, you could scarcely say the contents of this were equally sparse." The shelves of the cupboard were stacked with a profusion of make-up. Tubes of thick foundation jostled with palettes of eye shadow and blusher. Cans of hairspray vied for position with bottles of skin cleanser and depilatory creams. There was a set of electric curling tongs to accompany a hairbrush and tail-comb. A small ceramic pot had been pressed into service to hold a selection of eyebrow pencils and brushes. And a bottle of adhesive sat atop a stack of plastic cartons holding an array of talon-like false nails.

"Someone spends a lot of time with their look, boss," remarked the sergeant. Something on one of the shelves, almost hidden by the items in front of it, caught his eye. "Here, hang on. What's that?"

Copper rearranged to shelf's contents. "That, sergeant, is a can of shaving gel for sensitive skins."

"I thought it looked familiar. That's the same sort I use."

"For your delicate baby complexion, I assume," observed the inspector. "And there's a razor to go with it."

"And that's the same as mine too," marvelled Radley. "Coco de Roque must have pretty hairy legs."

"You may well be right." Copper gave a quiet smile. "What say we carry on looking? Take a glance in the wardrobe, while I …" He crouched down alongside the bed. "Aha! As I thought."

"What's that, boss?" enquired the sergeant, turning back from the open wardrobe.

"No suitcase to be seen, so where might it be? The obvious place – under the bed." Copper drew out the case. "And fortunately for us, unlocked." He threw back the lid to survey the contents, and his smile grew wider. "Well, well, well."

"What have you got, boss?" Radley came to peer over his shoulder. "It's just more of the same, isn't it? More pants and bras – well, padded bras, by the look of it. And gawd knows what those other pad things are for. And a couple of wigs. Our Miss de Roque obviously wasn't satisfied with her natural assets."

"I'm thinking not." Copper seemed to be struggling to hold in a laugh, to his colleague's slight bewilderment. He delved beneath the garments, to find a passport. He opened it, and let out a chuckle of delight. "And that'll do nicely." He brandished it in triumph. "That, sergeant, is what you call a fraud. Now, let's tuck everything away again, as you might say." He replaced the passport in the case, closed it, pushed it back under the bed, and stood. "And now let's see what else turns up next door."

*

"I don't get it, boss," said Pete Radley in slightly injured tones. "What was that all about?"

"You have led a very sheltered life, Peter," replied Dave Copper, still chuckling, "and I wouldn't dream of spoiling the surprise, once we've sorted everything out. Anyway, moving on. Tilly Wakes next, I think."

"That's right, boss. Let's hope she's not there. She's going to be a bit miffed if we just march in. Do you reckon I should knock?"

"Do so." Silence.

"Our luck's in." Radley opened the door. "After you."

Tilly's room was similar in furnishings to Coco's, but without the fripperies. In fact, the room was almost obsessively neat, with no clothing or shoes in evidence, the bed immaculately straightened, and the only sign of occupation a cut glass tumbler on the bedside table.

"Bit of an absence of personality," remarked the sergeant. He opened the wardrobe door. "And a bit of a contrast to Coco's wardrobe next door. That one was like an explosion in a paint factory, all bright colours and designerish patterns. This lot's just dull."

"True," agreed Copper, standing at his shoulder. "I bet you never knew there were so many shades of beige. She did strike me as something of a mouse when we first met her. But, according to what Denise overheard Velma say, there must be something interesting about her, or else why should there be talk of a secret?"

"She was in that newspaper story that Anna told us about," Radley reminded him. "If this surgeon was responsible for that patient's death, maybe Tilly knew something about him."

"Hmmm. Not convinced. Keep looking." Once again, Copper inspected the washing facilities concealed behind the screen in the corner, while Radley began to burrow through the contents of the chest of drawers. Again, the contrast with Coco's room was marked. Here, other than a toothbrush and toothpaste, there was nothing to be seen on any of the surfaces, while the inside of the cabinet yielded nothing more than a modest sponge-bag containing deodorant spray, some feminine items, and a bottle of over-the-counter painkillers. There was not a scrap of make-up to be found. "Well, that didn't take long," he reported, emerging. "Any luck?"

"Nothing unusual so far, boss. Just one drawer to

go." Radley pulled out the bottom drawer and riffled among the jumpers folded neatly within. Suddenly, he froze. "And just a little something to finish with." He turned and held up a bottle of tablets for his superior's inspection. "Wonder what these are. No label on the bottle. Headache pills, do you reckon?"

"Unlikely," replied Copper. "I've already found some of those in her wash bag." He looked more closely at the tablets. "They've got a code number of some sort pressed into them. If I had to make a guess, I'd say that these are some sort of professional medical supply, rather than your common-or-garden pills from a high street chemist shop. Make a note of this." He squinted at the bottle and quoted the reference number on the tablets. "Maybe Una can identify what they are."

"Tilly's certainly situated in the right place to get hold of something out of the ordinary, working in a hospital," pointed out Radley. "Hey, maybe they're something which could have been used to knock Spelman out as part of a plan to kill him."

"I very much doubt whether hospital pharmacies stock tablets consisting of concentrated essence of oleander," observed Copper, "so that suggestion probably won't take us very far."

Radley looked downcast. "Oh well, it was just a thought." But then he brightened. "Oh, hang on. There's something else here." He withdrew a carefully-wrapped bulky jumper, which he unfolded to reveal a half-empty bottle of whisky. "Somebody hasn't been sticking to Castor Spelman's rules about no booze on the premises, have they?" he grinned. "That's it! She's a secret alcoholic!"

"Let's not jump too quickly to that conclusion," said Copper, crossing to the bed. He picked up the tumbler and sniffed. "Although it's fair to deduce that she likes a nightcap on retiring. Well, it certainly seems as if she regards that as something to be kept secret. How that would relate to our murder victim's death is another question. So we'll park the knowledge and plough on."

Chapter 15

A tap on the door of Velma Van der Voor's room produced no response. "Looks as if our luck continues to hold," said Dave Copper, as he led the way in.

"Back to posh, I see," said Pete Radley. "No slumming it for our sweet old lady."

"Not necessarily so sweet," Copper reminded him. "Trained as a secret agent, with more ways to kill a man than you can shake a stick at, by her own testimony."

"And one of the other women told us that she was pretty good with the arrows. It makes you wonder whether one of those ways involved screwdrivering your target and then disguising it with an arrow to confuse your enemies."

"And intended to make no undue noise, which has to be a plus when you're involved in nefarious activities," added the inspector. "Fair point. Let's do a sweep and see if there's anything to back up your theory."

The room's furnishings were much more in accordance with accommodation intended for one of the Institute's co-owners. An imposing canopied bed with red velvet hangings held centre stage, with side cabinets, clothes press and blanket chest in matching Jacobean style, with a pair of elaborately-carved high-backed armchairs flanking a desk under the window. A Turkish carpet in rich deep colours lay on the broad polished dark oak floorboards, and portraits of pasty-faced and stiffly-posed anonymous ancestors graced the panelled walls. Next to the clothes press, artful use of similar panelling had created a small shower room, whose door stood open to show simple white tiling interspersed with occasional blue and white Dutch rural scenes in the Delft style.

"Looking at those tiles, Mrs. Van der Voor must have felt right at home," remarked Copper. "Lucky lady."

"That's not what I'm looking at, boss," said Radley, his attention elsewhere. "How about this?" He indicated a door almost concealed behind a tapestry hanging. "If I'm not much mistaken, Castor Spelman's room is right on the other side of that door."

"I can't think why I didn't notice it when I was in his room earlier with Una," said Copper. "And of course this used to be Rudy Day's room. Communicating doors for the two men. Not entirely to be wondered at, given their relationship."

"Communicating door for Velma Van der Voor to get access to Mr. Spelman during the night, more like," stated the sergeant. "She could have got in there any time she wanted." He turned the handle and eagerly pushed open the door. There was a loud clonk. "Oh." He peered through the crack and stepped back crestfallen. "Damn."

The doorway was blocked on the far side by a large and clearly very heavy wooden wardrobe, which had been firmly pushed up against the opening. "And that is obviously why I didn't notice the door from the other side," said Copper. "And I doubt very much whether Mrs. Van der Voor, for all her many talents, could have succeeded in moving that wardrobe surreptitiously in the middle of the night without alerting her potential victim. Sorry to rain on your parade, but there's another theory down the drain."

"Well, she's got to be hiding something," insisted Radley. "She's a spy, for crying out loud."

Copper laughed. "We'd better try to find it then, hadn't we? Right, you have a burrow through the wardrobe and what-have-you, and I'll see if this desk yields anything."

There was the sound of doors being opened, hangers being slid along rails, and lids being lifted, before the sergeant turned back to his superior. "Not a sausage," he reported. "Mostly just ordinary clothes and a load of old lady cardigans, plus a coat with a bit of a waft of mothballs. And I took a trick out of your book, and had a shufti under the bed to see if there was a case there. The good news is, there is. The bad news is, there's nothing in it but some big clumpy shoes."

"Bad luck," replied the inspector, his perusal of the desk having revealed little other than some blank sheets of writing paper embossed with the legend '*Holt Manor Institute*', and several ballpoint pens bearing the name and logo of a Canadian airline. "Pretty much the same here." He closed the desk drawer, and his eye fell upon something pushed back underneath the desk. "Except ..."

"Except what?"

"Except this." Copper pulled out a metal waste paper bin and peered inside. "Hello, hello, hello."

"Excuse me, boss," grinned Radley. "I know you tell me not to get too clichéd in my detecting, but did I just hear you say ...?"

"Never mind what you heard me say," retorted Copper, colouring slightly. "Come and take a look at this." He indicated the contents of the bin, which consisted of the burnt remnants of a sheet of paper. "You wanted evidence of something being hidden. What better way to hide something than to destroy it?"

"Whatever it is. We'll never know, unless Velma tells us, will we?"

Copper looked more closely. "Do you know, I wouldn't be too sure about that, sergeant." He reached into the bin and with his fingertips carefully extracted one item, evidently the one corner of the piece of paper which had survived the destruction. "Now, that's interesting."

"What is it, boss?"

"It looks to be a printout of a newspaper article." Copper squinted at the fragment. "And if I'm not much mistaken, it's in either German or Dutch."

"Bingo!" said Radley excitedly. "That'll be the one that Anna told us about. The one that Mr. Spelman was so interested in. The one that she printed off for him. So what's it doing here, burnt?"

"Evidently Mr. Spelman had that good long talk with Velma that he intended, and he must have confronted her with whatever information this article contained. And there must have been something other than the details of her marriage which Anna picked up on, and it looks to me as if it was something that Velma wasn't too keen to have widely known. Hence her little piece of arson."

"So," said Radley slowly, thinking it through, "could she have managed to get Mr. Spelman drugged and incapable and killed him, and then pinched the incriminating document from his room and destroyed it? Result, nobody would ever find out about her guilty secret. Whatever it was."

"Now that, sergeant, is more like a theory. I think we'll be taking a leaf out of Mr. Spelman's book, and having a good long talk with Mrs. Van der Voor."

*

"Do you want to take your second look at Castor Spelman's room, boss?" asked Pete Radley, as the detectives stood once more in the corridor. "I haven't been in there yet. Not that I'm saying you could have missed something which I might spot," he added quickly.

"And don't think I wouldn't appreciate it if you did," responded Dave Copper. "But for the moment, I think I'd rather carry on working down our list of suspects. Because at least there's one thing we can be sure of – Spelman didn't kill himself. We'll check his room last."

"In which case, a quick check on my list tells me that there's just Sue Pine and Charlotte-Anne Connor's rooms to tackle."

"As we're skipping the main man, let's take a look at his second-in-command first," decided the inspector.

"You're the boss, boss." The door of Charlotte-Anne's room opened with a rather unnerving squeak as Radley turned the handle. "Cor, that doesn't half put my teeth on edge," observed the sergeant. "That's even worse than fingernails down a blackboard."

"That's as may be, but it's useful in one respect," said Copper. "Anyone would have the devil of a job sneaking out of this room in the middle of the night without being heard. Perhaps a point in Ms. Connor's favour."

"Unless everybody in the vicinity is drugged, boss. Which Mr. Spelman could well have been by the time Charlotte-Anne crept out to put part two of her plan into operation," suggested Radley. "Or, of course, other people might have been in the habit of wearing earplugs at night. I mean, I had to at police college, because the guy I was sharing with had a snore like a buzz-saw."

"Let's stick all those in the 'maybe' column," replied the inspector, "and see if we can locate anything which points a more positive finger."

Charlotte-Anne's room was considerably more feminine than her initial businesslike appearance might have suggested. The half-tester bed had furnishings in a delicate pink-and-gold brocade, which was echoed in the upholstery of the spindly Regency sofa which stood at its foot. A delicate table with a lamp of an oriental design was positioned alongside the bed, and its character was matched by an elegant *bonheur-du-jour* with accompanying upright chair under the window. A double wardrobe painted in pale cream accentuated with gold stood against one wall, next to the now-familiar discreet door standing ajar to reveal a modest en-suite bathroom.

"Same again, boss?" enquired Radley. "I'll do the wardrobe and such, while you take a look in that bureau thing?"

"Why not?" said Copper, as Radley immediately set about his inspection. "And this bureau thing, as you call it, stands a very good chance of being the host of something helpful. It's the sort of place where every nineteenth-century lady would have kept her most precious secrets." Copper seated himself and began to open drawers and compartments.

After a few minutes of searching, and having moved on to a swift glance into the bathroom, Radley came to Copper's side. "Nothing peculiar that I can find," he reported. "Not even a case shoved under the bed, but I suppose, living here, she wouldn't have. How about you?"

Copper shook his head. "Sadly, nothing. Some bits and pieces of stationery, a catalogue for a seriously upmarket cosmetics company with a very smart address in Mayfair, some packs of tissues, and a diary for this year without a single entry in it."

"That's a bit odd, isn't it, boss?" remarked the sergeant. "If Charlotte-Anne's supposed to be in charge of the organisation of schedules around here, she must keep some sort of records. And she hasn't got a separate office, according to Anna. So where are they?"

"Where indeed?" Copper reflected for a few moments, but then a light came into his eyes. "I've just thought of something. I remember one Sunday evening. Una and I were sat at home watching one of those antiques programmes, and they had a piece of furniture rather like this on it. And the expert said that, very often, there would be a hidden compartment where the afore-mentioned lady would keep her afore-mentioned secrets. And I just wonder ..." Copper reached into crevices, pressed pieces of decorative moulding, and ran his fingers along underneath the frame of the desk, while Radley looked on in expectation. Eventually, the inspector sighed. "Nothing. Well, I suppose it was a long shot." And just at that moment, as he absent-mindedly pressed a piece of trim alongside the front of a compartment, he was rewarded with a loud click, and a shallow drawer concealed in the thickness of the desktop slid open.

"Boss, you're a genius," said Radley, grinning in admiration.

"Not so fast," said Copper. "Let's see what we've got first." He gently lifted out the drawer's contents. They consisted of a slim buff file, and two matching red ledger books. He opened the first. "This is a bit old-fashioned," he commented. "Paper accounts? My old guv'nor was a bit of a technophobe, but I think he'd at least moved on to internet banking. And our Ms. Connor seems pretty sharp and on the ball. So let's see ..." He ran a finger down the first page. "As far as I can see, it's a tally of fees paid in by the guests – Mr. Spelman's so-called 'seekers' – and a rundown of expenditure. Payments to suppliers, that sort of thing." He flipped open the second ledger. "Hmmm. Much the same."

"Oh no it ain't, boss," said Radley over his shoulder. "Look." He pointed. "There are more names on that second list of guests than on the first, and some of them have got asterisks."

"Well spotted."

"And on the other side of the page, some of the payments are different. Look at that – 'Westchester Property Maintenance Services' – six hundred quid in one book, but twelve hundred in the other."

Copper leaned back and sighed in satisfaction. "And there's an explanation for some of the comments we've been told about."

"So what's in that other file, boss?" asked Radley.

The inspector opened the file. "Just bank statements from a bunch of accounts, by the look of it." He surveyed the papers more closely. "Oh, that's clever," he said in grudging admiration.

"How, clever?" wondered Radley.

"These account names. The first one – 'Halt Manor'. The second one – 'Castle Spelmore'." A riffle of papers. "And there are others." A wintery smile. "I think 'sharp and on the ball' doesn't begin to describe our Ms. Connor. We'll put these back for now, but I look forward to a very interesting conversation with her later."

*

"And that just leaves Sue Pine, boss." As Pete Radley tapped on the door of the final room and, receiving no reply, pushed it open, he almost stumbled as he avoided treading on a piece of paper lying just inside. He picked it up. "And someone's been shoving notes under her door."

"What is it, the last piece of the jigsaw?" enquired Dave Copper facetiously. "'*I know you did it – bring £1000 to the Coven Tree at midnight to buy my silence*'?"

"Nothing so exciting," said Radley. "It just says '*My bedside lamp's not working. I think it needs a new fuse. Please fix it. And my door hinges need oiling, and my hot tap is STILL dripping.*'"

"Signed?"

"Just 'C'. C for Castor, do you think? Is the undead spirit of Castor Spelman stalking the halls?"

"Unlikely. Dead men tell no tales, and they certainly don't write notes. Let me see." Radley passed the note to his superior. "No mystery, I'm afraid. That's the same handwriting as in those accounts books. C for Charlotte, the lady with the squeaky hinges."

"That's another one of my theories on the duff pile then, boss."

"I fear so, sergeant."

"Oh well." Radley sighed. "Back to reality." He looked around the room. "So, our put-upon Miss Pine seems to be the maid-of-all-work around here," he remarked. "And not glamorously rewarded for it, by the look of things."

The room was indeed unremittingly plain. Probably originally an actual maid's room, thought Copper. The unpanelled walls were painted in an unprepossessing dull green, with a modern single bed against one wall, and a bedside cabinet, wardrobe, and chest of drawers whose appearance hinted at flat-pack Scandinavian ancestry. Below the window stood an ordinary metal office desk bearing a desktop computer with dark and silent screen, and a tall metal filing cabinet alongside it.

"Plainly Sue's workstation as well as her bedroom," said Copper. "Something of a far cry from her employer's smart study. This was clearly the engine-room of the operation, while Castor Spelman swanked about behind his extremely elegant antique desk."

"Shame the computer's not on, boss," remarked Radley. "That could probably tell us a lot about what was going on in this Institute place. Do you want me to see if I can get into it?" he enquired hopefully. "I mean, my hacking's probably not up to Anna's standards, but I could have a go."

Copper shook his head. "Let's leave that for the moment. We can always enlist Anna's help if it turns out to be necessary. But in the meantime, you can do your customary burrow through the personal effects, while I check on the contents of the filing cabinet. Which, I notice, has been left with the key sitting invitingly in the lock. Maybe there are no secrets worth protecting. But we'll take a look." He opened the top drawer and began to browse through the hanging files, as Radley turned his attention to the wardrobe.

The paperwork in the top two drawers of the filing cabinet revealed nothing of a suspicious nature, consisting mostly of correspondence with visitors to the manor, reaching back several years and dealing with arrangements for forthcoming visits, or letters of appreciation following a guest's stay. The tone of the letters was complimentary in the vast majority of cases, and on a few occasions positively gushing, although there was a small leavening of disappointment from some writers, whose lives had evidently not been transformed in the way they had anticipated. But there was certainly nothing to indicate a level of animosity towards Castor Spelman which might have precipitated his death.

Moving down to the third drawer, Copper discovered files of a more financial nature, and as he leafed through the folders, one in particular caught his eye, and he pulled it out for a closer look, seating himself at the desk.

"Found something interesting, boss?" asked Radley, coming to his side. "I hope you have, because I've got nothing. And I have to say, it's getting a bit boring, going through drawers of women's knickers. A man could get a complex."

"There's this, sergeant." Copper held the file out for Radley's inspection. "Do you remember those entries in the ledgers in Charlotte-Anne's room? The ones with the different amounts? I noticed this because the company name stuck in my mind - 'Westchester Property Maintenance Services'. And here's the file of bills that it related to. Obviously Charlotte-Anne passed the paperwork to Sue to file, once she'd processed the payments. And this top one here is the six-hundred-pound invoice which you drew to my attention. No mention of a twelve-hundred-pound one to go with it. So here's some nice corroboration of what we've already found."

"And you reckon Sue could have been in on this fiddle?"

"That I can't say," demurred Copper. "There are

plenty more company-named files here to take a look at, if only we had the leisure or the expertise. That's a job for somebody else in due course, perhaps. But there is one objection, as far as I can see. If Sue Pine is so glowing in her admiration for Castor Spelman, would she be the sort of person who would engage in an enterprise to rob him?"

"It's a thought," conceded Radley. "So really, we're not actually any further forward."

"Not so far." The inspector closed the file and pushed the chair back from the desk. As he did so, there was a soft metallic clang. He peered under the desk. "Another waste bin."

"Any more interesting goodies like in Velma's bin?" enquired the sergeant eagerly.

Copper pulled the bin out and looked inside. "Probably not. But we would be remiss not to check." He extracted several of the crumpled sheets of paper and smoothed them out. "Offers of credit cards ... leaflets from the water company on how to economise ... promotional letter from a firm of funeral directors ..."

"She'll probably be wishing she'd kept that one."

"But nothing personal at all so far," concluded Copper. He rootled around among the remaining contents, producing a slight rattle. "Aha! And a nice little glass jar with some tea leaves in it."

"It's not the fatal mixture that did for Castor Spelman, is it, boss?" enquired Radley excitedly.

Copper took an experimental sniff of the contents. "No. It's just some herbal mix with heavy tones of orange peel." He sneezed. "And pepper," he added. "But I doubt if it would kill you. Probably just not to her taste."

"Does everyone around here drink weird potions?" wondered Radley.

"Evidently," replied the inspector, replacing the jar in the bin, to an accompanying 'clink'. "Oh. And underneath everything, the pieces of a smashed coffee mug."

"She obviously has to clear up after people as well as fixing their fuses," remarked Radley. "Not a job I'd fancy."

"No," smiled Copper grimly. "We just clear up after people murder other people." He gave a philosophical shrug. "Well, somebody has to do it. So let's get on with it."

Chapter 16

Dave Copper stood in thought in the bedroom corridor. "One question now is, I suppose, is it worth having a second look at Castor Spelman's room?" he murmured.

"Second look for you, boss," pointed out Pete Radley. "I haven't seen it yet. And I wouldn't mind taking a dekko at the scene of the crime. Or presumably part of it, anyway."

"Then that's what we'll do," agreed Copper, and pushed open the door.

Radley gazed around the bedroom with some amusement. "Well, it's not quite so much of a harlot's parlour as Coco's lair, but it's not far short," he remarked. "I must say, I wouldn't find it too easy getting to sleep with all those fat little cherubs peering down at me. And look at the height of that bed. You'd need a stepladder to get up into it."

Copper meanwhile was examining the wardrobe behind the door, which had effectively concealed the connecting door to the adjacent room on his previous inspection. "I was right about this wardrobe," he said over his shoulder. "There's no way anyone could have moved it from the far side to get access to this room. It's far too heavy. And there's also no way someone could have somehow introduced anything into this room for some purpose or other. The amount the door opens is far too small."

"Well, there you go," responded Radley, his attention elsewhere. "What's this, boss?"

Copper turned. "What's what?"

"This." The sergeant had picked up a small book which had been lying open at the foot of the bed. It was bound in faded and somewhat scuffed brown leather, with dull gold lettering on the spine. He turned it over.

"It's called '*An Historie of the Ancient Countie of Wessex*'," he reported. "And it's pretty ancient itself, by the look of it. Although somebody is in desperate need of a spellchecker."

"What, I wonder, is it doing here now?" queried Copper, moving to his colleague's side. "It certainly wasn't here earlier. So where's it come from, who's been in here, and why has it been left?"

"Couldn't say, boss. Although it looks as if it's been done on purpose, because that little ribbon bookmark thing has been used to mark the open page." Radley took a closer look. "And maybe here's why. This place gets a mention."

"What, Witch's Holt, or Holt Manor itself?"

"Both, boss. Just let me ..." Radley perused the page for a few moments, and then cleared his throat. "According to this, '*There be manie tayles ...*' - oh, stuff this. Can I just give you the gist?"

"Please do," replied Copper, amused. "I don't think we necessarily need the full Laurence Olivier recitation."

"Thank goodness," said a relieved sergeant. "I was never any good at drama at school. Anyway, the book reckons that there is a long history of witchcraft in Witch's Holt going back to before the Normans came, and that when the original manor was built in thirteen hundred and something, the lord of the manor set out to drive the witches away, and set up all sorts of trials to root them out."

"I've heard about those," said Copper. "'Trial by ordeal', they were called. If you believe someone's a witch, you tie her up and throw her into the village pond. If she floats, she's a witch, so she gets hanged. If she sinks, she's innocent. The unfortunate side effect of that is that, by the time you've got her out of the pond, she's probably drowned anyway."

"Pretty much lose-lose then," reflected Radley.

"Although I reckon some of our local minor villains would benefit from being chucked in a pond to teach them the error of their ways."

"I fear the magistrates might take a dim view of that kind of rough justice," smiled Copper. "You'd hope we've moved on a little since the middle ages. But all this doesn't explain what that book is doing here in the first place."

"I'm just coming to that, boss. It seems that one of these so-called witches who floated was about to be hanged from the Coven Tree, and just before she dropped, she put a curse on the lord of the manor."

"A curse?" echoed Copper incredulously. "Oh, spare me! You can't expect me to believe in that."

"Ah, but isn't it not about what you believe, but what somebody else might believe?" pointed out Radley.

"Fair enough," admitted the inspector.

"And it goes on to say this," continued his colleague. "This curse said that the lord of the manor would, and I quote ...," He took another look at the page. "... '*feel the sharpe stynge of Death's dart for all Eternitie*'."

"Very dramatic."

"Yes, but think about it, boss. The lord of the manor – well, these days, that would be Castor Spelman, wouldn't it? And '*Death's dart*' sounds an awful lot like the fatal arrow to me."

"I hope nobody is seriously expecting us to believe that Castor Spelman's death was brought about by some ancient curse," said Copper.

"Of course not. But somebody obviously knows about this curse. And they've put this book here for us to find. So they're trying to muddy the waters, and steer us up some side alley, away from the actual crime."

Copper chuckled. "My guv'nor used to send me up for mixing my metaphors. It must be a sergeant thing. But you're absolutely right. This is meant to be a distraction, and I don't intend to be distracted."

"So what do you want to do next, boss?"

Copper surveyed the room. "I don't think there's anything fresh here, other than that book. Which, although it may be a little late in the day to think about this, you'd better bag up. Then we'll check where it's come from, and who knows anything about it. And that will doubtless emerge during the series of conversations which I intend to have with our remaining ladies." He took a deep breath. "So we'd better get on with it."

*

Back downstairs, the detectives entered the library to find several of the manor's residents in the room, with the atmosphere seeming far from relaxed. One or two murmured conversations were taking place, but they were suddenly hushed as Copper appeared.

"I'm glad to find so many of you here," announced the inspector, "because I wanted to have a further word with several of you." He surveyed those present. "Perhaps I could begin with you, Mr. Day."

Rudy looked apprehensive, but quickly recovered. "Of course, inspector. In the study, do you mean?"

"I think that would probably be best, sir." Copper turned to Charlotte-Anne. "And perhaps, Ms. Connor, you'd be kind enough to arrange for those not already here to be standing by. I'll be speaking to you next, but I'll also want to see Mrs. Van der Voor, Miss Pine, Miss Wakes, and Miss de Roque, so if you could track down any of those who aren't already here, I'd be grateful."

Charlotte-Anne rose to her feet and, with just a short nod of acquiescence, exited into the hall, while Copper and Radley followed Rudy into the study.

The inspector resumed his seat behind the desk. "Your relationship with Castor Spelman was not altogether in a happy state, was it, Mr. Day?" he began bluntly, before Rudy had scarcely had time to settle himself in the chair opposite.

"I'm not entirely sure what you mean, inspector," replied Rudy evasively.

"Let's not beat about the bush, Mr. Day. What I mean is that you and Mr. Spelman had been in a long-term personal relationship, alongside that of your business partnership. Nothing wrong at all in that, and I'm not here to pry into your personal life. Except, that is, as far as it relates to this murder investigation. And we have compelling evidence that this relationship of yours was very much on the rocks. You were no longer sharing a room. You were heard by one of the guests here saying that you wished you'd never got involved with Mr. Spelman in the first place. That of course could be taken two ways – either that you regretted setting up the Institute, or that the shine had come off your romance. Now, as to the first, we know you were heard to talk about the worth of the manor, so it's possible that we're speaking about finances. But, having taken advantage of your very kind permission to carry out a search of the premises, we felt at liberty to interpret that in its widest possible sense. The result – we noticed some pictures on your phone which showed you in a very friendly situation with another man in Canada. The pictures are recent. So, Mr. Day, you can see why we might believe that you had tired of Mr. Spelman and wanted to move on. And one very permanent way of disentangling yourself from your relationship with him would be to remove him by bringing about his death."

Rudy seemed to be at a loss as to whether he should be outraged, offended, or dumbfounded. "You looked at my personal pictures without my permission?" he spluttered. "How dare you? What right do you have to pry into my private affairs?"

The inspector was not to be ruffled. "An interesting choice of words, Mr. Day. Certainly, infidelity is not a crime. And as long as this new love affair of yours was private, we would have no interest in it. Although, as I say, we had your permission to make a search. My sergeant will confirm that from his notes. And your phone was lying around, open to be viewed. Perhaps you should do something about that. But the ramifications surrounding any break-up between you and Mr. Spelman make things more complicated. We come back to the financial question. You have money invested, and you might not have found it easy to extract that in the event of a dissolution of the business. Quicker and easier to inherit the entire operation, after which you could do whatever you liked."

"And you think I dragged Castor out against his will in the middle of the night, sat him down against the Coven Tree, and then calmly shot him with an arrow, while he did nothing about it?" Rudy sounded incredulous. "That's absurd."

"Quite so," agreed Copper. "But, you see, nobody dragged anybody anywhere. Because Mr. Spelman was drugged into a co-operative state."

"What? I don't understand."

"According to forensic evidence, a narcotic was administered to Mr. Spelman, which would have rendered him confused and unprotesting." Copper declined to volunteer any further explanation.

"How do you mean, administered? What, somebody injected him with some drug or other?"

"No, Mr. Day. He appears to have consumed something."

Rudy gazed unfocussed for a moment, obviously thinking furiously. Suddenly, he looked up. "You mean – oh, not that tea of his, surely?"

"And what makes you think that, Mr. Day?" asked Copper.

"What else could you mean? He never drank

alcohol, he only ate what we all did at dinner, he hated taking tablets of any kind because he said they poisoned the mind. The only thing it could be was that weird tea that he drank every night. He kept the mixture in our ... in his room. Lord only knows what it was. It smelt foul, but he said that it helped cleanse his mind for sleep, and he had a cup last thing every night. Religiously."

Copper raised his eyebrows. "And was this generally known?"

"I'll say. He tried to get other people to try it from time to time, but nobody would touch it. But everyone knew about it."

"And did everyone have access to it?"

Rudy shrugged. "I don't know. I guess so. Nobody locks any doors around here. Castor said it was bad Feng Shui. But anyway, it can't have been that. He always drank it. So if I wanted to get rid of him, as you so ridiculously think, I couldn't have used that. Why would I? If things had gotten really bad, I could have just gone, and then Sue could have had him. She was welcome to him."

"You think Sue Pine had amorous designs on Mr. Spelman?"

"Oh, come on," scoffed Rudy. "Call yourselves detectives? Anyone with half an eye could see that. But that dog was never going to hunt."

"Then I have just one last question, Mr. Day. I'd like to establish people's exact movements at the end of yesterday evening, as the party dispersed to bed. Can you help me with that?"

"I have absolutely no idea," said Rudy. "I don't keep tabs on people. I went up early, and I think the de Roque woman was ahead of me. After that, who knows?" He stood. "And now, if you don't mind, inspector, if we're done here, I'm going up to my room to put some security on my phone." Rudy stalked out through the door to the hall.

*

"Check if Charlotte-Anne Connor has reappeared, would you, sergeant?" requested Dave Copper, as the door closed behind Rudy.

"Planning on ruffling some more feathers, boss?" grinned Pete Radley.

"If that's what it takes."

Radley stuck his head out through the door to the library. "She's back," he confirmed. "And it looks as if we've got a full house."

"Good. Let's have her in."

Charlotte-Anne took the seat facing Copper, her apparent calm self-control somewhat betrayed by the fitful twisting of her hands together in her lap. "Have you found out what happened, inspector?" she asked, her voice level and low.

"We've found out many things, Ms. Connor," responded Copper cheerfully. "Sadly not, at this stage, who was responsible for Mr. Spelman's death. But we have been able to gather quite a substantial amount of information as to who might have had reason to wish him harm."

"Oh?"

"Indeed yes. You, for instance."

Charlotte-Anne seemed taken aback at the inspector's brusque statement. "I ...? But why should I ...? I mean, I wouldn't ..." She floundered for words.

"Well, let's just examine what you would, Ms. Connor," said Copper comfortably. "You see, we've had permission to carry out searches of certain parts of the premises, and we've come up with some very interesting items. Some of them in your own room, in fact."

Charlotte-Anne suddenly became very still. "I don't quite understand, inspector."

"Mr. Spelman gave you a very responsible job here

at the Institute," said Copper, with a change of tack. "According to your own account, that is." He smiled quietly to himself at his choice of words. "Although when it comes to accounts, Miss Pine seems to think that she takes quite a proportion of the work off your shoulders."

"She's wrong," retorted Charlotte-Anne dismissively. "The books are mine, and mine alone. I allow Sue to do some of the less demanding work related to the running of operations." She sighed. "I'm afraid Sue is something of a 'poor me', inspector. She always has an air of being put upon. It's a little sad. But responsibility?" A dry smile. "No."

"Well, it's good to have that cleared up," said Copper. "And, in fact, it chimes with one or two things which people have told us they overheard in conversations between yourself and the two directors of the Institute. At different times, that is. For instance, you were heard in a very interesting exchange with Mr. Day concerning the worth of this establishment."

Charlotte began to look a little defensive. "I don't see why that would be of any interest to you, inspector. He would tend to speak to me about the finances whenever he visited. That's perfectly normal."

"Although," countered Copper, "what I suspect wouldn't be perfectly normal would be a suggestion by Mr. Spelman that he should have the books looked at by someone more familiar with financial affairs than he was."

"Castor was quite at liberty to inspect the books at any time he wished," blustered Charlotte-Anne.

"And which books would those be?" enquired Copper smoothly. "The books which we discovered concealed in the desk in your room? The ones which you describe as yours, and yours alone? The ones bearing two differing sets of figures? The ones which might, in the hands of someone knowledgeable, indicate that a financial fraud had been perpetrated?" Charlotte-Anne regarded the inspector dumbly. "You can see, Ms. Connor, why someone investigating Mr. Spelman's murder might find a very plausible motive for killing him in a desire to protect oneself from exposure and arrest."

Charlotte-Anne's head went up. "And are you going to arrest me now, inspector?"

Copper smiled quietly. "At this stage, Ms. Connor, no." He sat back and regarded her.

"Then I have nothing more to say without a solicitor."

"As you wish, Ms. Connor. Unless you can answer just one more thing for me. Do you happen to recall the order in which people dispersed last thing last night?"

Charlotte-Anne looked confused. "Not really. Most people were still downstairs when I went up. I know Castor came in here, and Rudy had gone off somewhere, but apart from that ..." She shrugged.

"In which case, I don't believe there is any point in prolonging this interview at present," said the inspector. "But I assure you, I shall be speaking to you again later. And in the meantime, I advise you not to make any attempt to leave the premises."

"I can't quite make that one out, boss," said Radley, as the door closed behind Charlotte-Anne. "At one time she's cool as a cucumber, and then at another she's as jumpy as a cat. She would be, of course, if she had something to hide, which she obviously does with this business of the finances. But do you reckon it's just the money?"

"Money can lead many people to extremes," declared Copper. "But whether her guilt extends to something darker is not something I'm prepared to make up my mind on at present. There are too many loose ends from too many people left to tie up."

"I'd better get another one of those loose ends in

here then, hadn't I, boss?" grinned Copper. "How about the Dutch lady? She was nearest the door, I think."

"Carry on, sergeant."

Chapter 17

Velma Van der Voor settled herself in the chair across the desk with a slight grunt of effort. "You'll have to excuse me, gentlemen," she said. "At my age, one tends not to be as nimble as in one's youth."

"I'm afraid it's probably going to come to all of us in the fullness of time," said Dave Copper with an understanding smile. His face grew more solemn. "But, in fact, it's your youth that I'd like to have a word with you about."

Velma seemed surprised. "But that's all such a long time ago. I wouldn't have thought you'd be interested in ancient history, inspector."

"It interests me very much when it has a bearing on a murder case I'm investigating, Mrs. Van der Voor. Particularly since, as you yourself told us, it was the circumstances of your past which brought you to Holt Manor now."

Velma nodded. "True. But I'm afraid you'll have to explain to me what bearing you think it has."

Copper paused for a moment to marshal his thoughts. "Several things strike me. First among those was a rather startling piece of conversation overheard by one of your fellow guests. You were speaking to Alisha Barnes, I think, on the subject of secrets, and you were heard to say that you knew of many different ways to kill someone. And here we are, with a murder victim discovered on the premises. You can see why such a statement as yours might attract my attention."

"But surely you understand what I was talking about, inspector," protested Velma. "I may have not been entirely truthful with Mr. Spelman about why I wanted to come back here to the manor, but I told you the truth about my own history. You know I trained here in the war as an agent, and we were taught many skills which we might need to use when we were dropped into enemy territory." She shook her head. "But I have tried to forget them since those terrible days. There are some things you do not wish to remember."

"Which all brings together my next point, Mrs. Van der Voor. Castor Spelman, because of who knows what kind of intuition, seems not to have believed in your account of your reasons for coming here, and as a result, he asked his young researcher to see what she could uncover about your background. And she did find a certain amount about you, with the result that, as one might say, your cover was blown." Velma reacted with a slight flinch, which Copper did not fully understand. "Mr. Spelman knew that you were not quite who you pretended to be. And he had been given documentary evidence, which I imagine he confronted you with. And in your room, we found the burnt remains of this evidence. But what I don't yet understand is, how damning could this be?"

After a moment, Velma gave a serene smile. "You want to know why I would have a good reason to kill Castor Spelman? Very well, inspector. I will tell you. And it was all so long ago that I suppose it does not matter now." She sighed. "Yes, he did discover the truth about me. And I'm afraid I did not tell you the whole story before. Yes, my parents and I did come to England just before the war, but other members of my father's family did not. And as it turned out, we were the lucky ones, and they weren't. Because when the invasion of Holland came, they had to go into hiding to protect themselves."

"Is that because they were ...?" Copper hesitated, not knowing quite how to phrase it. "... a persecuted group?"

"Yes. I see you understand, inspector. And that was one of the reasons why, when the chance came to help free my country, I seized it. After our training was complete, we were sent over to meet up with a resistance group."

"We?"

"A ... friend and I. A very good friend. A Dutch boy. Paul Van der Voor." Velma took a deep breath and blinked as if to hold back tears. "We were in love, inspector. Oh, these things were not encouraged at the manor, so we had to keep it secret. But as soon as we arrived in Holland, Paul said we should be married at once, because you never knew what the next day would bring. He was right. Two days after our wedding I was arrested."

"But ..." Copper looked puzzled. "But you're here now. You evidently survived. So did you escape?"

Velma shook her head. "I was permitted to escape, inspector. But there were conditions. You see, when the occupation authorities found out who I was, they brought me some news. My father's family were still alive, and it was in my power to save them. All I had to do was betray my friends."

"How?" asked Copper quietly.

"There was an ambush of our group," replied Velma, her voice low and subdued. "No survivors, except me. They didn't even allow me to save ..." She bit her lip. "And after all that, my family disappeared. They were never heard from again. So it was all for nothing." She slumped in her chair. "After the war, documents were discovered showing what I had done. I went to prison. And this was what Mr. Spelman had found. And he could have told everyone about my secret, which I have tried so hard to forget. He could have ruined what is left of my life. And that is why I would have wanted to kill him." She looked Copper straight in the eye. "Except that I did not."

"Despite the fact that you had learnt to have no feelings?" queried Copper. "That's what you told Sue Pine, wasn't it, according to something Sheryl Icke heard? Or did your lack of feelings mean that you no longer cared?"

Velma gave a bleak smile. "Neither, inspector. I had no need to kill Castor. Oh, he had in his hands my whole story. It was raked up again when I was released from prison. But he had no intention of giving that information to anyone else. He spoke to me of his understanding of the turmoil in a person's mind when they are faced with an impossible choice. He said that his whole mission in life was to bring peace and calmness to people's spirits, and he would do whatever he could to help me. And then he gave me the paperwork in his possession. He told me to destroy it, and he would treat it as if it had never been. And so, up in my room, I burnt the papers. I looked forward to a fresh start without guilt. And someone has robbed me of that by killing Castor. So you see," she concluded, "I was the last person to wish him dead."

*

There was a long silence after Velma had left the room.

"Do you believe her, boss?" asked Pete Radley eventually.

Dave Copper let out a gusty sigh. "Do you know, sergeant, I rather think I do."

"Even though she must have had years trying to keep the truth hidden? After all, she had all the training to deceive the enemy. It was probably the only way to stay alive."

"And I have had years of looking into a criminal's eyes, trying to discover the truth," countered Copper. "I usually know when I'm being lied to. And I don't believe that this was one of those occasions."

"We'd better scrub her off the list then, hadn't we, boss," said Radley, attempting a grin in an effort to lighten the mood. "Should we see if we have any better luck with the next one?"

"Which would be ...?"

Radley checked his list. "Sue Pine, boss." He groaned. "Oh, not another tale of woe."

Copper smiled in sympathy. "Things can only get better. Go on, fetch her in."

As Sue took her place facing the inspector, exuding her usual atmosphere of nervousness, the inspector felt the need to put her at her ease. "I think you'll be able to help me more that I at first realised, Miss Pine," he began cheerfully. "I hadn't known you were such a local girl, so I'm sure you'll be able to give me a lot more background information about the manor. You were brought up around here, I believe."

"Yes," said Sue. "In Holt End – that's the nearest village."

"And you went to school there?"

"Yes."

"Tell me, when you were young, did you and your friends ever come over to Witch's Holt to play? I've been told that it was something of a magnet for local children out for some adventure."

"Well, yes, we did."

"Climbing over the wall to visit the witch's cave? I hear that was the thing to do, something of a dare."

Sue gave a shamefaced nod. "We did, inspector. But the manor was all shut up and deserted then. I know we shouldn't have, but ..."

"Oh, don't worry about that, Miss Pine," interrupted Copper jovially. "I know what children can be like. I'm sure no harm was intended. But I expect you must know all the local tales. And this would have been well before Mr. Spelman and Mr. Day bought the manor and set up the Institute, I assume?"

"Oh yes."

"And then, by a happy coincidence, you later came to work here. Tell me, how did that come about?"

Sue seemed to gain a little more confidence. "I was working in Holt End, and I saw an advertisement in the local paper," she began.

"I think Miss Benz mentioned that you had been teaching in the local school before you came here. Quite another happy coincidence, working at your old school."

"I wasn't actually a teacher," said Sue, with something approaching a smile. "More of an assistant. A little bit of everything – playtime supervision, lab assistant, librarian ..."

"Ah, now that last must have come in handy when Mr. Spelman asked you to catalogue all the library contents here. Which means, of course, that you'd very likely recognise this book." He held up the plastic bag containing the book discovered in Castor Spelman's room.

Sue held her hand out to take the book, but Copper swiftly pulled it back out of her reach. "I'm afraid you can't touch it, Miss Pine, because we're intending to send it for forensic examination. There may be prints. So can you just take a look and tell me if you've seen it before."

Sue leaned forward. "Of course, inspector. It's one from the library here." She looked directly into Copper's eyes. "But if you're worried about me touching it, I can tell you now that I'm sure it will have plenty of my fingerprints on it. I must have handled it many times."

"Then you'll know what it contains. Among other things, stories about Witch's Holt. Stories which you of course would have been familiar with already." In the absence of any comment from Sue, Copper paused for a few moments in thought. "You were quite an admirer of Mr. Spelman's, weren't you, Miss Pine?" he said. "But I gather that sometimes, that admiration wasn't reciprocated."

"I ... I don't know what you mean." Sue's nervousness had returned.

"It was something that Mrs. Cord mentioned. Apparently you and Mr. Spelman came into the kitchen when she was there, and he was saying that you were wasting your time. What was that about, I wonder?"

"Oh." Sue thought for a moment. "Oh yes, I remember. It was nothing. It was just that I'd written up some notes for him, but I'd made a silly mistake, so I'd have to do them again. It wasn't anything serious."

"I'm glad to hear it, Miss Pine. I wouldn't like to think that you and your employer were at odds. In fact, Mrs. Cord told us that someone heard Mr. Spelman laughing when you were in the study with him last thing last night, so I imagine you would be happy that you would at least have parted on good terms. Even though you couldn't have known that it was the last time you'd see him."

Sue pulled out a handkerchief from her sleeve to wipe away the tears which threatened to flow again. "But who would have wanted to kill Castor? I keep asking myself. Which of those people hated him so much?"

*

"She's a wreck, boss," commented Pete Radley, as he subsided on to his chair after escorting a weeping Sue from the room. "So much for a change of atmosphere."

"Let's hope things brighten up with our next interview," said Dave Copper. "Although, on reflection, I have my doubts. It's going to be Tilly Wakes, isn't it?"

"You're not wrong, boss."

"Well, she started out with tales of stress when we first spoke, and now, after what Anna managed to dig up, we have an inkling as to why. Go on – wheel her in, and we'll see what emerges."

Tilly's calm demeanour, a repeat of her behaviour during her first conversation with the detectives, came as a refreshing change from the previous few minutes. "Is there more information, inspector?" she asked.

"From me?" replied Copper. "No, not at this stage, Miss Wakes. Our enquiries are continuing. But I'm wondering whether you might be able to provide me with more information in order to move things forward."

"Me?" queried Tilly. "But I don't see how. I've told you all I know."

"That's not entirely true," said the inspector. "I know you gave us an account of how you came to be here at the manor. You described the stresses involved with your job, which I can quite well understand. But what you didn't mention was anything by way of a secret."

Tilly caught her breath. "What ... I mean, which ... I don't ..." Her voice faded away.

"Let me explain, Miss Wakes. You see, you were heard in conversation with Mrs. Van der Voor. Or rather, she was heard speaking to you, and in that exchange she assured you that your secret was safe with her."

"Well, yes," admitted Tilly. "Because I'd told her about trying to keep control over the pressures I was feeling at work."

"Good try, Miss Wakes," responded Copper. "But unfortunately, she then went on to talk about ways of killing someone. Now we know how that relates to Mrs. Van der Voor's rather surprising history – she's been quite open with us about that. What that doesn't explain is how that comment related to you. Or rather, it didn't explain it, until we were told about some research which filled in a little more detail about your own personal story."

After a long pause, Tilly gave a deep sigh. "I suppose you mean ... about that patient."

"About that patient, indeed," confirmed Copper. "There was a death during an operation in which you were involved, wasn't there?" A nod. "And quite a large amount of notoriety arose as a result. Accusations flew between yourself and the surgeon in charge, I gather.

Both careers were affected, I understand, although you are back in your position now, I think?" Another nod. "And one would hope, with Mr. Spelman's assistance, you would be emerging from the stressful situation you found yourself in."

"He said ... he said that the past could be wiped away," faltered Tilly.

"Quite so," said the inspector drily. "However, there is more than one way to attempt to wipe away awareness of the past. Or indeed the present. People take refuge in many different ways. One might be to seek some sort of therapy, such as that offered by Mr. Spelman. Some people take to drugs. Others find oblivion in the bottle. And occasionally, both. Any thoughts on that, Miss Wakes?"

Tilly regarded him dumbly, a look of apprehension on her face.

"We've been carrying out some searches of the premises," continued Copper. "And in your room we found concealed both a bottle of as-yet-unidentified tablets, and a bottle of whisky. Perhaps you'd like to tell me about both of those."

Tilly wilted under the inspector's gaze. "I don't sleep. Not since ... you know. One of my friends at the hospital got me the pills. She wasn't supposed to."

"And you wash them down last thing at night with whisky? That's a pretty lethal cocktail. So evidently your conversations with Mr. Spelman weren't having the desired effect. Did he know about your drinking?"

"He said the only way to get through was to tell him everything," said Tilly. "So I did. I told him ..." She took a huge breath. "I told him I was drunk that day. That it was all my fault. I'd misjudged the dose I'd given the patient, and he'd died on the operating table. And I did all I could to pass the blame on to the surgeon, but he knew that the mistake was mine, although he couldn't prove it.

It nearly cost him his career. And that thought had tormented me ever since, because he was a really brilliant man. I confessed everything to Castor in the hope that he could make it all go away, but it didn't. And I ended up wishing I'd never told him in the first place."

"And did you take steps to remedy that situation, Miss Wakes?" demanded Copper sternly. "Did you drug him with pills and alcohol, and then stab him to death with an arrow?"

"No!" insisted Tilly, panic in her eyes. "I could never do a thing like that. I know what it's like to have killed someone. I'm supposed to be the one who helps to cure people. How could I face myself if I took another life?"

Chapter 18

"You don't actually believe a word of all that guff, do you, boss?" accused Pete Radley, as the detectives found themselves alone once again after Tilly Wakes' rather shaky departure.

"Which guff would that be exactly, sergeant?" wondered Dave Copper, his expression amused.

"That stuff about her giving him pills and booze so's she could manipulate him down to that tree," said Radley. "We know for definite that she didn't, because Una didn't find a sniff of any such thing in Spelman's body."

"Quite true," replied Copper. "I just wanted to gauge her reaction to the suggestion. And I couldn't detect anything resembling the right sort of guilt in it. No," he mused, "I have a feeling that both the alcohol and the pills were there for her own use. I think the alcohol was there to provide at least a temporary softening of her feelings of anguish at what she'd done, and perhaps the pills might have given her a more permanent solution, should Castor Spelman have failed to work his magic."

"Figure of speech, I assume, boss?"

Copper nodded. "Of course. I don't think there's likely to be anything supernatural about the death of our heavenly twin."

"You what?"

Copper sighed. "That school of yours seems to have been very remiss in the teaching of classical myth, sergeant. I'm feeling a great deal of sympathy for my old guv'nor when he used to have to fill in gaps in my knowledge. He always had something of a mission to educate." A fond smile of remembrance. "Surely you remember when you first queried Castor Spelman's name with Rudy Day? He said Castor's name wasn't like the oil, but like one of the Heavenly Twins, Castor and Pollux." His colleague still looked perplexed. "Greek myth. The constellation Gemini is named after them."

"Sounds like a right load of old Pollux to me," muttered Radley under his breath.

Copper affected not to hear his colleague's comment. "Anyway, if I'm right, that just leaves Coco de Roque to speak to. At least that should provide us with a touch of light relief," he added with a quiet smile.

"How so, boss?" Radley sounded puzzled.

"Oh, you'll see," responded the inspector breezily. "You'd better issue that invitation."

Coco de Roque appeared in the doorway and paused for a moment in a self-consciously elegant pose. "What can I do for you gentlemen?"

Copper stood. "Ah, Miss de Roque. Thank you for joining us. Sergeant, please hold the chair for our visitor." Radley did so, his expression faintly bemused at his superior's behaviour. "Now, please take a seat ... sir."

Coco froze for a moment, before sinking gracefully on to the chair being held. A wry smile swept across the carefully-made-up features, and a small laugh issued from the scarlet lips. "When did you find out, inspector?" The voice was several tones lower than during previous conversations.

"I have to say, the illusion was almost perfect," said Copper, resuming his seat. "Although I did from the start feel that there was something artificial about your persona, but I put that down to the world of fashion in which you move. But then, we carried out a search of your room, Sergeant Radley and I." He nodded in the direction of his colleague, who had subsided on to his own chair, his face etched with an expression of startled disbelief. "We found a certain amount of your ... paraphernalia, together with your passport. And the photograph, if I may say so, is a very good likeness, whichever persona you are adopting. So, sir, why don't you tell me all about it? At least for the benefit of the sergeant here. Who by now, I would have thought, should be used to surprising revelations." He sat back and regarded Coco with anticipation.

After a moment, Coco relaxed, the body language becoming indefinably more masculine. "My name is Colin Rockingham," said the newcomer. He turned to Radley. "Tell me, sergeant, have you ever tried to establish a career as a fashion designer?"

Radley cleared his throat gruffly. "Er ... as it happens, no ... sir," he replied, still somewhat nonplussed.

Colin permitted himself a smile. "Then let me tell you, sergeant, it isn't easy. Oh, I had all the opportunities open before me. My teachers at school picked up on the fact that I had a real flair for unusual imagery, and I went on to an extremely good college of art and design. I majored in fashion. My tutors couldn't sing my praises highly enough, and whenever we did an end-of-year show, my designs were always put front and centre. I thought the world was open before me. And then ... nothing."

"Don't see what you mean, sir."

"I mean exactly that, sergeant. Nothing happened. Do you have any idea how many people there are coming out of art colleges and scrambling for the few places on offer in the industry? Precious few. I could have contented myself doing grunt work, churning out dull designs for somebody to manufacture in the Far East, but I wanted better than that. So I sent portfolio after portfolio to all manner of people, always with the same result. Girls with green hair and piercings, or guys swathed in black plastic with dubious South American accents, would always beat me to it. So I was at something of a loss, and deeply frustrated. That is, until I got drunk in a gay pub one night with a friend from my old college course."

"I'm not sure we need to delve too deeply into the details of your private life, sir," interrupted Copper.

Colin laughed. "Don't worry, inspector. It wasn't that kind of drunken escapade. In fact, the third member of our party was my then girlfriend. As it turned out, she was a great help to me."

"In what way, sir," asked Copper, intrigued.

"I'd better explain. You see, my friend from college works part-time as a drag queen. Karl had about as much success as I did in breaking into the fashion business, so he was working in an insurance company's call centre in Croydon. Hardly glamorous, and a job that meant there wasn't a great deal left over after he'd paid the rent. But as a make-up artist he was brilliant, and he could make wonderful dresses, so he'd created a drag diva called Ivy Eff, and he used to take a cabaret act round the pubs and clubs. That's his billing – '*Ivy Eff – And Science Created Woman!*'. Absolutely outrageous, but the punters lapped it up. Not just the gay clubs either – he went down a storm in some really rough pubs in the East End. Anyway, long story short, he suggested that I ought to take a leaf out of his book, and magic up some phoney French fashionista to see if I could make a mark on the fashion scene that way. Of course, it was the booze talking, and we all fell about laughing, but Ellie and I got talking the next day, and we ended up thinking 'Well, why not? What's to lose?'."

"I think I begin to see where this is going, Mr. Rockingham."

"Pretty obvious, isn't it, inspector?" said Colin. "I made up my mind to take Karl's advice. We got back in touch with him, and he let me in on all sorts of the tricks of the trade to create a natural-looking appearance. The last thing I wanted was to look like a bloke in a frock and high heels, with the stubble showing through, so he taught me all about padding and so on, and coached me in body language. I'd done a bit of acting at school, so that helped. And Ellie tutored me with the make-up, and researched wig suppliers. And shops that sold size 9 high heels! Between the three of us we created a back-story for the character. Someone who knew she could be the best. And then, with a deep breath, we launched Coco de Roque on the world."

"And this worked?" marvelled a disbelieving Radley.

"Apparently so, sergeant," pointed out Copper. "He had you fooled, for one. But go on, Mr. Rockingham. This is fascinating, if bizarre."

"We couldn't believe how well it worked," continued Colin. "All I had to do was gatecrash a couple of premières wearing something astonishing, and the cameras started clicking. And then it was 'Who's that girl?', and 'Who designed that amazing dress?', and everything snowballed from there. Coco took off, and suddenly I was in demand."

"And your then girlfriend?" enquired the inspector delicately. "How did all this sit with her?"

"Actually, she's now my fiancée," smiled Colin. "I could never do all this without her help. It's a double life, but we manage. We're getting married next year. And I've designed her wedding dress."

"But there's a fly in the ointment, isn't there, sir?" observed Copper. "Because all this construction is under threat from Castor Spelman. Or was, until his death. He was heard to say to you, if I'm quoting correctly, that he could smell a fraud a mile off, and that you were finished. And in a conversation with Denise Benz, you told her that Mr. Spelman knew, and that you needed help. She didn't understand what you meant, and you were interrupted before you could explain. But it's clear that Mr. Spelman had penetrated your disguise. I'm wondering how."

"Me too, inspector," admitted Colin. "I have no idea how he figured it out. And the reason I spoke to Denise was … well, she's not exactly the most girlie girl, is she? In fact, I did wonder just a little if she might be …" Copper regarded the other curiously, eyebrows raised. "Well, never mind. But perhaps Castor actually was psychic, because I'm sure I never gave him any reason to suspect that I was anybody other than Coco, his favourite designer. But the fact was, it seems he knew. Presumably he took offence because he felt he'd been deceived. But I couldn't risk exposure. There's a whole article about me due to appear in the next edition of '*Vague*' …"

"Don't you mean '*Vogue*', sir?" put in Radley.

"No, sergeant. '*Vague*' is a French magazine about the new wave of designers. 'Vague' is the French word for 'wave'. And this article would have been my international launch. I couldn't risk anything jeopardising that."

"You do realise that you've given me a perfect motive as to why you would have wanted to kill Mr. Spelman, sir," said Copper sternly.

"Except that I'm not a violent man, inspector. Murdering somebody is the last thing I'd ever do. I'd have tried to persuade him not to reveal the truth about me. I'd have gone down on my knees and begged him, if that's what it took. Hell, I'd even have tried to bribe him with the offer of free robes for life."

"A life cut dramatically short," remarked Copper.

"But I never got the chance to do any of that," concluded Colin. "I would have tried to speak to him last thing last night, but he disappeared into the study here, so I didn't have the chance. I went up to bed, thinking over and over how I might talk him round. And I would have spoken to him first thing this morning … but I never had the opportunity."

"And you didn't leave your room after you went upstairs?"

"No. I heard some other people out in the corridor, but I don't know who. And nobody came in to see me, so I can't prove anything, I'm afraid."

*

"Why ... I mean how ... Oh, I don't get it, boss," spluttered Pete Radley, after Colin had been dismissed back into the library.

"You should have seen your face," chuckled Dave Copper. "I shall treasure that memory for a long time. Wait until I tell Una."

"Anyway, boss," said Radley, with an embarrassed throat-clearing, "we're not here to enjoy ourselves, are we? Isn't there a murder investigation we should be getting on with?"

"You're absolutely right," agreed Copper, sobering. "And there's one thing we haven't yet managed to winkle out, and that's the sequence in which people dispersed last night. I have a feeling that somebody must be able to tell us."

"You could always ask," pointed out Radley reasonably. "They're all next door."

"Fair point, sergeant," said Copper, getting to his feet. "The simplest answer is often the quickest." He opened the library door, stepped forward, and addressed the room. "Excuse me, ladies and ... ladies. I'm hoping one of you can assist me. I'd like to be sure of people's movements last thing last night, as you all dispersed to bed. I wonder, can any of you recall the order in which you left the group?"

After a moment during which all those present exchanged looks, Sheila Peel hesitantly put up a hand. "I think I can, inspector," she said. "At least, I can remember who was gone before I went to bed myself."

"That may prove very helpful, Mrs. Peel. Sergeant,

perhaps you'd like to make a note."

"Will do, boss." A riffle of paper as Radley leafed through his notebook.

Sheila considered for a few seconds. "I think Castor had gone into the study," she began. "And Coco was the first one to go upstairs, and I think Rudy followed shortly afterwards. Then ..." She closed her eyes in an effort to recall. "Then it was Charlotte-Anne, and Maia left after her. And I believe Velma was the next, and Tilly was just before I went through to my room in the stables, and of course I don't know what happened after that."

"I've got details here of Mrs. Peel and the other ladies," murmured Radley in Copper's ear. "You know, from Anna's camera."

"Then that's fine, Mrs. Peel," declared Copper. "I think that's all I need. Now, I'd just like a word with all of you, in order to clarify the current situation." His gaze swept around the room. "Except that not everyone is here, of course."

"Mr. Day did mention that he was going upstairs, boss," Radley reminded his superior.

"He did. I remember."

"Actually, I think that's where Maia's gone," volunteered Sheryl. "I was talking to her about how Rudy must be knocked a bit sideways by Castor's death, what with them being ... well, you know ... close, and we'd seen Rudy go past the door, and Maia said she'd slip up and have a little chat with him. You know, words of professional advice and all. She's not long been gone."

"And Sue's popped out to the kitchen," put in Anna. "She said she needed a cup of something for her nerves."

At that moment, Sue Pine appeared from the direction of the Great Hall, bearing a steaming mug. "Did somebody want me?" she asked.

"I wanted to speak to everybody, Miss Pine," explained Copper, "and the others were saying that you and Mrs. Cord were elsewhere."

"She's gone upstairs, hasn't she?" said Sue. "Do you want me to go up and get her?"

"That would be very helpful, Miss Pine. Thank you."

Sue deposited her mug on a side table and disappeared in the direction of the staircase.

The uneasy silence that settled over everyone else was suddenly shattered by the penetrating ringtone of Radley's mobile.

"Hello ... oh, hi, Una ... yeah, he's a bit in the middle of something at the moment ... what, no prints at all? ... okay, I'll hand you over." Radley reached out and passed the phone to his colleague, but at that moment all those gathered in the library were startled by a piercing scream, shortly followed by a cry and the sound of a series of thumps. Everyone rushed to the hall passage, Copper and Radley in the lead, to discover Sue huddled in a heap on the landing, sobbing and clutching a knee.

"She's dead!" Sue managed to gasp out between groans and sobs. "And ... and he pushed me!"

Leaving Radley to look after Sue, Copper bounded up the rest of the staircase and surveyed the bedroom corridor. Halfway along it, lying with her head in a pool of blood, stretched the motionless body of Maia Cord. And frozen in the doorway of Castor Spelman's room, his face a mask of horror, stood Rudy Day.

*

After a second of utter silence, punctuated only by the tinny *'Hello ... hello'* emanating from Pete Radley's mobile in his hand, Dave Copper turned back to his colleague. "Sergeant, we have another situation up here. Leave Miss Pine for the moment, and come up and check on Mrs. Cord." As Radley surged past him to kneel at Maia's side, Copper put the phone to his ear. "Hello, Una ... yes, there is actually quite a lot going on here. We've got another casualty." The inspector looked towards his junior, to be greeted by a solemn expression and a mute shake of the head. He sighed. "Make that another fatality, by the looks of it. I need you and Suzanne back here as soon as you can manage." A grim half-smile. "You'd better let Sooz do the driving. You can bring me up to date with whatever you've come up with when you get here? Okay? See you soon." He rang off without waiting for a reply.

By this time, Radley had joined him at his side. "Looks as if she's gone, boss. I'm not getting a pulse."

"Right." Copper looked up, to see Rudy taking a tentative step towards Maia's recumbent form. "Stay exactly where you are, Mr. Day!" he barked. He handed the mobile back to Radley. "You'd better summon an ambulance double quick, just in case there's something to be done for Mrs. Cord, and they can take a look at Miss Pine as well. Then I want Uniform back here straight away. Khan and her oppo should still be somewhere in the area, plus you'd better get another car at the gate to seal off the premises." He raised his voice towards the group congregated at the foot of the staircase. "And everyone else downstairs, please go back to the library and wait there." He moved to kneel alongside Sue. "How are you feeling, Miss Pine?"

"I ... I think I'm all right, inspector," she quavered.

"Does it feel as if you've broken anything?"

Sue gave a few tentative flexes. "I don't think so."

Copper looked up at Radley, who was just replacing his phone in his pocket.

"All done, boss," reported the sergeant. "The cavalry's on its way."

"Good. In that case, perhaps you'd like to help Miss Pine down to the study. I'll be down as soon as I can, and she can tell us what happened." Copper lowered his voice. "And keep an eye on all the others. Don't let anyone stray."

"Will do, boss."

"I'm going to have a word with Mr. Day." The inspector's tone was determined and, as Radley helped Sue to her feet and the pair began to move gingerly down the stairs, Copper advanced on the still shocked-looking Rudy.

Chapter 19

"I ... I don't know what happened, inspector," said Rudy. He appeared thoroughly shaken by the turn of events. "I just heard a scream, and I came out and saw ..." He looked down at Maia's body and gulped.

"Perhaps you'd like to step back into Mr. Spelman's room," suggested Dave Copper. "I assume that's where you came out from." He quirked an eyebrow. "Although I'm asking myself why." He ushered the other into the bedroom and closed the door behind them. "So, please explain what you were doing here."

Rudy subsided to perch on the end of the bed. "This is going to sound pathetic, inspector." He took a breath and seemed to steady himself. "You know that line in the song – *'You don't know what you've got till it's gone'*? That's what I was thinking, about Castor and me. Okay, we'd had bumps along the road, and yes, I admit, the latest bump was a pretty big one, but ..." A wistful ghost of a smile. "You can't throw away the years just like that. Maia understood that. Well, she would, in her job. That's why she came looking for me. She realised that, for all that the situation hadn't been the best lately, I must be hurting. She just wanted to be a shoulder for me to cry on."

"But I still don't follow why you should be in here. You have a room of your own."

"And that's where she came looking for me. I was in here, but I heard her knocking at the door of my room and calling out my name, so I looked out, and she came in here with me."

"But why here, Mr. Day?" persisted Copper.

Rudy shrugged helplessly. "I don't quite know. Maybe I just wanted to soak up a few memories of the good times with Castor. Breathe the same air. Anyway, Maia came in and we spoke for a few minutes. She said, when all this was over, if I needed to talk everything through at length, she could be there for me. And then I said I wanted to be alone for a while, and she left. And I just lay down on the bed for a minute or two – look, you can see where I did ..." Rudy indicated the impression left on top of the bedclothes. "I don't know. Maybe I wanted to feel at one with Castor somehow. And then, suddenly, there was a scream, and I jumped up and went to the door. And that's when you appeared."

"So you're saying that you weren't in your own room at any point since you came upstairs after leaving the study? Not at all?"

"No, inspector." Rudy's tone was firm. "Not for a minute."

"But when you left the study, you said you were intending to go to your room to alter the settings on your phone," challenged Copper. "So which version is true?"

"I changed my mind," said Rudy simply. "I thought, what's the rush? You already know about those pictures. And maybe thinking about them kick-started my conscience somehow. So I came right in here. And the rest, I've told you."

"I see." Copper's voice indicated that he was reserving judgement. "Then we will go back downstairs, Mr. Day. I will leave you with the others while I speak to Miss Pine to see what she can tell me, and we will go from there." Copper held the door for Rudy, who skirted Maia's body while making a desperate effort not to look at it, and the two descended and entered the library, where the group scattered around the room under Radley's watchful eye looked up to regard them with varying degrees of apprehension and uncertainty.

"Sue's in the study, boss," murmured Radley. "I've given her back her mug of whatever-it-was. It smelt horrible, but I think she needed it, although in her place I'd have settled for a large Scotch. Shame about the no-booze rule. Still, I suppose we could always have raided Tilly's secret stash."

"Let's not complicate matters further," replied Copper quietly. "I'd rather have everyone sober." He addressed the other occupants of the room. "Please remain here, all of you, while Sergeant Radley and I are speaking to Miss Pine. We have other colleagues on the way to assist us and some of them may wish to ask you some questions." The remark was met with an exchange of uneasy glances from the gathering. With a nod of the head to Radley to indicate that he should follow him, the inspector pushed open the door to the study, to find Sue Pine hunched in a chair, draped in a blanket, sipping at her mug.

"Mrs. Van der Voor grabbed a throw off one of the sofas," explained the sergeant. "She said Miss Pine ought to keep warm, on account of the shock."

"Good thinking," approved Copper. He brought the chair around from behind the desk to sit alongside Sue. "How are you feeling, Miss Pine? Are you up to answering a few questions?"

"I think so, inspector," replied Sue. Her voice quavered. "But it was all such a surprise."

"I can understand that. So, in your own words, please just tell us what happened after you'd left us to come upstairs."

"I got to the top landing," said Sue, "and I remembered just in time that Rudy wasn't in his usual room, because they'd given it to Velma, because ... well, Castor ... I mean, Mr. Spelman and he were not together any more ... and so I was just about to knock on his door when I happened to look along the corridor, and I saw Maia lying there. I could see the blood, and I just screamed. And then I turned round to come downstairs, and just as I did, I felt a push in my back, and I fell. I couldn't stop myself." She wore a horrified expression. "I could have been killed."

Copper reflected for a moment. "Now when I reached you, Miss Pine, you said to me 'He pushed me'. So why did you say 'he'? Does that mean that you saw who was responsible?"

"No," admitted Sue, "but it must have been Rudy, mustn't it? He's the only one who was there. He must have opened the door of his room and pushed me." She began to sniffle. "But why should he want to kill me, inspector? What have I ever done to him?"

"That, Miss Pine," said the inspector, "is a very good question. And one I intend to give a great deal of thought to." He looked up, alerted by the reflection of blue flashing lights in the mirror opposite the window. "But in the meantime, it looks as if our police and forensic colleagues are arriving, so I shall need to give them my attention. For the moment I think it would be best if you rejoin your friends in the library. Sergeant, would you please settle Miss Pine with the others? I'm going out to meet the new arrivals."

"Righty-ho, boss," said Radley cheerfully, receiving a slightly suspicious look from his superior as Copper made his way out towards the front door of the manor.

*

"You like to keep us busy, don't you?" observed Una with a dry smile, as she and Suzanne unloaded their cases of equipment from the back of their vehicle.

"Not my doing," responded Copper grimly. "If I dare get dangerously close to quoting 'The Scottish Play', something wicked has definitely come this way."

"And are your thumbs pricking yet?" Una started to climb into her white overalls.

"They're beginning to. But I still need all the input you can give me."

"Glad to help. You'd better point me in the direction of your latest victim."

"Up the stairs, first floor bedroom corridor."

"And who are we looking at?"

"A woman by the name of Maia Cord. She's some sort of marriage counsellor, and she was one of the attendees at the current session at the Institute. Although to me, she seemed like one of the more sensible ones. She could probably have given Castor Spelman a tip or two," Copper added wryly.

"We'll take a look. Come on, Sooz."

Copper turned to the paramedics who were emerging from the ambulance which had followed the forensic team up the drive. "Thank you for getting here so quickly, gentlemen. I'm D.I. Copper, in charge of this investigation. Would you like to follow Sergeant Singleton here, please. She'll take you to the casualty, who I'm very much afraid is in fact a fatality, but I'd be glad of your professional confirmation that she's beyond your help. And then there's a young lady in the house who needs your attention. Fortunately this one isn't so serious – we're talking about a fall downstairs. My sergeant is indoors – he'll show you where to go."

"Leave it with us, sir," said the lead ambulance-man. He opened the back of his vehicle and reached in to collect a huge shoulder-bag. "After you, miss." He and his colleague followed Una and Suzanne into the manor.

Copper then switched his attention to Jazz Khan, whose patrol car had just pulled up behind the ambulance. "Good timing, Khan," he greeted her. "I wondered if you might have got over to the other side of your patch by now."

"We were just finishing a circuit before going off shift, actually, sir," replied Jazz. "We'd gone through Holt End on our way back to Westchester when Control came on the radio, so we said we might as well come back here as we were the nearest. You've got more problems, they said."

"You might describe it as that." Copper smiled without humour. "There's been another attack. It looks as if our murderer has claimed a second victim. Forensics are checking things out now. But what I'd like you and your colleague ..." The inspector screwed up his face in an effort of memory.

"Brad, sir. Well ... Constable Bradford, actually."

"Fine. You and he can resume your former watching brief around the entrance to the building ..." Another police patrol car could be seen making its way up the drive. "... and we'll get the officers in that other car to station themselves at the gates of the estate to stop any unauthorised arrivals or departures."

"That's our relief shift, sir," said Khan. "I can tell them, if you're busy."

"Just a tad, Khan. Thank you for that. If anyone needs me, I'll be inside." Copper made his way in through the manor's front door and climbed the stairs to the first floor.

Una was kneeling alongside Maia Cord's body, as the ambulance crew stood to one side. She looked up as Copper approached. "No surprises here, I'm afraid. The chaps here and I are in agreement – the lady is good and dead. Nothing to be done for her."

The inspector sighed. "Well, it was rather a forlorn hope. Thank you gentlemen anyway. But I'm sure your services will be of much more help to the young lady downstairs. She should be in the library. If you head downstairs to the hall, there's an officer down there who can direct you."

"Right, sir." The ambulance crew disappeared in the direction of the staircase.

"So, tell all."

Una sat back on her heels. "A very conventional blunt force trauma to the head. A single blow which has fractured the skull. Death was more or less instantaneous."

"Any idea as to the weapon?"

"Speak to Sooz." Una nodded towards her fellow forensic investigator, who was occupying herself a little further along the corridor. "I'm still checking the victim over to see if there are any other obvious injuries. But nothing jumps out so far."

Copper stepped delicately past Maia's body and approached Suzanne. "Una says you've got something for me."

"Well, the trauma might have been conventional," said Suzanne. "But the choice of weapon certainly wasn't. Take a look here." She pointed.

"I remember those," said Copper. He regarded the bowl of artificial fruit which had attracted the attention of Pete Radley earlier. A sombre chuckle. "Peter was feeling a bit peckish, and he was on the verge of sinking his teeth into one of those apples, until a member of the staff here pointed out the error of his ways."

"He'd certainly have been taking a quick trip to the dentist if he'd tried it," smiled Suzanne. "They're all made of onyx, tinted to look real. Very solid, and very heavy."

"And ...?"

"And just the thing to pick up and clout someone on the back of the head with. Which, it appears, your perpetrator has done. Look." Suzanne pointed to traces of blood, swiftly drying, on one of the pieces of artificial fruit. "I haven't touched it yet, because I wanted you to see it, but I'd be very surprised if, once we've tested it, that blood isn't your victim's."

"So, spur of the moment? Grab the nearest handy lump of something and whack the victim on the back of the head? And then replace the fruit, which fortuitously happens to be a red apple, and hope it won't be noticed?"

"Spur of the moment perhaps," mused Suzanne, "but not heat of the moment, I'd guess. The blow is to the back of the head, so the victim was facing away from the attacker. You wouldn't think this happened in the midst of an argument."

"Good point," said Copper admiringly. He looked back. "Una, did you hear that? What do you reckon?"

"No sign of any defensive injuries," said Una. "I think Sooz is right."

"Bag it up then, Suzanne, and we'll add it to the heap." The inspector joined his wife beside the body. "Anything else you can tell me at this stage?"

Una grimaced. "Not really. Other than the fact that she's only been dead a very short while …"

"Which we knew already," interrupted Copper. "Her movements are accounted for up to a few minutes before she was found."

"So then there's nothing other than the obvious at this stage. No incongruous items in the vicinity of the dead woman. The attack seems to have been quick and decisive. There may be something else when we get her back to the lab but …" Una shrugged. "For now, who knows? So I've pretty much finished here. With your permission, I'll phone in and get someone to come and collect her."

"Go ahead." Copper surveyed Maia's body. "For the moment, can we at least cover her up? It doesn't seem right just leaving her here exposed."

"No problem," replied Una. "I expect we can find a clean spare sheet in one of these bedrooms. Leave it with us." She reached for her phone.

As the inspector prepared to leave, a thought occurred to him. "While you're at it, could you and Suzanne give all the bedrooms along the corridor the once-over. I know you and I have taken a look already, but Suzanne may pick up on something. As Radley said to me, fresh pair of eyes, and all that."

"Of course," agreed Una. "You carry on, and we'll

come and find you when we're done."

Back downstairs, Copper found Radley standing guard at the study door. "The paramedics are taking a look at Sue Pine in here, boss," reported the sergeant. "They had a quick word with her, and they didn't seem to think it was necessary to take her out to the ambulance, but they reckoned a bit of privacy was in order, so I put them in the study."

"I'd better find out what their thoughts are."

As Copper was about to knock on the study door, it opened, and the paramedics emerged. "Well, we've checked her over, inspector," declared the leader. "And she seems to have been very lucky. No broken bones, and no evidence of concussion that we can see. She says she doesn't remember hitting her head anyway, so all she's come away with are a few bruises. It could have been a lot worse. So she's gone back into the library with her friends. And if you don't need us for anything else ..."

"No, you get on your way. I dare say you've got plenty of calls on your time."

"That we have, sir," smiled the other paramedic.

"Then thank you again." Amidst a round of handshakes, the crew of the ambulance made their way out of the front door.

"What next then, boss?" enquired Radley. "Anything useful so far from Una and Sooz?"

"They've identified the weapon," replied Copper. "One of those pieces of stone fruit that you had your eye on when we were upstairs with Anna. Other than that, nothing at the moment. The ladies are taking another look around upstairs to see if they spot anything useful. Oh, and Una's called in for the mortuary van. You'd better notify the front gate patrol car to let them through."

"I'll sort that out with Jazz and Brad, boss. And how about you?"

"I'm going to shut myself away in the study for

some quiet solo reflection," said Copper. "There are some odd factors in this case, and I want to chew them over."

"You bash on, boss. I know you like to do your thinking thing, just like you told me Mr. Constable used to. And I'll guard the door against all-comers," grinned Radley.

"Good. And perhaps you'd loom menacingly over the group in the library from time to time. No harm in making whoever's done this feel nervous."

"I can loom, boss."

"Excellent. But you'd better let Una in when she reappears."

"I wouldn't dare try to keep her out," responded the sergeant. "From all I know, she's a very determined woman."

With a smile of acknowledgement, Copper passed into the study and softly closed the door behind him.

Chapter 20

What sort of a man was Castor Spelman? That's the question Dave Copper began to turn over in his mind as he settled himself behind the study desk once more. Because, as his old boss Andy Constable had never tired of quoting to him, 'know the man and you know his murderer'. So what did he know about Castor Spelman?

The first question that sprang to mind was, how genuine was he? Everyone had heard innumerable tales of fake faith-healers and bogus evangelists who pointed the way to a cure and salvation, and perhaps even a combination of the two. Usually there was a fat fee involved somewhere along the line, and by a strange quirk of circumstance, the practitioners of these organisations always seemed to travel around in a

very expensive car or a private jet. Obviously Castor Spelman didn't fall into that category. All the accounts given to the detectives told of a modest, almost abstemious lifestyle. The man's living quarters were comfortable but not outrageously luxurious. His only extravagance that the inspector could identify was a penchant for the elaborate robes which he affected for the rather curious rituals which he conducted. And besides, the people he attracted to his Institute seemed to be of very ordinary means. There was no fleecing of the gullible wealthy. So the establishment had clearly not been created by Castor as a money-making machine.

Did that mean that he actually believed in what he was doing and, more to the point, did those who attended his courses feel that the activities of all sorts were beneficial? It appeared that the answer was yes. The manor's reputation had obviously gone before it, and several of the current participants had come, or been sent, on recommendation. Several members of the staff had attested to Castor's abilities to guide people towards finding an inner path to the solutions to their problems. He was said to be an inspirational speaker. And would Rudy Day, an astute businessman and clearly no fool, have been taken in by, and invested a substantial amount of money into, a venture which was designed to deceive, irrespective of his personal feelings towards his partner? It seemed unlikely.

But why the theatrics? What was the motivation behind the ceremony at the Coven Tree at dead of night? Copper gave a grim inward smile at the unintended pun. Presumably Castor Spelman was aware of the reputation of the little community of Witch's Holt, and particularly the manor itself, with regard to supernatural goings-on. There was a very informative book in the library on the subject. Had that influenced the choice of site for his Institute, or was it merely a bizarre coincidence? Did he think there was any basis in fact for the tales? And did he therefore hope somehow to be able to tap into the mystic powers said to be flowing around the property? Or was the whole business of the midnight gathering merely a gentle sort of joke, a reinforcement to help the susceptible believe in what he was offering? There was no particular evidence of a sense of humour on Castor's part. Why, if he believed in his theories and methods, would he indulge in self-mockery?

So how significant was the choice of the murder site? Was it chosen by the murderer as some form of revenge because they felt that they had somehow been deceived by a fake? Surely that question had been answered already – nobody had been found to say a particularly bad word against Castor among those currently present, and no theoretical former disgruntled guest could have penetrated the property without detection. But what if the murder scene had been concocted as an elaborate charade, whose mystical elements were intended to disguise the actual motives for the crime?

If the motive for the murder did not appear to lie in the character of Castor Spelman, Copper concluded, then it surely lay in what he knew about others. The series of interviews which he and Pete Radley had conducted among the manor's residents provided much more fertile ground for consideration here. The inspector sent up a silent prayer of thanks for the intervention of Anna Logue and her closed-circuit TV surveillance system. A list of a dozen potential suspects would have proved daunting, but at least the evidence of her video recordings was enough to put many of those in residence out of contention. There remained only six people who could have had the opportunity to bring about Castor's death, and between them, they offered a fine selection of motives, some stronger than others.

Copper set himself to consider how Castor's knowledge of the suspect individuals presented a threat to them, which they might have felt was sufficient to contemplate taking drastic measures to remove. Start at the top of the organisation, he decided. Rudy Day clearly offered several strands of thought. First, and most obvious, was the fact that his personal relationship with Castor Spelman was no longer what it had been, and that there was a new relationship with another person in prospect. Did Castor know about Rudy's new man? Was that really enough to prompt Rudy to kill his partner? Of course, there were two aspects to the partnership, personal and commercial. Rudy had been heard to mention the value of the Institute, presumably in money terms. With Castor dead, the ownership would probably devolve on to Rudy as the surviving partner. And the lure of money is always a powerful incentive. But how then to account for the killing of Maia Cord? Could there be two murderers? Rudy appeared to have been the last person to see Maia alive. Had her visit to him provoked a clash, an outburst of rage which had caused him to attack her? With her professional skills as a conciliator, was she the sort of person who would have allowed such a confrontation to arise? Surely not.

The inspector moved on to contemplate the second-in-command at the Institute. He thought back to his reflections on the lure of money. This was clearly the principal factor in analysing Charlotte-Anne Connor's motivation for committing the crime. Castor Spelman's remarks to her indicated that his suspicions were aroused, and the discovery of the financial records in her room showed that he had grounds for his concerns. And Rudy had also touched on the subject in a conversation overheard by Alisha Barnes. Could the two of them have been working together in a conspiracy to defraud?

The third of the members of staff who had to be considered, if only because of the placing of their accommodation, was Sue Pine. Sue's relationship with Castor seemed to have been a fluctuating one. On the one hand, she voiced almost unequivocal admiration for his character and his philosophy, and he seemed to have relied on her to a considerable extent when it came to the transformation of his sometimes random thoughts into a coherent programme of classes. On the other, he was evidently not always appreciative of her efforts, as witnessed by Maia Cord during a moment of tension between the two. But against that, Sue herself had been the victim of an attack. Could that have been because a killer believed her to be in possession of some damning piece of evidence which would point the finger in their direction? Copper shook his head in puzzlement. It was difficult to imagine what that might have been.

Copper switched his thoughts to the other occupants of the bedroom corridor, who were the only others who could have had access to Castor Spelman at the crucial period. Again, there was fertile ground here when it came to motivation. The inspector visualised the corridor, moving from room to room in turn. Behind the first door was the self-styled Coco de Roque. Copper couldn't help smiling to himself as he considered the elaborate persona which Colin Rockingham had succeeded in creating for himself. He chuckled quietly as he recalled Pete Radley's reaction to the revelation of Coco's true identity, and was suddenly reminded of the scene at the end of the film 'Some Like It Hot', when one of the lead characters announces to 'her' suitor, '*I'm a man, dammit!*'. And the reaction – '*Well, nobody's perfect*'. But Coco's perfect plans would have been destroyed if Castor had revealed the truth to the world. Could Colin have contemplated the destruction of all his hopes without doing something about it? Even something as drastic as murder?

Who next? Tilly Wakes. By her own admission, she had been directly responsible for one death, and although she had made every effort to avoid responsibility at the time, she had admitted the truth to Castor Spelman, and subsequently to the detectives. But was what she had admitted to, the entire truth? Might there have been other factors, as yet unknown to Copper, which meant that the death of the patient had been, not a terrible accident, but the result of a deliberate act on Tilly's part? In the absence of anything to support it, was this a speculation too far? How much had she confessed to Castor, and did she subsequently regret it? Did she fear that he might break confidentiality? Because if she had initially got away with murder, as it were, what would have stopped her resorting to a further murder in order to conceal the fact? She certainly had the as-yet-unidentified tablets in her possession, which might have been used to bring about Castor's drugged state, although the initial post-mortem seemed to show that he had no narcotics in his system. Might the intake of oleander have disguised their presence? And if Tilly had confided in Castor, might she not have done the same to Maia Cord, evidently a ready listener, and then also regretted that action, leading her to kill the counsellor to preserve her secret?

And finally came Velma Van der Voor, the woman who had said, almost boastfully, that she knew more ways to kill a man than Tilly had dreamed of. It was still hard to reconcile the image of a white-haired old lady with the necessarily ruthless secret agent which Velma had been trained to become during the war, even though she still displayed the kind of vigour which would be the envy of many women twenty years younger. Did she still retain the ruthless streak which she would have had to possess as a spy in daily danger of death? Death was certainly a constant companion to her, and if her ghastly admission that she had sacrificed her Resistance colleagues in an ultimately futile attempt to save her family had become known, she would very likely have been shunned for the rest of her days. To kill again to protect that secret might not have come easily to her, but who knew what some people might do when they believed that circumstance was forcing them into a certain course of action?

Copper leaned back in his chair, closed his eyes, and let his mind wander unfocussed through the forest of facts. Was everything he had been told actually a fact? He had been a detective for long enough to know that the same event, observed by two witnesses, could easily provide two completely contradictory versions of the same thing. People did not necessarily mislead deliberately, but often their perceptions of what they had seen or heard were coloured by their own situations. The answer was usually – and how often had this been dinned into him by his former superior? - look for the incongruities. Where there were two contradictory facts presented to him, both could not possibly be true. So in the mass of testimony that had been placed before him, where did these incongruities lie? Who was where, and when? As the musings circulated in the inspector's mind, time drifted past.

Suddenly, Copper's eyes jerked open, a curious light in them, and only seconds later there came a gentle tap at the study door. He swung himself upright with a brisk 'Come in!', and in response to the summons, Una Singleton and Suzanne Heming entered from the hall passage.

"We've done as much as we can for the moment," announced Una. "We've both double-checked over the body and the corridor, and we're both as certain as we can be that there's nothing more to be found there, subject to the victim's internals ..."

"Which I'm perfectly happy for you not to go into too much detail about," interrupted Copper with a faintly queasy look on his face.

"Una says you were never that good with the squishier aspects of our profession, were you, David?" smiled Suzanne. "What a good job she doesn't bring her work home. My husband's a bit the same. I never get greeted by a cheerful 'Have a nice day at the office, dear?' when I get back in the evening."

"We men obviously have more delicate constitutions," remarked Copper wryly. "So, no news?"

"On the contrary," replied Una. "We have interesting things to tell you. For a start, there's what I was attempting to tell Peter over the phone when this latest crisis arose."

"And what was that? Didn't he say something about fingerprints?"

"He did. And that was the point. You remember the tray of tea-making equipment in Castor Spelman's room? You wanted it checked for prints, in case the perpetrator had very kindly left some incriminating traces when brewing the fatal cup."

"And ...?"

"Nothing. Which in fact tells us everything."

"I suspect I know why, but I'd hate to steal your thunder, love. It tells us everything because ...?"

"Because you'd expect the tea things to be covered all over with Castor Spelman's prints from all the times he'd made himself a cup of this concoction of his. Likewise that little glass jar, which Sooz confirms does have traces of oleander in it. The fact that there isn't a print to be seen, everything having been meticulously wiped clean, shows that the person who made the oleander brew wanted to be very careful not to leave any evidence that they had been there. Proof of intent."

Copper nodded, a quiet smile beginning to form on his features. "Then that fits quite nicely into place with ..." His voice tailed off as he seemed to be thinking something through.

"With what?" prompted Una.

The inspector avoided answering the question, and instead posed another of his own. "Did you and Suzanne happen to come across anything else noteworthy while you were browsing around? A phone, maybe?" he asked airily.

Una looked at her husband quizzically. "I think you know we did. There was a mobile lying on the bedside table in the end room ..."

"Rudy Day's."

"Presumably. Because Sooz took a quick glance at it, and it just opened on a selfie of him and another chap. We didn't fiddle about with it any more than that."

"You didn't need to," said Copper. "I just wondered if you'd seen it." He declined to explain further. "Anything else?"

"Oh, just one thing." Una began to echo the growing

smile on Copper's face. "In one of the waste paper bins in another room. Sooz has a nice evidence bag with the contents. Go on, Sooz – show David what you found."

Sooz held up the plastic bag in her hand. "One or two tests when I get this back to the lab, and I can probably tell you what you want to know."

Copper got to his feet. He radiated resolution. "No need for that."

Una looked him up and down. "You know already, don't you?" she said, her tone gently accusing. "You've worked it out, haven't you?"

"Do you know, love, I rather think I have." The satisfaction was plain to hear in the inspector's voice. "So if you and Suzanne would like to get back to the lab and let me have confirmation of those results as soon as you can."

"As you would say, '*To make assurance doubly sure*'?" smiled Una. "I can never resist quoting you back to you."

"Why not?" said Copper. He rubbed his hands together briskly, and held the door to the hall open for the two women to exit. "And I'll see you at home later, love. Although don't be too surprised if I'm a little late. I have a couple of arrests to organise."

The forensic team made their way out of the manor's front door, passing Jazz Khan who was hovering just inside.

"Khan, just the person I need," declared the inspector. "Do you know where Sergeant Radley is?"

"He went through to the library when Sergeant Singleton came downstairs, sir," replied Jazz. "He said he was going to loom." She looked puzzled.

"Good for him," smiled Copper. "And your friend P.C. Bradford?"

"He's just outside on the forecourt keeping an eye on things, sir."

"Fine. Fetch him in, And then perhaps the two of you can come through and station yourselves at the entrance to the library."

"Yes, sir."

"Oh, just one thing before you go, Khan. Have either of you ever made an arrest before?"

Jazz seemed slightly taken aback at the question. "Brad has, sir. Not me." An edge of disappointment was in her voice. "Not so far."

"Then you'd better prepare yourself for a new experience, constable," said Copper, turning and heading for the library door.

Chapter 21

As Dave Copper pushed open the door to the library, leaving it ajar behind him, a sea of faces turned towards him, only for many to look away swiftly with varying expressions of embarrassment and unease, while others continued to regard him with undisguised curiosity. The inspector moved to the side of Pete Radley, who stood next to the fireplace, leaning on the mantel and scanning the room with every appearance of nonchalance, an impression belied by the alert expression in his eyes.

"Any breaking news on the forensic front, boss?" murmured the sergeant to his superior. "Una looked a tad sparkly when she and Sooz came down. Are we any further on?"

"I think we can safely say that we are," responded Copper in similarly lowered tones. "A great deal further, as it happens."

Radley took in the look of quiet satisfaction on the inspector's face. "You've got it, haven't you, boss?" he said. "You've done that thinking thing of yours, and then Una's come in and given you the final piece of the jigsaw."

"Something of the sort," agreed Copper. "We'll call it a team effort." He took a breath. "Well, no sense in prolonging the situation. We'd better get on with it."

"Shall I start jingling handcuffs?" enquired Radley with a grin.

"Not just yet. And I've got Khan and Bradford standing by, so I think we can let the junior ranks have some of the excitement." Copper's eye was caught by movement in the doorway. "And speak of the devil." He raised his voice. "Come inside, you two. Constables Khan and Bradford, perhaps you'd like to wait just by the door there. I may have something for you to do in a little while."

The two junior officers obeyed, while exchanging speculative glances, as Copper turned to address the room. "Everyone! May I have your attention, please. I'd like to thank you all for your patience while my colleagues and I have been engaged in our work. And I know that the process has been unsettling for some of you, but I'm glad to be able to tell you that your ordeal will shortly be over. In one way or another."

Rudy Day stood. "What's this, inspector? Are you telling us that you know who's killed Castor? And poor Maia too," he added as a slightly guilty afterthought.

"I believe I do, Mr. Day," replied Copper.

"Then who?" Rudy's voice betrayed urgency.

"I hope you'll all bear with me if I approach the matter slightly indirectly," began Copper. "Because one of the first things I need to do is to reassure those present who we are not considering in our investigation that they are clear of suspicion. And the person I, and you, chiefly have to thank for that is the Institute's I.T. specialist, Anna Logue." All eyes swivelled to look at Anna, who flushed at the sudden attention. "Thanks to Miss Logue's closed-circuit surveillance system, we can definitely prove that many of you were well out of the way when Castor Spelman was last seen alive and well."

"Well, who?" demanded Charlotte-Anne Connor. "Don't keep us in suspense."

"Not yourself, unfortunately, Ms. Connor," replied Copper. "I'm speaking of the ladies who were accommodated in the rooms in the stable wing. In other words, Anna Logue herself, as well as her colleague Denise Benz, and three clients of the Institute – Miss Alisha Barnes, Mrs. Sheryl Icke, and Mrs. Sheila Peel." A note of regret entered the inspector's voice. "And I would have been only too happy to include the unfortunate Mrs. Maia Cord, whose sad death has in fact been ultimately responsible in leading me towards my solution of this crime."

"I don't follow, inspector," said Sheila Peel. "Are you saying that Maia was the one who murdered Castor, and that she's been killed in some sort of revenge attack? I can't believe that."

"By no means, Mrs. Peel," responded the inspector. "As I've already said, Mrs. Cord could not have killed Mr. Spelman. Nor, in fact, do I believe that she herself knew who was responsible, so it is not possible to say that she was killed for what she knew." He paused to correct himself. "Actually, that isn't quite true. It would be more correct to say that she was killed because she didn't realise what she knew. But the killer couldn't run the risk that the truth might dawn on her."

Sheryl Icke shook her head in bewilderment. "None of this makes any sense, inspector. I don't understand what you're saying about who knew what about whom."

Copper smiled. "I apologise, Mrs. Icke. I'm afraid I'm being a little oblique. But you've put your finger on the central point of the entire case. Because what the whole matter revolves around is what Castor Spelman knew about certain of his 'Seekers', as he called them. In fact, in one way, he was a seeker himself – he sought to know as much as possible about those who were here at his Institute, and as a result, he came into possession of some very sensitive information. Information which presented a threat to those it concerned. Information which, under extreme circumstances, might lead them to wish him dead, in order to preserve their secrets.

"On top of the question of motive, there was also the question of opportunity. We swiftly came to the conclusion that, because of the way the crime was committed, there could only be a limited number of people who were in the right place at the right time. These were the people who had rooms in the first floor corridor of the main manor building, where Mr.

Spelman's own room was situated." Copper regarded the co-owner of the establishment. "I'm speaking of you, Mr. Day." Before the other could react, his gaze moved on. "You too ..." A slight hesitation. "You too, Miss de Roque." The expression in Colin's eyes was a mixture of trepidation and relief. "And then, moving along the corridor, we come to Miss Wakes, and then Mrs. Van der Voor, after which we have Mr. Spelman's very comfortable suite. Then it's Miss Pine's room after that, and finally Ms. Connor's at the end. And all of you could have had access to Mr. Spelman's room at the relevant time."

"But why should we?" asked Sue Pine. "What's all this talk of secrets?"

"There are many different kinds of secrets, Miss Pine," replied Copper. "And some are more powerful than others. They almost always involve guilt of one sort or another. Some can have the power to destroy a person's life beyond repair. Let me take one example. Let us imagine, for instance, that someone holds the life of another person in their hands." Tilly Wakes gave a tiny start, unnoticed by the others but detected by the inspector. "Or perhaps more than one person. Perhaps an entire group." Velma gazed steadily at Copper, her immobile features betraying nothing. "If Castor Spelman came to know the facts of a particular instance, and made it known that he was in possession of that information, then is it beyond the bounds of possibility that the individual concerned might seek to bury that knowledge by bringing about his death, however much he may have assured them that he would never reveal the truth?

"And what about deceit? Deceit can take many forms, some of them highly personal. Take, for instance, a relationship between two individuals." Rudy Day seemed to be making a conscious effort to remain unconcerned, despite the one or two curious glances thrown in his direction. "At the start, everything in the garden may be rosy, but occasionally, as time passes, the bloom can come off the rose. And one of those individuals, possibly through no fault of their own, possibly without any deliberate intention, finds themselves drawn to another person. If that fact becomes known to their partner – and let's just imagine, for purely hypothetical reasons, that the partner is also linked in the business sense – then all manner of trouble might ensue. There could be financial repercussions, to say nothing of the anguish and recriminations which follow when a relationship falls apart. In the midst of such a situation, might not a person think the unthinkable, and resort to murder to remove the cause of that trouble?

"Then there was another aspect of deceit, the question of fraud, which Mr. Spelman was heard to mention on more than one occasion. Again, more than one reading of the word is possible. Let's consider the possibility that Mr. Spelman discovered that there was an individual present who was not in fact what they presented themselves to be. Perhaps a person in whom Castor had invested a great deal of credibility. If this discovery so outraged him, because he felt that he had been taken for a fool, might he not have reacted to expose the fraudulent person, irrespective of the damage caused to their future prospects? We have testimony that, for all his healing instincts, he was not immune to the occasional outburst of anger. And under those circumstances, mightn't the threatened person believe that the only way to avert disaster was to remove Mr. Spelman himself?

"But there's another more obvious meaning to the word 'fraud', that of financial malpractice. If Mr. Spelman came across evidence that he was being deceived, and he suspected that somebody he had trusted to handle his finances had betrayed that trust, what might his reaction have been? He would certainly have taken steps to check whether his suspicions were justified – he was heard to state that intention – and to forestall the imminent discovery, could the fraudster have acted swiftly and decisively by murdering their employer?"

Copper looked directly at Charlotte-Anne Connor. "You asked me not to keep you all in suspense, Ms. Connor," he said. "Very well. I'll oblige. You are already aware, although the rest of the company may not be, that we discovered two conflicting sets of the Institute's accounts in your room, and that these seem to provide unmistakeable evidence of fraud on your part. My colleagues in the Fraud Department, whose expertise in these matters is far greater than my own, will doubtless be able to put some flesh on the bones of my suspicion. You also asked, during your most recent interview, whether I intended to arrest you. I replied no, not at that time. But now the circumstances are different." The inspector turned to Jazz. "Constable Khan, would you be so kind as to place Ms. Charlotte-Anne Connor under arrest, pending further investigations. The charge is fraudulent accounting."

Jazz Khan, blushing slightly as she suddenly became the focus of all eyes, stepped forward uncertainly. "If you're sure, sir." At Copper's encouraging nod, her voice became firmer. "Of course, sir." She moved to Charlotte-Anne, cleared her throat, and began, "Charlotte-Anne Connor, I am placing you under arrest on suspicion of fraud." As the young officer proceeded through the formula of words, the inspector continued to nod approvingly, a quiet smile of almost pride on his face. As she finished, Jazz turned back to Copper. "Do you want us to put her in the car now, sir?"

"Not straight away," he replied. "We still have matters to resolve."

Alisha Barnes spoke up. "Does that mean that it

was Charlotte-Anne who killed Castor, inspector?" she queried. "And then she killed poor Maia because she knew she'd done it?" She gave a shudder.

"Not at all, Miss Barnes," replied Copper. "Because although serious, Ms Connor's crime is by far the less drastic of the two we are considering. And if we review the circumstances of Mrs. Cord's death, the list of those who could be responsible is much reduced. Look at the timing. Virtually everyone was gathered here in the library when I had finished my most recent round of interviews. Only three were absent. Mr. Day had gone upstairs, with the stated aim of making some changes to his phone's security. Mrs. Cord later went up after him, with the intention of offering him some words of comfort and advice to deal with his assumed grief. And Miss Pine had gone through to the kitchen to make herself a hot drink. And then, when I requested that everyone be brought together, she offered to go upstairs in order to bring Mr. Day and Mrs. Cord down to rejoin the group."

"And I did," said Sue. "You were here. You saw me. I went up, and that's when I found Maia dead."

"Indeed," said Copper. "You left us. We heard you scream. We heard the noise made as you fell down the stairs. And you stated, quite firmly, that your fall was no accident. 'He pushed me,' you said. And the assumption was that it could only have been Mr. Day who was responsible." The inspector held up a hand to silence Rudy Day, who seemed about to protest.

"It must have been him," asserted Sue. "He was in his room. He only had to open the door, and I was right in front of him."

"Except," responded Copper quietly, "that he wasn't in his own room. When I arrived on the top landing, Mr. Day was standing in the doorway of Mr. Spelman's room. There is no way that he could have caused your fall and reached the position I saw in the

232

time."

"But he was the only one," insisted Sue.

"Not so," said the inspector. "There is one other person who could have engineered your fall downstairs. You yourself."

Chapter 22

There was a sudden hush.

"But ... but that's mad," said Sue, her voice ragged. "Why would I do such a thing?"

"To divert attention away from yourself. To throw suspicion on to someone else for the killing of Maia Cord. And ultimately, for the murder of Castor Spelman."

"But I couldn't have," stressed Sue, beginning to look hunted. "I was downstairs when Maia was killed. And what reason could I have for killing either of them? I worshipped Castor. And what was Maia Cord to me?"

"A danger," replied Copper simply. "She was the one person who contradicted your account of last evening. And she even mentioned her knowledge in front of everyone, except that nobody noticed. Nobody, that is, except you."

The inspector paused, took a deep breath, and began afresh. "It is a sad fact, but one that I have noticed many times in my career, that murder can occur when the omens were, from the outset, very much to the contrary. The statistics of violent killing within marriage are tragic evidence of that. And you, Miss Pine, are an unfortunate illustration of the principle. You say you worshipped Castor Spelman, and I believe you. Whether it was on account of his physical attractiveness, or whether you were filled with admiration for his charismatic desire to cure people's inner maladies through his psychological procedures, you idolised him. Unfortunately for you ... how shall I put this? ... Mr. Spelman's affections were engaged elsewhere. His relationship with Mr. Day was a long-standing one, and left no room for you. So you were reduced to worshipping from afar, but I'm guessing that all hope that Castor might see the error of his ways, as you may have regarded it, was not lost. And so you continued to serve him in your lowly capacity, a handmaiden to his high priest.

"But then there came a change. You became aware that Mr. Spelman and Mr. Day had had a falling-out. Perhaps you even knew the circumstances – that Mr. Day had met someone else, and that his partnership with Mr. Spelman was jeopardised. Could this be your chance? I'm guessing that matters began with the dropping of simple and subtle hints. '*If ever you have any problems, I'm only too happy to help.*' Graduating on to '*I'll always be here for you*' – that kind of thing. I'm speculating, of course, but then we come on to a concrete piece of evidence, provided by Maia Cord herself, who told me that she'd witnessed an encounter between Castor and yourself which had ended up with him saying to you, in no uncertain terms, that you would always be wasting your time. I'm guessing that this was only the culmination of an increasing series of approaches from yourself, and a mounting series of rebuffs by him, until you were in no doubt that your affections were futile. Perhaps it was at that point that you were heard by Sheryl Icke to warn Castor of the danger he was in. You told him how love can turn to hate. He mistakenly thought you were referring to Rudy." Copper shook his head sadly. "How such an intuitive man could miss your meaning is a mystery, but evidently he did. And so I believe that you formed the resolve that, if you could not have him, nobody should.

"We know that you had a certain amount of scientific experience from your work as a teaching assistant at the local school. How you encountered the information regarding the poisonous qualities of the oleander bushes growing so plentifully on the estate I can only guess at – perhaps from the many researches you carried out among the books in this very library. But you had both the skill and the wherewithal to concoct a poison. Not one which would kill your victim immediately. No – it was one which would render him sufficiently malleable so that you could stage a bizarre final scenario, perhaps some twisted demonstration that all his mysticism was not sufficient to save him from death. But you gave him one last chance. You went to him in his study, last thing last night, and made your final offer of love and support. And he laughed in your face. We know this, because Sheryl Icke overheard it, and she mentioned it to Maia Cord. Sheryl told us that you were the last of the group to disperse last night, although you had stated that you didn't see Castor after dinner. A lie. But Mrs. Cord misunderstood the laugh – she took it to mean that the two of you were on good terms. How wrong she was.

"So now, I believe, you decided to act. When everyone else had settled for the night, you must have called in to Castor's room, next to yours as it was. I imagine you probably feigned embarrassment at the earlier scene between the two of you. You probably promised that you would never trouble him again with your importuning. And you suggested, as a peace offering, that you might make him a cup of his favourite herbal tea, which you knew he always took last thing at night. In forgiving frame of mind, he accepted. But you had, concealed about you, the jar of oleander, identical to Castor's own jar of herbs. You exchanged the two. And that is how you came to administer the dose of poison to him.

"I dare say you went back to your own room at that point, leaving the oleander to take effect. But after an interval, you must have returned and manoeuvred Castor, now in a pliant drugged state, out towards the Coven Tree. Not by the main staircase – the creaky treads might have attracted unwelcome attention, and who knew who might still be wakeful? Instead, you used the old servants' stairs down to the kitchen, whose access is conveniently just opposite your own room, pausing on your way out to collect the murder weapon from the storeroom in the hall passage. We now know, from a note left for you by Ms. Connor, that you, as the person usually charged with attending to minor repairs around the house, would have the most obvious access to the toolbox in that storeroom. Here you collected the screwdriver, the actual murder weapon with which you stabbed Mr. Spelman to his unresponsive heart, once you had positioned him at the foot of the Coven Tree. And then, to disguise your work and throw suspicion on to one or other of the manor's residents, you forced one of Denise Benz's arrows into the wound. I imagine, if we check the contents of the toolbox carefully, we shall find a recently-cleaned screwdriver buried at the bottom. You then went back to Castor's room and attempted to remove any trace of your presence there, replacing the tainted cup with a clean one from your own room. And then all you needed to do was return quietly to your quarters, smashing and discarding the dirty cup in your own waste paper bin, and prepare to be shocked when the body was discovered."

Copper stepped back and looked at Sue, who regarded him steadily, no trace of emotion on her face.

"Sue deliberately wanted me to take the blame for the murder?" Denise sounded as if she could still not quite believe it. "But why kill Maia? And how could she do it? She was down here when it happened."

"As to why," replied Copper, "we already know. Maia was one who could demolish her account of her movements at the end of yesterday." He sighed heavily. "And I'm afraid I have to take my share of the blame for Sue Pine becoming aware that Maia had learnt of Castor's laughter at her expense. Because if she was shown to have lied about that, we would be bound to be asking why. And as to the second question, she did what so many murderers do. She repeated an action which had proved successful beforehand. She used the kitchen servants' stairs. And she had to act swiftly. What might Maia reveal on her return downstairs? So Sue made an excuse to go to the kitchen, quickly went up to the first floor, and as soon as Maia emerged from Castor's room, probably slightly to Sue's surprise, she hit her with the most convenient heavy object, one of the pieces of ornamental stone fruit on the corridor table. She then came back down the way she had gone, reappeared here as if nothing had happened, and innocently volunteered to go up to fetch Rudy and Maia, all too well aware of what she would find in the corridor. But what she did not know was that Rudy was not in his own room, so when she fabricated the fall downstairs, attempting to divert attention from herself and place the blame on him, the cracks in her story began to form."

The silence persisted for several long seconds as those present took in the inspector's account. Eventually, Sue stood and scanned the room, the sneering expression on her face a far cry from her hitherto diffident manner. "Look at you all," she said, an odd light in her eyes. "There's not one of you who was worthy of Castor. Rudy and Charlotte-Anne – you both betrayed him. You others – either you feared him because you believed the worst of him, or else you were like sheep, following him along a path you couldn't begin to understand. I was the only one who valued him for what he was, what he could be. And if he could have shaken off his dependency on the weaklings who crowded round him, he could have been so much greater. And I told him so. I told him that, with the real devotion that only I could give him, nothing would ever stand in his way again. And what did he do? He threw it in my face. He couldn't comprehend what I was offering. He told me I was deluded. He laughed." She took a deep breath, and her voice fell from the high pitch it had reached. "Nobody should laugh at an expression of true love. If he could reject me, then I could reject him. And if he couldn't come with me along the path I was offering him, then he wasn't worthy to go on living to receive the affection of others."

As Sue remained standing, panting slightly with emotion, her nostrils flared, Copper gave a quiet nod to Pete Radley.

The sergeant moved forward and placed a hand on Sue's arm. "Susan Pine," he said, "you are under arrest for the murders of Castor Spelman and Maia Cord. You do not have to say anything ..."

It was at this point that Sue Pine began to scream.

*

As the two police patrol cars drove away, each bearing their arrested cargo in the rather self-conscious custody of the local officers, Dave Copper stood alongside Rudy Day in the shelter of Holt Manor's entrance porch. "So, what are your plans now, Mr. Day?" he enquired.

Rudy shrugged. "I'm not exactly sure, inspector. I imagine the first thing I'm going to have to do is sit down with you and make a formal statement about everything."

"We'll make that a priority, sir," smiled Copper. "And then?"

"I'll be getting on the first flight to Canada. There's somebody there I'm going to need to spend some time with, and I don't intend to waste a minute. Everybody deserves a little happiness, right?"

"Right," nodded the inspector. "And what about the Institute? Where does that go from here?"

"Exactly nowhere," replied Rudy. "Without Castor, the whole idea is dead ..." He caught himself. "Sorry. That was an utterly crass thing to say. What I mean is ..."

"I know what you mean, Mr. Day," Copper

reassured him.

"So I'll need to check the legal situation, but I guess the whole establishment is mine now. Lord knows what state the finances are in after Charlotte-Anne's activities, but when everything is sorted out, I guess I'll just close things down and put the place up for sale. After all, I do have some experience in doing property deals. Don't these old places tend to get turned into spas or hotels?"

"They do, sir. Although whether recent events will add to the manor's attractiveness to a buyer is anyone's guess. Perhaps you should have a chat with Alisha Barnes."

"The notoriety might even hike up the value," mused Rudy, a speculative gleam in his eye. "Who knows?"

"I shall watch with interest, Mr. Day," said Copper with a smile. "You can update me when you come back to the U.K. We shall need you here for the court cases in due course."

"I'll be there. And now, if you'll excuse me, I have to go and tell some guests that their stay is at an end. And I have to give out the bad news to some people about their jobs." Rudy turned and re-entered the manor.

After a few minutes of quiet reflection, Copper followed him, to find Pete Radley in conversation with Anna Logue in the hall passage. "Anna," said the inspector, "I'm glad you're here. I just wanted to thank you again for all the help you gave us. I don't think we'd have managed to arrive at a conclusion half as quickly without your input."

"Just doing my job, inspector," she smiled. "I'm only too pleased I could help you two do yours."

Copper's face grew serious. "Sadly, from what Mr. Day has just been saying to me, things don't look too good on the job front for the staff here at the Institute. He's probably planning on closing it down."

"No great shock there," said Anna. "I couldn't see it carrying on without Castor anyway. But don't worry about me. There are plenty of jobs in computing out there. I'll just have to go and do my researching somewhere else."

Pete Radley cleared his throat. "Er ... boss ..."

"Yes?"

"You know I used to be in Intelligence, before I got bumped up to C.I.D.?"

"Of course."

"Well, I've still got some mates down there. And one of the I.T. girls is leaving next month to have a baby. I don't think they've advertised for a replacement yet ..." Radley let the suggestion hang in the air.

"And you think, if I put a word in ...?" said Copper. "Well, Anna? Is that the sort of thing that might appeal to you?"

"Sounds great," responded Anna enthusiastically. "I've really enjoyed seeing how you've gone about doing the detecting thing. I mean, if it wouldn't be an imposition ..."

"Leave it with me," chuckled the inspector. "I'll see what I can do."

"See you at the coal face, Anna," whispered Radley with a smile. "And don't forget to bring the teacakes."

*

Dave Copper threw himself untidily into the chair behind his desk and let out a long slow sigh of relief. "Well, that's done. All I've got to do now is write it up." He looked across at his junior colleague, who was also lowering himself into his own chair with a slight grunt. "For which I am going to be relying heavily on the copious notes which I am confident you have been making."

"Course I have, boss," replied Pete Radley cheerily. "Trust me. My notebook's full of scrawl, some of which you're going to have a job reading." He produced it from a pocket. "I suppose you're going to want to make a start now."

Copper shook his head with a weary smile. "Not at this hour. We'll make a start in the morning."

"Can't say I'm sorry, boss," said Radley. "Not after two great long sessions in the interview rooms. I don't know about you, but I'm starved." He started to burrow through his desk drawers. "I'm sure I had a doughnut and some crisps in here. It's been so long since I've had something proper to eat that my stomach thinks my throat's been cut."

"Not the happiest of images, sergeant," remarked Copper.

"Sorry, boss," grinned an unrepentant Radley. "Still, we got 'em. Well, you got 'em," he amended.

"Teamwork, Peter. Everybody contributed. Una, Suzanne, Anna, Khan with her snippets of local knowledge ... even you with your occasional off-colour remarks." A smile showed that the criticism was not intended to be taken seriously. "Which, actually, used to be my trademark, according to Mr. Constable," he confessed.

"Funny old mixture, wasn't it?" mused Radley. "I mean, a nice simple case of fraud such as you might find anywhere, and if it hadn't been for Castor Spelman's murder, Charlotte-Anne Connor might have got away with it for heaven knows how long. And then you've got the weird one ... Sue Pine."

"Indeed. But once you strip away all the extraneous nonsense about supernatural influences swirling around the manor, and all the jargon and New Age theories that Castor Spelman was peddling, whether sincerely or not, it does come down to a very old story. Love rejected can have some very unpleasant consequences."

"A touch of the old *'Hell hath no fury'*, eh, boss?

Shakespeare got it right again."

"Actually," said Copper, "it isn't Shakespeare at all, although most people make that mistake. I did, until my old guv'nor put me right. It's from William Congreve. The actual quote is *'Heaven has no rage, like love to hatred turned, Nor Hell a fury, like a woman scorned'*. Which, oddly, is exactly what Sheryl Icke said she heard Sue say to Castor. Prophetic words. But I'm sure he never for a moment imagined that the warning needed to be taken seriously."

"I still don't get how you can murder someone you're supposed to be in love with," said Radley. "Unless you've gone completely round the twist. I mean, Sue wasn't exactly one hundred percent rational during that interview, was she, boss?"

"I suppose it's the result of having unrealistic hopes, and then seeing them dashed before your eyes. I think we can believe what Sue told us to start with. She was utterly enchanted with Castor Spelman. In a way, he bewitched her. She built up her hopes, and when the break with Rudy came, she thought her moment had arrived. But then the brutal truth hit her, and she cracked." The inspector sat up and pushed himself briskly to his feet. "Anyway, enough for today. It's been a very long session, and you should get yourself home. Get a proper meal inside you, and relax in the bosom of your family."

"As long as that sprog of mine lets me have five minutes peace," grinned the sergeant. "How about you, boss?"

"I intend to have a long hot bath, a large glass of wine, and some quality time with my darling wife," said Copper. "And not necessarily in that order. And we will do our best to forget all about crime."

"Until tomorrow, that is, boss."

Copper chuckled. "You're absolutely right, Peter.

Until tomorrow."

***

also by Roger Keevil

The Inspector Constable Murder Mysteries

Murderer's Fête
Who could have foreseen the murder of a clairvoyant at a country fête?

Murder Unearthed
Sun, sangria and suspects during a supposed holiday in Spain

Death Sails In The Sunset
Murder ensues when a journalist won't let guilty secrets be buried at sea

Murder Comes To Call
Three short stories to tax the talents of our detectives

Murder Most Frequent
Another trilogy of intriguing cases for Constable and Copper

The Odds On Murder
Who is riding for a fall when a prominent racehorse trainer is killed?

No Bar To Murder
Complicated relationships make a potent and lethal cocktail

The Murder Cabinet
A return to Dammett Hall leaves the nation's fate in the team's hands

The Game Of Murder
Sudden death at the TV studio as entertainment turns to murder;
PLUS a bonus short story, 'Exit A Murderer', and a full index to all the Inspector Constable mysteries

The Copper & Co Murder Mysteries

Murderer's Honeymoon
Even on an idyllic tropical island, murder never takes a holiday

***

Printed in Great Britain
by Amazon